## About the Author

**Margaret Woodhouse** is the author of over thirty titles. Her books include the best-selling *Know Your Cat's Purr Points*, for which Miu Sakamoto composed music to accompany the Japanese edition, and her satirical take on Westminster politics, children's title *Jim Bleat for Prime Minister*, which, when published, attracted surprisingly earnest political debate on BBC 2's Newsnight.

*Miriam McGregor's Shadow* is her second novel.

Margaret Woodhouse lives beside the lake on the Central Plateau in New Zealand.

Also by Margaret Woodhouse

The Uncertain Measure of Success
Jim Bleat for Prime Minister
The Rise and Fall of Weaseldomderry
Know Your Cat's Purr Points
The 9-Life Habits of Highly Successful Cats
Cat's Tales from Shakespeare
The Latex Cat
Feline Cuisine
The Female Semaphore
The Secrets of Elephant Wisdom

# Miriam McGregor's Shadow

## Margaret Woodhouse

MAGARI PUBLISHING

MIRIAM MCGREGOR'S SHADOW

Published by Magari Publishing, PO Box 104, Taupo, 3351, New Zealand

E-mail: frontdesk@magari.co.nz

ISBN: 978-0-908801-70-1

www.magari.co.nz

This book is dedicated to
all embattled neighbours

# Contents

# CHAPTER ONE
## WATCHED

Miriam McGregor never bothered getting to know someone before passing judgement on them. She was far too sure of her own excellent instincts, her superior assessment of personality. And so it was, even before she met Carrie Thompson, she decided her new neighbour was trouble.

Glade Heights had often been rattled by scandal. But now, deep in its most private corners a disturbing tremble was beginning. And not even Miriam could have predicted the extent to which it was about to shake her pretty neighbourhood.

Miriam put the binoculars to her eyes and released a fast downward snort. Already she was expressing disapproval. Below her, Glade Heights Estate fanned out. And beyond, the lake rolled east, caught by the wind in a continuous pitching of blue and white. The occasional boat braved the waves, sending up great white sprays. Back on the estate the wind dealt to the trees in the same buffeting manner, whirling their leaves into Mexican waves as it clipped the tops. Rushed, urgent, and excited.

Yet despite the frenzy of the outside elements, the day had a lazy feel about it, as if the sun and water and rushing air had sapped all other energies. From the protection of her sitting room Miriam stood wrapped in her cloak of self-satisfaction. She scanned the scene below. There was plenty of time to analyse the situation. No need to hurry. The binoculars made slow sweeps across Glade Heights' bow. And stopped.

Miriam stiffened. She had found her target.

For several minutes Miriam's binoculars focused on a single point. Then, still clutching them in her left hand, she picked up a pen from the table beside her and began a hurried writing into a notebook. Her notes proceeded with tremendous energy. They were detailed, copious, as she allowed herself only an occasional halt to take another look through the binoculars and to mutter the odd, "Honestly!" and an impatient, "Frightful!".

On the other side of the room sat Angus McGregor, Miriam's husband. The old floral-liveried armchair he sat in almost consumed him it was so deep and linen-y and old world-y. It was as if he were barely present.

As Miriam scribbled, Angus watched. But he did not dare interrupt his wife's industry. He peeped over the arm of the chair just as she looked up, and as their eyes met, a wash of sadness flowed over him. Hers were not eyes he chose to linger on any more. Once they had drawn him in, allured him with a message of warmth and kindness. Or so he had felt. These days they tended to cast blame and resentment.

He averted his gaze until she was busy again, then he spied on her from under the cover of his eyelashes. Lately she had started wearing her hair tied up like some bun affair from a by-gone era. He supposed it made for efficient management. And it was greying. Not just at the edges, but in one by one strands of approaching old age. She had broadened over the years, too. Particularly around her chest and girth. If he was honest, she was getting fat.

And that was strange, he thought. Because her more recent behaviour made her seem lean; gaunt, in fact, and hungry for something. Was it hunger for gossip? Miriam did have an insatiable appetite for gossip. He didn't mind the gossip so much. He had always found it quite nourishing. The juicy titbits Miriam provided had in fact sustained him for years. He was always given his share of her scandalous pickings and even contributed to them from time to time. But he was far from the consummate gatherer of gossip Miriam was. Her ability to delve into everybody's business whether she was welcome or not – that was what made her seem lean.

Yet here she was taking on the proportions of a steamroller.

Angus McGregor reflected for a moment on steamrollers. Things of the past. Giant and cumbersome and not at all something one wanted to be married to. He hadn't meant to marry a steamroller. The young Miriam had been worth falling in love with. His lips lifted in a wan smile as he remembered his lively, inquisitive, and really rather attractive young wife. She had been a sparkle in his grey world. What had happened, then? To her, to him, to their marriage? He could sense his life losing its control. And in his wife, lively was becoming sharp, inquisitive degenerating into nosy. He felt pushed over and steamrollered. A squashed shadow of his former self.

Angus sighed. Miriam scribbled.

The scratching of Miriam's pen intruded further on Angus's comfort. He yearned for the happy old days when he and Miriam laughed and conspired, conducting innocent debriefs after a night out socialising.

That was before Cynthia died. Their Cynthia. They had both been scoured out by the deluge of grief that followed her death. And not only were they racked by grief. They had been left exhausted by the unremitting emotion spent trying to coax health from their daughter's frail little body. Automatons. That's what they became. They functioned but they had no awareness of their surroundings.

In time, Angus managed to shake himself back to the present. Malcolm was, after all, also young and he needed his parents every bit as much as Cynthia had. And finally, after months, Miriam appeared to rally also. There was an intensity about her, though, Angus had not seen before. A relentlessness. Grief then hurt then resentment; one had thrown up the other as she wrestled for control of her life. She was suddenly so hungry for control – of everything – compensating, he supposed, for the impotence she had experienced as Cynthia's life had slowly expired.

Angus shot another furtive glance in her direction. She was huddled over her notebook, protected by her own furious industry.

He remembered so clearly the first time he had seen her lose proportion. *The In-law Tale*, that was how he always thought of it.

He liked to think she had been motivated by kindness – at first, anyway. Her brother's wife had been suffering from postnatal depression after the birth of their daughter, and while Miriam was still raw following Cynthia's death, her wish to help Elise seemed genuine.

Angus had assumed she was yearning to be close to a newborn baby, a symbol of hope. Her brother, Maurice, was not keen to have her so involved but he was unable to resist her. It was extraordinary to watch. At first Angus, who could read his brother-in-law's worry, tried to counsel Miriam to leave them to sort out their own troubles. He approached her gently only to recoil at the ferocity of her response.

"You just back off, Angus. I know how to deal with this situation," she had railed at him through narrowed eyes. "Elise will pull through with my experience. I don't need anyone else's hopeless input, thank you very much."

Leaving Angus to cope with Malcolm, Miriam moved in with Maurice and Elise and assumed the mantle of sole caregiver. In the same breath as she assured Maurice it was nothing, all the time she sought his praise and gratitude.

Angus had watched, silenced into horrified fascination as Elise became more and more irrelevant, as did her baby. It was all about Miriam. Elise withdrew further. Still Angus tried his gentle counsel, but Miriam would turn her look of steel on him for a moment, then plough on.

Finally, Elise crumbled – completely; unable to speak, unable to stop crying. Only then did Maurice manage to shake himself free from the web Miriam had trapped him in. His pent up emotion and frustration exploded as he attacked his sister, at last exerting some control over his tattered family life, telling Miriam to leave and never return.

Angus had braced to pick up the pieces, but the Miriam who returned home was not going to be seen to be broken. The casual manner in which she dismissed her brother and sister-in-law and justified her own position stunned Angus.

From that day she cast Maurice and Elise aside, and while Angus still saw them from time to time out of a mixed sense of duty and apology, Miriam only ever saw them at the occasional extended family get-togethers, and never to acknowledge their hurt, let alone her own.

Angus looked again at the woman who had once been so young and convincing.

He had begun to feel his own energy sapped from the time of Cynthia's death, and with it, his ability to withstand Miriam.

As the years slipped by Miriam became more and more driven to mould life into a shape she could manage. Wrestling for control, which began as her protection, was now her lifeblood. And the most important tool in maintaining its flow was her *Itemizations*. These were detailed entries in her notebooks. They were the spring for her river of gossip. Angus knew they kept her happy and they at least kept her attention diverted from him, but at times they contained social dynamite. And despite this bustling sunny day, the thought of Miriam's *Itemizations* sent a cold chill down Angus McGregor's spine.

"Those notebooks are getting thicker by the day," he thought. "They are growing into chunks as unwieldy as

Miriam's hips. Why do I stay with her? I did promise to hang in there until death, I suppose. So why do I now always feel so eaten up and spat out?"

Miriam stopped writing and turned to her husband.

"I'm not sure about that young woman. She's very lax with those children. And her backyard, Angus. It's a shocking mess. If this behaviour keeps up, it will bring the neighbourhood a bad name. We must not let standards drop. To be honest, I can't understand how she can afford to be living here. Look. Look at this. The way she deals with those little children. Come and look at this setup, Angus."

"Must I?" he asked.

"Of course you must. How else will you know what I'm talking about?"

He prised himself out of the chair and walked over to take up the binoculars. As he focused on the house in question, his interest was stimulated by the sight of a naked woman darting into her garden to gather up two young boys.

"You're right, Miriam. This could be construed as a dirty backyard, although I don't mind it so very much."

Miriam snatched the binoculars back and re-focused in time to see a shapely bare bottom disappear inside the back door.

"Oh really," she gasped. "How could you Angus?"

"It was you who asked me to look, Miriam."

For a second his wife glared at him. Then she lifted her head and with a loud huff, dismissed him with the back of her hand. Once more she picked up her notebook.

Scribble scribble. Her beleaguered husband returned to the safety of his chair and ruminated. "I don't know why I go along with it. I could move, I suppose. Find a small place of my own and leave her to her own devices. Then what? I quite like looking out over this lake, this glorious view. Particularly if curvaceous neighbours oblige like that. The girl's probably quite delightful."

*"Tuesday 10:31am: Children taken out to front lawn. Toddler left without supervision for minutes on end. Older boy with garden fork. She reappears and takes toddler off garden. Toddler stumbles over to wheelbarrow. Appears to have fallen into contents. She lifts older child out of tree and retrieves secateurs from toddler. Goes back inside while children remain in garden unsupervised. Toddler starts off down the drive."*

*10:32am: Toddler is rescued from the road - having made its way there once again without supervision. No apparent control on part of mother. She disappears inside leaving children in garden – again.*

*Mission: Must sort out this unusual girl. Don't agree with way she mistreats those children."*

Miriam was oblivious to Angus's treacherous thoughts. Her scribblings over for the moment, she slapped her pen down on the table. The phone was the tool she needed now. She sighed with the weight of neighbourhood responsibility as she moved across the room to pick up the only type of phone she would allow in the house, a landline. She tapped in a number.

"Hello? ... Hello, Carrie? Miriam-McGregor-up-the-road, dear. *Number 73*. Carolyn Smith at the Glade Flats shop told me we had a new entrant in our little spot. She happened to have your number. How are you settling in?"

Her voice dripped sweet-scented oil.

"...Oh, I'm sorry, did I get you out of the shower? Dear, Angus and I were just discussing the fact that it's high time we met you. Have you up here to meet your neighbours and so on. We have a potluck dinner coming up next week. Wednesday, actually. Why don't you join us? ... Oh splendid. We're mostly all organised, but would you like to bring starters? ... Perfect. Soooo looking forward to meeting you. Seven o'clock then. Bye. ... Yes, bye."

"What was all that about? What potluck dinner?" her husband asked.

Miriam dusted off her hands. "Time for a get-together, Angus. Needs must. I'll get to the bottom of what she's all about, just you see."

"Bottom?"

"Oh for heaven's sake, you stupid man. Go outside and do something useful. I have enough to organise without you getting under my feet."

Angus was obedient. The garden escape was a well practiced routine for them both. She liked to think he would go. He was always relieved to have the opportunity to do so.

He was looking forward to the release a pipe would provide. Smoking in the house was outlawed, so he had created a pleasant shrubbery overlooking Glade Heights and the lake that was his alone. Today it was chilly despite the sun. All the better to blow out the unpleasant cobwebs Miriam had woven since breakfast.

The shrubbery was Angus's contrivance. The rest of the garden Miriam controlled, but here Angus had been allowed to plant for silence and release. It was a positive blip in the McGregor domain, and the only grating in its otherwise velvet environment was the fact Miriam called it *The Hidey-hole*. What was it about his wife?

He settled down on the garden seat and drew on his pipe. Perhaps he wouldn't leave Miriam just yet. But one day he just might go. And if he did, it would be for good.

He closed his eyes and turned his head to the sun – if he could just shut out the growing sense of unease.

# CHAPTER TWO
## HIDDEN

Carrie Thompson put her phone down on the bed and dressed quickly. It was kind of her neighbour to call and invite her to a meal, so why was she left feeling quite so disconcerted? She pulled a jersey on over her head and flicked her hair free. For a moment, she stood and sized herself up in the mirror. But her attempt at a smile soon folded into a frown and her shoulders slumped. Perhaps she should call back. Say she had forgotten she had another engagement. But that would do no good, the McGregors would simply ask her another time.

She could hear her young sons playing in the living room and as she moved to go check on them, she managed a quick laugh at herself. She couldn't hide forever.

Jake knelt in a tight huddle with Tom, arranging their pick-up trucks. Carrie bent to give them each a quick hug.

What a relief to have got the lease on the house at Glade Heights. At last the three of them had their haven. She had not been able to endure Craig's treatment any longer, his frightening fierce blows. His storms would gather in a thunderous moment and with little warning he would unleash his lightening temper. She would have been willing to stay, to work things out. If he had only been prepared to move out for a while. Then he could have kept in contact with their sons without all the noise and bustle that clearly set his nerves on a razor edge.

With a shiver Carrie stood up and went to organise a snack for the boys. Craig had wanted no compromise. Her husband had insisted – he would stay and she must stay. The mere mention of her yearning for separation and peace had ignited a terrible violence. When he had finally screamed his threat – he would take the boys away from her where she would never find them – that was the moment steel replaced fear and Carrie decided to act first.

She waited until he was away for a few days, then she took the children herself, to where he could not find them, fearing for their safety as well as her own. It was typical of her, she realised. The impulsive decisions she had made over the years had so complicated her life. This was the right decision, though. Given time she would meet Craig through her lawyer and try to sort the mess out. Meanwhile the peace and beauty of this place promised to restore some sanity and give the children time to recover from the concussion their parents' violent arguments had wrought. Certainly, being in a gated estate gave Carrie an added sense of security.

She stood at the kitchen bench and gazed across the tree tops to the lake. The leaves danced as the wind caught them, obscuring the view for a moment. Then they fell back to let the water sparkle a full smile. At last she felt alive again.

She had made some foolish choices in her life, had some bad luck. But she had also had some wonderful luck. A picture of Astra lit up her mind. How could her parents have called that an unwanted pregnancy? Her loving Astra, so warm and full of hope. They had such different temperaments, she and her daughter. Astra tackled life's problems head on, and not always without anger. Carrie preferred to keep her head low and attempt reconciliation. Perhaps that was why she made such hasty decisions – it helped her escape confrontation. But she had a thing or two to learn from her daughter's approach – Astra would never have put up with Craig for as long as Carrie had.

Shrieks of delight broke out from Jake and Tom, making her turn. She smiled again. Of course, being with Craig had brought her the two boys. Not one but three wonderful children had been born out of difficult times.

Carrie finished buttering the bread. "Would you like an apple, too, you naughty boys? Come on. Time to fuel up."

They rushed to the table, and as she sat and joined in their lively chat she acknowledged to herself it really was time to move on. The invitation to meet the neighbours at the McGregors had to be a good thing.

Back up the road, Miriam had been busy issuing invitations to the potluck dinner. The Holbeins had accepted. Wonderful. That meant the occasion was now a certainty. She just needed two more couples to give it the appearance of an organised party.

From the moment Carrie Thompson had arrived within range of her binoculars Miriam had felt uneasy. How could a casual woman like that care for two small sons? Where was the husband? No. Carrie did not suit the Heights. Miriam needed to meet her, find out more about her and her liberal ways. And a potluck dinner would be the perfect place to start.

Miriam phoned Sally Brimsmead.

"Hello Sally? Miriam McGregor here ... Hello? ... Is anyone there? ... Oh yes, Sally. Miriam McGregor. How are you? It really is time we caught up with your wonderful company ... Quite. Well, Angus and I thought we truly ought to introduce you to Carrie Thompson. She's the new entrant in *Number 12*. You should get to know h... Oh you have? Already? ... I see." Miriam's voice fell slightly then rallied.

"Delightful, isn't she? Well look, it's just that we have organised a neighbourhood potluck dinner for the coming Wednesday. Loads of the neighbourhood coming already. We thought you and James would like to come too. You know, show the Heights flag and that sort of thing. Most of the meal is organised already but perhaps if you did a pudding. Nothing too fattening. Ha-ha! ... What, busy? Oh, I am sorry. Perhaps next time ... Right. Bye for now."

"Stupid woman," Miriam muttered as she thumped the phone down. She scratched the name Brimsmead off her list. One...two...three hard strokes of the pen. "Don't like that husband of hers either. And when I think of how much trouble I went to in order to help settle them into the Heights. Who's next?"

Despite her mutterings about Sally Brimsmead, Miriam struggled for a moment. People perplexed her. She liked it when they arrived in her presence easy to categorise and remain where they belonged. She did not like it when they strayed outside the compartment she assigned them. How close had she come to being taken in by Sally Brimsmead? Sally's true colours had been discovered in the nick of time.

"That Brimsmead woman voted Labour, apparently," she had recently told Angus. "Can you believe it? How appalling. So what if her husband has made money. The man is nothing. He, I'm afraid, is coloured by her ribbons."

Miriam consulted her list once more and continued to call around the neighbours. Her list had grown smaller over the years. Names had not been replaced as it had been rationalised and redrawn. But there were still the stalwarts who, having been wooed into Miriam's web, were too enmeshed to stagger out. At the end of an hour, she had successfully asked the Ryans, the Pattersons – who were going to bring along her sister who was visiting from Italy (rather a coup, Miriam considered) – and Stephen Tiehurst.

"Stephen Tiehurst," Miriam whispered to the room with breathy import. "Dear, dear Stephen. He will show Carrie Thompson the sort of person we welcome around here."

Stephen Tiehurst was the epitome for Miriam. He was polite, had money, good looks, and above all, access to others who had *Names*.

Miriam was keen on *Names*. *Names* lead you to more *Names* and all that knowing *Names* entailed. She was careful never to enquire too closely into Stephen's credentials just in case she found a fault which might compromise her high opinion of his social station. He was, in truth, the one person who overawed her, who evoked an honest emotion in her. Money in this case did indeed override all else. In any event, Miriam was positive his credentials were without blemish. Stephen had, after all, been to a good school.

If Miriam had any genuine claim to social respectability herself, it was that she too had gone to a 'good' school, endowing her, as it did, with some tenuous connections. Possible *Names*. To some extent it was this 'good' schooling that had left her somewhat of a social snob. As the years had passed, snobbery had led Miriam to become more and more a capital C Conservative. And being a capital C Conservative had caused Miriam to become even more of a snob.

Miriam married Angus soon after leaving school. He had been an insurance broker. Of the old style. While their marriage had been challenged by the death of their young daughter and Miriam's consequent controlling behaviour, it had so far remained intact. He worked for the same firm for years, making a respectable living – enough anyway to buy a piece of land at Glade Heights Estate and build a pleasant home for his family. In time he accumulated enough brownie points at work to qualify for a gold watch and a firm handshake when he retired.

He wasn't a bad sort, Angus. Old school. Dependable. But he had allowed his forehead to become well and truly indented by Miriam's increasingly sizeable thumb print.

They were now well into their seventies. And Miriam was very certain of her standing in the community. When being introduced she was always charming. She would hold court, deign to greet people, give them her advice. She would smile at them and, invariably, she would potluck dine them. However, if Miriam was crossed, her retribution could be forbidding – as Sally Brimsmead was already well aware.

This social struggle was how Miriam barricaded herself away from her own painful thoughts. As she isolated her emotional self, so her empathy for others diminished. She had become determined purely on her own ends. She was a proverbial curtain shifter, highly trained in the use of binoculars, an expert at the gathering of dirt. And while she wove her social web around targets and cast her spell about fellow conspirators, at the end of the day the success of her weaving had to be hers alone to enjoy.

For Miriam, it was survival.

Angus had smoked enough pipe and he sauntered back inside. Miriam's scratchy humour still needed a little sandpapering, he noticed, but it had softened enough to tempt him to remain in her presence.

Apparently, Miriam's invitation had now been turned down not only by Sally Brimsmead, but also by the new people next door at *Number 71*. Angus was unsure whether this would be good news or bad news. Miriam preferred it if neighbours accepted an invitation if she proffered one. She considered it easier to control the neighbourhood if the neighbours co-operated in her endeavours.

However, she often told her husband, "While allies are necessary, it is just as important to develop a good base of enemies. *Us* is nothing, Angus, unless you have *Them.*"

Consequently, Angus hoped Miriam's being turned down by *Number 71* would produce a positive result. It would give her the excuse to indulge in a little scandal, and if he were lucky, she was about to share some with him.

"Do you know, Angus, those women in *Number 71* applied to run a massage business from their house. Too busy, she said, to come to potluck dinners. I ask you. They would never have been allowed to go ahead with some project which lowers the tone when I was chair of the Residents Committee. Before you know it, they'll be having the lower socioeconomic classes visiting the Heights. And outside our house. Mark my words. We must be vigilant.

"That will be a job for you in the future, Angus. Needs must. You'll need to monitor how many cars park outside the house. And we need to keep a detailed dossier on who arrives and who leaves and at what times. We'll see about a massage parlour."

"I understood it was to be some sort of sports therapy thing. Isn't that it?" Angus didn't want to disappoint or be disappointed, but there was no getting past the rather more ordinary outcome such a business implied.

"Do you mean to say you knew about this all the time and you didn't say anything to me or attempt to do something about it?"

"I think it's a fairly respectable business, Miriam. What do you imagine might happen?"

Angus was genuinely a little puzzled, but his bemusement acted like flint to ignite his wife's temperamental fire.

She exploded in a mass of irritated air, leaving Angus in no doubt his comments, far from being soothing, were proving provocative in the extreme.

He knew better than to say more. The pursuit would be long and the outcome inevitable. Miriam had achieved successes with this sort of situation before. She knew all the Council pitfalls, most of the Council regulations, and to secure the result she wanted, Miriam could be as tenacious as a pit bull terrier intent on securing a share of the postman's ankle.

Angus was reminded of that poor chap Franklin Mitchell. *Franklin's Tale* he called it. Franklin had moved into a house down the hill. Miriam had been so charming at first. Chummy, in fact. She even paid him to mow their lawns, but that was where the trouble started. His role had changed. He had gone from friend to tradesman, and suddenly he was living too close to Miriam. Before long he was demoted further, from tradesman to one of the great unwashed. As far as Miriam was concerned, he and his frequent visitors had become a menace and they simply had to go.

A couple of weeks of intense *Itemization* followed. Miriam approached Franklin with what she had discovered, though her manner was full of sugar.

"All those dear little people who keep turning up at your house, Franklin. Are they buying spare parts for motorbikes from your garage? What ingenuity."

But to Angus she sneered, "He's running a spare parts business from his garage. How ghastly. We can't have that around here. How do those people get the Heights gate code? He must be handing it out to all and sundry."

She rang the Glade District Council to complain. "No, no, I don't want to cause a fuss, but it's such a shame oil spills on Glade Heights streets are eroding the tarmac so badly."

When, after a number of weeks, no Council inspector arrived to sort Franklin out, Miriam was livid. Taking Angus in tow, she went to the Council in person.

She spoke to the Public Enquiry Clerk. Helpful chap, Angus remembered. Very patient with Miriam as she pointed out that oil spillage was a pollutant and it was particularly unfortunate in a marvellous residential area such as hers.

Determined to imprint her point further, Miriam had leant across his desk, pushing her face forward.

"And when did you last examine Clause 4.9(b)(i) sub-subsection ix of the Glade District Council town plan?"

she asked, her voice growing louder and louder. "I, myself, know it well. And did you know Mr Franklin Mitchell is intent on creating a light industry in a residential area? And when is there going to be an inspection before a major pollution incident happened? And who is your superior, because I am not going to accept the word of some two bit, half-baked, second-rate, clerical nobody?"

This last unladylike crescendo of Miriam's secured capitulation. If she would put her concerns in writing to the Council, he, the exhausted Public Enquiry Clerk, would himself ensure the matter was brought to the attention of the appropriate officer.

"Although I can't promise anything, Mrs McGregor."

"Promise. I don't need your promise young man. I need action."

Miriam had duly transcribed her concerns in writing and action was what she got. It wasn't Franklin's fault the Council inspector had been so keen to know Franklin's business, but it was Franklin's fault Franklin socked him one on the nose and the police had been called.

It transpired Franklin had been growing marijuana in his shed. With lights and everything. Hydroponic whacky backy. With the police involved, that had been that. Franklin had been whisked away from Miriam's domain and had gone to live rent-free for a time at Her Majesty's pleasure.

With his mind full of sympathy for Franklin, Angus retreated to the kitchen.

"Just how is it Miriam can worry an issue to within

an inch of its life," he muttered to himself, "yet remain impervious while the world around her gets torn apart? I hate to think what's in store for that poor young Carrie Thompson down the road now Miriam's chosen to sink her teeth into her."

CHAPTER FOUR
## BALANCE I

While Angus pondered his wife's exploits, next door at *Number 71* Mary Naysmith and her sister, Judith, were busy painting one of their massage rooms. Both had worked as nurses but retrained as masseuses. Judith had been through the marriage-that-didn't-work thing. Mary had never been married. And having watched the disintegration of her sister's marriage from the sidelines, Mary decided she liked her single state of affairs.

They were a practical uncomplicated pair. Together they had bought the house at Glade Heights with money their deceased parents had left them. Here was the perfect setting; a quiet neighbourhood where they could be private and be allowed to get on with life without interruption.

To be able to work from the house was also perfect. The Glade Heights Estate rules said they simply had to follow Council regulations. The Residents Committee had sent a letter of approval. And the Glade District Council had no objection. Such a helpful little chap behind the Public Enquiry desk.

"No undue noise as a consequence of the business," he had told them. "Keep the number of cars outside the house – for the business, I mean – to a minimum. Oh, and could you keep the level of oil spillage to a minimum also."

"Sorry?" Mary had asked, truly puzzled. "The what to a minimum?"

But this was never explained.

Well, noise was not going to feature in their business. Therapeutic massage was a respectable and necessary source of medical relief these days. Quiet and acceptable. And it was administered to one client at a time per sister. Two cars? Not a problem. They were pleased with the soothing results of their decorating, too. The phone call had been the only intrusion on their peace that morning.

"Who was that on the phone, Mares?" Judith asked her sister.

"That McGregor woman from next door."

"Oh, she's all right Mares. Maybe a bit of a busybody at times but she's probably fine. Her husband says hello nicely."

"His problem, young Judith, is that he is married to her. I'm not sure I trust her. I'm not sure why, but I don't. I mentioned the massage thing and there was this stony silence at the end of the phone. I wouldn't put it past her to object."

"But she can't."

"Well, she can. She won't get anywhere 'cause we've already had it all OK'ed. But trust me, we'll be hearing from Council over this."

Judith's contentment was jarred. "What did she want?"

"The old dragon is organising some god-forsaken potluck dinner. Apparently to introduce Carrie Thompson to the neighbours. I told her we don't do potluck dinners."

"Mar-y."

"It's all right sis, I was pleasant enough. Feel sorry for Carrie, though."

As Mary spoke, her roller strokes of paint darted all over the place. She didn't let on to Judith, but Miriam McGregor had touched a raw nerve.

"Do you think we should warn her?" Judith asked.

"Who?"

"Carrie Thompson. You know. We met her, remember, down by the lake. Not Miriam's sort at all. Do you think we should tell her Miriam does seem to be inordinately interested in other people's business?"

"Won't do her any good and she may be in with a chance if she gets on side with Miriam. Mind you, she's rather good looking and Miriam won't take kindly to that husband of hers enjoying Carrie's company – as he is bound to."

Mary added an extra flourish to the wall and got down off the ladder. As she brushed her hair away from her eyes, she smeared a long streak of Wild Rice paint across her cheek. It made her sister laugh.

"War paint, now, is it?"

And Mary shrugged back in good humour. "Idiot. Come on, I've had enough. Let's go for a walk."

The sisters packed up their gear and headed into the sunshine. As they passed their neighbour's house they could not avoid seeing Miriam inside the sitting room window, binoculars to her eyes.

"What do you think she's doing?" Judith asked.

"I hate to think. We must make absolutely certain the blinds we put up on their side are impregnable. I'm telling you, Judith, that woman's trouble."

They walked off down the road, enjoying the rush of

wind past their faces. Sunshine does wonders to lighten the soul. Sunshine coupled with wind makes it radiate, and they, two women of the elements, were not about to fret their way around the Glade Heights circuit. They upped their pace and headed for the lake, their troubles left well behind them.

Miriam McGregor flicked her binoculars around. She watched the Naysmith sisters disappear down the road, then dropped her surveillance equipment on the table and called out to her husband.

"Just going out for a quick breath of fresh air, Angus."

She sneaked out the front door before he had a chance to ask where she was going and made a bee line for *Number 71*, arriving at the gate breathless. She stopped briefly, bent well backwards to cast a few furtive glances left and right, and scuttled up the drive and across the lawn to her neighbour's windows. The view she had of the room the sisters were decorating was excellent, and she made mental notes of its size and probable use, which she would formalise as an *Itemization* once she got home. The colour of the room didn't immediately suggest itself. Had she been expecting bordello red? This was a disappointment. It was muted, quite peaceful.

Miriam wanted to find something. She darted around the back of the house unearthing nothing more noisome than a compost bin full of fresh scraps. The unpleasant hot smells that greeted her as she lifted the lid made her nose wrinkle and she let the lid fall back. Quickly she bent and wiped her hands on the grass to scrape off any traces of compost, then bustled back up her own path and darted through her front door.

"Where have you been, Miriam? You look hot and bothered," her husband asked.

Miriam had the grace to look a little sheepish. "I've been to check out that den of licentiousness," she panted.

"What? Den of where?"

"Next door. At *Number 71*. I'm worried about that business, Angus. We cannot have our property undermined by two snips of girls. Leave me in peace, will you, while I go and make an *Itemization*. Then I want you to take some mail to the post for me."

As Miriam made to pick up her notebook she was stopped short. Another movement in the lower part of Glade Heights had caught her eye. She snatched up the binoculars. A furniture truck worked its way down the road and came to a halt opposite Carrie Thompson's house.

"More new blood, Angus," Miriam said, unable to keep the excitement out of her voice.

Without taking her eyes off the activity below, she flapped her hand behind her to ensure Angus did not interrupt. "Moving into the house opposite that irresponsible mother. Could be useful. I wonder who they are?"

"Surely you can't make out any details, even with that snooper glass of yours?"

"Don't be so rude." She silenced him again with another dismissive wave. "You are just as interested as I am. Admit it.

"Oh look. There goes a bed. It's a king size. A couple then. Doesn't look like madly attractive furniture. No antiques, I shouldn't think. I can see a man giving instructions, Angus. Can't tell whether he might be the new resident. How on earth they'll fit all that stuff into that house, I do not know."

"I'm sure you'll let them know how if they haven't worked it out by the end of the week."

Miriam lowered the binoculars and spun round. "Really, Angus, I don't know what's eating you these days. You used to be on your knees for information. Now all you can do is make unfortunate remarks. And, heaven forbid, even disapproving ones. You'd be nowhere without me you know. There would be nothing to lift that boring mind of yours."

"Steady on. The only boring thing about my life is you boring in."

"Well – you know if you don't like the way I run things, Angus, you should just leave."

"And well I might."

With his courageous stance stared to an end by his wife's searing gaze, Angus turned to take himself back to the garden. He fired one last brave round.

"You know what, Miriam, I've always obliged and yet this is the way you treat me. If you want letters posted," he defied her, "you can damned well do it yourself."

Miriam was not phased by this exchange for long. Angus had been acting strangely – going through some late-life retirement crisis, probably. What did it matter? She was the powerhouse behind the battle-faring, the general in charge of the forces. He was just a minor foot soldier, tired and out of step and quite capable of being kept in order.

Much more interesting was the drama unfolding this sparkling morning. In tune with the day's vitality, numerous targets had yawned, stretched and revealed themselves. Might not all be problems. Could be an ally unpacking itself from that removal van. And close to home there was a neat little diversion developing at *Number 71* that would fuel her controlling spirit with just the right amount of drive she needed to tackle Carrie Thompson. For there was no doubt, Carrie Thompson was a considerable problem.

Ah yes, it was a joyous day indeed. Miriam picked up her notebook. Time for some energising *Itemizations* before lunch, then what could offer a more invigorating afternoon than a bedding session in the garden?

It was time to till some dirt.

CHAPTER FIVE

## POTLUCK I

Angus watched Potluck Wednesday draw up faster than a cat's claw. There was much to look forward to – the scandalised exchange of local information; enough guests to help him disguise from his wife his generous quaffings of wine.

The spectre of Miriam at full calculating throttle was not so appealing, however. Miriam's potluck dinners were always entertaining. But quite how they entertained varied. On this occasion Miriam would be intent on discovering truths about Carrie Thompson. And knowing Miriam's track record, he was concerned she might end up causing the girl harm.

As he moved about the room doing his wife's bidding he recalled an earlier potluck dinner. *The Tale of the Raw Recruit* was how he thought of it. It was the first time he had been aware of a rather vicious side to Miriam that, up to that point, she had managed to hide – even from him.

She had met the Raw Recruit at some mayoral function in town. She was called Miriam-Smith-but-do-call-me-Mimi. Angus supposed the name in common got them talking and Miriam decided Mimi might be a useful aide in the waging of her community crusades without amounting to competition. Mimi was on the small side, thin even, with a very tight mouth and straight, cropped, unadorned hair. No buttocks to speak of, Angus recalled.

"Such plain people make ideal adjutants, Angus," Miriam had told him. "Good at *Itemization*. Mark my words."

She invited Mimi to a potluck dinner. The evening started well enough. Everyone was plied with alcohol and the conversation gathered apace as Miriam rallied the forces to fight for the exclusion of day-trippers from the lake shore below Glade Heights Estate.

"If we can organise a convenient no-parking zone, outsiders won't want to visit and consequently won't crowd out our beach," she told them. "We must keep the rabble out."

As the evening wore on, Mimi, stirred by General Miriam's fight and Angus's generous ministrations of alcohol, had become loquacious. Each time Miriam rose to conduct, Mimi would over-reach her rank and grab Miriam's baton, spilling out her opinions and counter arguments like there was no tomorrow.

While the other guests had been oblivious to the dark clouds hovering over Miriam's forehead, Angus could not help but notice the brewing storm. When it was time for the guests to go, Mimi was given the last of the smirching farewells.

"So good of you to come, Mimi," Miriam had cooed. "Sample our little abode. Ha-ha!"

"Thank you so much Miriam. Really too kind. I tell you what…"

The wine had emboldened Mimi. She tiptoed so she could be eyeball to eyeball with Miriam, and with her arm half-wrapped over her hostess's shoulder, she creased her brow.

"…don't you worry your pretty little head about the next get together," she stage-whispered with eye-watering breath. "I'll organise it. They are fun, aren't they?"

The second the door was shut on Mimi, the indignation that had pustulated just beneath Miriam's skin all evening burst over Angus like an erupting pimple.

"What a nerve," she cried. "How she ever imagines she'll succeed in life, Angus, is a mystery. Did you hear her? The audacity. And at my soirée. Mine! Never again, Angus. Mark my words. I'll never speak to her again."

"She'll hear you, Miriam," he whispered with a look of genuine concern.

"Hear me?" Miriam raised her voice higher. "The woman's not heard a word from anyone all night. How dare she think she can run a campaign like this. No skills. No experience. Just the look of her puts you off."

Despite her criticism, the following day Miriam expected the phone to ring.

"The least the ungrateful woman could do is ring to say thank you," she complained to her husband that evening.

"Perhaps she overheard your – um – words," he suggested.

"What nonsense. Ring her up, Angus. If you want an excuse, ask her if she saw where that knife of mine went – you know, the one we had out at the bar-b-que. Can't find it anywhere. It will give her a chance to do what she's not had the decency to initiate herself."

Despite her seething contempt for Mimi's behaviour, Miriam still needed to be acknowledged as the social superior. So Angus did as he was asked and made the call.

"Angus here, Mimi. Miriam was just wondering if you happened to know what happened to her bar-b-que knife last night."

"Her knife? Oh I know where that went, Angus," had been Mimi's clipped and distant reply. "Tell her I found it in my back where she left it."

And that had been the last they had seen of the Raw Recruit.

Angus winced as he remembered his wife's crude display of emotion. It was so puzzling. Clearly beneath that exterior of hale embrace Miriam carried a terrible resentment. She hid it admirably – perhaps she even concealed it from herself. But it was there. A silent disturbing animus.

He shivered and went to place a few requisite bowls of peanuts on side-tables in the sitting room. The room was buffed into high polish. It was Miriam's 'best room' where she could display her ornate trophies. She wore it a little like her best clothes to show herself off to best advantage.

Angus did a quick check before strolling outside for a reflective smoke. He wondered what Carrie would be like, what Miriam could possibly have taken such an exception to.

At that moment her confident warble broke out from

the kitchen, destroying his brief moment of contentment and warning of looming conflict.

Oblivious to the winds of war, Carrie finished brushing her hair and checked herself in the mirror. She had chosen a simple stylish dress to cover her slender frame. Her attempt at a confident toss of her head didn't help, however. Her face clouded. Why she had not cancelled this evening she couldn't explain, and it was now too late to back out.

In the living room Jake sat straight-backed on his teenage babysitter's lap. She held a book up for him to look at, but he wanted nothing to do with it. He was much more interested her bright green hair.

Carrie smiled at them both. "Thanks, Tracey. I won't be late."

She collected a basket off the coffee table, which contained the contribution she had thrown together for the night's dinner.

"Tom will probably sleep through now. And Jake – you're to be in bed in half an hour. Right. Come on, big hug. Don't let him convince you otherwise, Tracey. Bed as soon as the story's finished."

With her basket balanced on one hip, she crouched down, steadying herself for a brief and boisterous hug. She managed to get in her own affectionate squeeze before he darted back to the entertainment on the sofa.

"We'll do just fine, Mrs Thompson. I love looking after the boys. Have fun."

Mrs Thompson. That's a laugh, she thought. No Mr Thompson around any longer though, is there? Poor kids. Carrie had decided to walk up the road to her neighbour's dinner party. It would do her good to get the fresh air, and she might need some fortification if the evening got too unbearable. Better she walk home.

She climbed the hill effortlessly and paused to look back to the water. Off on the lake's far edge the fine ink line of strengthening wind spread wider. Nearer Glade Heights, lighter wind shifts ruffled the lake into a patchwork of slates and ice-blues. She squeezed herself. This was what represented her take on life, not that besieged and brutal existence she had experienced with Craig. Yes, impulsive she might be. Impetuous. But she was also an optimist. How lucky. To find such a place as this. All she had to do was keep her head down and remain an obliging enough neighbour and develop some new friendships. Perhaps Mary and Judith Naysmith would be at the dinner. She had liked them the one time they had met. It wouldn't hurt to meet some of the locals. She might even make some good friends.

It was dusk by the time Carrie walked up the McGregor pathway. She stiffened a little as she took in the garden. It seemed to have been designed so the plants could be disciplined, reprimanded if they grew too loosely; a statement of curbing and edging and confinement. Marigolds manned the front line, their petals bending in supplication in the gloom. Behind them, serried rows of portulaca plants had begun to break rank and were letting their mauves wander through the gold. Carrie giggled. She half expected to see a municipal floral clock ticking in the circular garden nearer the house. Instead she found the dutiful swirls and whirls of pansies and scarlet salvia. The most remarkable thing about bedding plants of this kind, she thought as she stopped to stare at them for a moment, was that people actually liked them. Perhaps they brought colour into lives that otherwise lacked it. For Carrie, their limited height and limited age-span was depressing.

"Limited imagination," she told them out loud, then cursed quietly.

Why did she feel so uncomfortable about the evening? Miriam had been friendly enough on the phone, if rather organising. The trouble was, it was risky to become too involved in the neighbourhood. If somehow Craig found out she was here – but that did not bear thinking about.

She looked up at the McGregors' house and felt a wave of panic. It was too late to turn away. The curtains had already shifted and her arrival had been noted.

# CHAPTER SIX

## UNSEEMLY INTEREST

Carrie allowed herself to be sucked up the McGregors' crazy paving to the front door. As she pressed the door bell, a frenzied chiming of *Home, Home on the Range* rang out. Yet, despite seeming to be anticipated, it was some time before footsteps were heard and the door was flung open.

"You must be Carrie. Come in, dear." Miriam's voice rang out like the door bell.

Carrie managed to smile and hand over her contribution. "It's good of you to ask me."

"Not at all. We're a very matey group around here. Help each other out and that sort of thing. Thank you for bringing this leee-tle contribution. Every morsel is a welcome stab at the outside world. Sign of solidarity and so on."

Miriam lifted the cover on Carrie's basket and sniffed. "What have we here? Rice crackers and baba ganoush dip. Never mind, dear. We'll be able to bolster that lot up in no time."

Miriam's sting had the required effect and Carrie was

rendered speechless as she was guided inside.

"We live elevated, here, to command a marvellous view of everything Glade Heights has to offer," Miriam began, and applied an incessant chat-chat-chatter that continued to silence Carrie as she was led up the stairs and into the McGregors' formal sitting room.

As they entered, a pharynx of expectant eyes challenged her. Her heart sank. She was to be on show. She tried to take it all in, the dazzle of wood polish, the porcelain figurines, the incongruous mix of paintings chosen, she found herself thinking, for their colour coordination rather than any intrinsic good taste. But she was not distracted by the furnishings for long. Miriam was demanding her attention with a most unusual introduction.

"John and Maisie Holbein – *Number 25* down the way not far from you, Carrie. Maisie's the worker. John is in charge of their leee-tle abode these days, aren't you John, but we all understand why. And from *Number 46*, although we won't hold it against you, will we, Peter and Helen, ha-ha! – Peter and Helen Ryan – actually it's a dear little house. And these are our local can't-do-withouts, Mike and Patricia Patterson from two doors up, and Patricia's sister, Maria Holworthy – you're living in Italy, aren't you dear. So nice. You must pop in any time you feel the need to breathe in a little culture, by the way."

It was a rapid delivery, and there was more to come.

"And this is my husband Angus. This is Carrie Thompson, everyone, who has recently moved into our glorious little nook. You'll find us a modest but happy group, Carrie. No pretensions. Just honest good taste and behaviour. And now, Carrie dear, tell us all about yourself."

Carrie was stage struck. What on earth could she say?

While she was sorting out her thoughts and finding her voice, her modest and unpretentious neighbours took the opportunity to gather in a tight semi-circle about her, tilting forward so as not to miss a word.

"Um. I come from poor but honest parents," she ventured and gave a quick laugh. But instead of amusing them, her observation seemed simply to cause them to lean in further.

"Ahh…it's very nice at Glade Heights, isn't it Mrs McGregor? I must say I am very happy to be here."

"Miriam, dear. Call me Miriam. So where was home before this?"

Her neighbours leant in yet a little closer. And as eighteen eyes drilled in and nine mouths tweaked themselves into lines of unseemly interest, Miriam wedged herself in so close Carrie thought for a moment she might gag on her hostess's intrusive breath. She feigned an itch on her cheek in order to brush her hand across the front of her nose, and managed to stifle her irritation. She loathed this kind of social interrogation. Had no wish to relate any of her personal history, not to a group of strangers. She stood her ground.

"Oh, it wasn't nearly as nice. Honestly." She offered a thin smile, hoping to distract.

"I meant, dear, was it north of here, perhaps?"

"No, not north."

"Oh. Then south?"

"Ah, no. No, as it happens, not south." Carrie was unsure how long she could hold out. She enjoyed learning about others. But this kind of curiosity was surely not healthy. Above all, she must not let these people know where she had been living before. The next thing, they would find out about Craig and tell him where he could find her.

It was Patricia Patterson who first returned to the perpendicular, having apparently registered Miriam's growing impatience.

"A town not far from here, then; where you lived?" Patricia asked Carrie with great self-assurance.

But it was hardly a skilled attempt at information gathering and it provided Carrie's escape route. She immediately turned to Maria Holworthy, looking for support from the only other outsider.

"Not as far as you, of course, Maria. How long have you been back in New Zealand?"

And just like that, Miriam's moment was lost. Short of asking for Carrie's last physical address, which even for Miriam and the potluck crew would be awkward, nothing else could now provide the information Miriam desired.

Carrie ignored the look Miriam shot Patricia. The poor woman withdrew in a fluster, while Carrie turned to concentrate on Maria. As a polite conversation struck up between the two single women, the others fell back on the conversations interrupted by Carrie's entrance. Out of the corner of her eye, she could see Angus moving amongst his guests, filling glasses and bestowing his hopeful little smiles. She felt his eyes land on her as he made his way closer and she turned to smile at him. To her amusement his drinks tray tilted for an alarming moment before he collected himself and took up the apparent invitation to join her and Maria.

"Maria, would you like a top-up?" he asked.

Maria smiled and held her glass out. "Thanks, Angus. Carrie was just saying she has a child at university already. That's hard to believe, Carrie. You look so young."

"Thanks. I wish I felt it."

Angus expressed genuine interest. "You have a child at university, Carrie? But your boys aren't even at school yet."

"Oh. I didn't know you knew I had sons, Mr McGregor."

He looked at his feet for a moment and cleared his throat. "Call me Angus, Carrie, please. But your older child – boy or a girl?"

"Astra? She's a girl."

"Who's a girl?" Miriam appeared out of nowhere and shoved Angus aside.

"Carrie has a daughter at university, Miriam," Angus told her as he steadied the drinks tray.

"Good heavens, Carrie," Miriam's shrill voice pierced the room, immediately silencing the other guests. "You must have been a child yourself when she was born."

Even Angus was moved to look embarrassed. He coughed to divert attention, but Miriam was now unable to quell her curiosity.

She ploughed on. "How old were you, then?"

Carrie, assessing the danger she was in, fortified herself with a sip of wine. How was she going to get out of this one?

"Well, put it this way," she ventured with a weak smile, hoping at least to disguise the answer. "As I said, Astra's at university, already."

Miriam slowly lifted her left eyebrow and cast a narrow sideways glance at Angus.

"Oh heavens," she cried. "Do excuse me a moment, everyone. I think something's burning. Ha-ha!"·

Carrie watched, fascinated, as Miriam dashed out to the kitchen and scooped up a notebook. She turned back to continue her conversation with Maria, but the oppression she had felt since her arrival began to seep deeper. Nor was her ability to concentrate made any easier by seeing her 'leee-tle contribution' now being passed around the guests, the rice crackers removed and replaced by sculptured crostini, her dip redecorated in swathes of lemon slices and parsley. How could she have let herself into such a lion's den?

She thought suddenly of Craig. He had instilled in her the same awful anticipation. Everything seemed so perfectly civilised at the moment, but she knew only too well; the storm was not far behind.

# CHAPTER SEVEN

## STEWING THE BREW

In the kitchen Miriam trembled. She stared out the window, out past her reflection and into the night. Her body lifted to the thrill. There was more to this girl than had met even the lens of her binoculars. There was no way she was fit to be a mother. Not only was she on her own – what was the girl up to having babies in this thoughtless way – but she had a *Past*. A *Past*! Having a *Past* was almost more remarkable to Miriam than having a *Name*.

She took a long savouring gulp of wine and let it marinate her imagination. These were rich pickings, indeed, and she allowed the heady mix of social spice and wine to mull and intoxicate for many more minutes before she was stirred sufficiently to go back into the sitting room.

With a clap of her hands Miriam summoned her guests to the meal.

"Let's eat on our laps. I always feel it gives a picnic atmosphere. So relaxed."

"And uncomfortable," her husband muttered under his breath.

Angus was right. Far from loosening up, Miriam's potluck guests helped themselves to food and went to sit stilted and mostly mute on the edge of their chairs. Plates perched. Glasses precarious on the McGregors' too-piled pink carpet. Short sorties into conversation were made in turn by different members of the party but they were weak attempts to disguise the embarrassment that comes with too much silence during a meal. There was no relief until Miriam had sorted out everyone else, begun her own meal, and taken over the conversation once more.

"We've had to start without dear Stephen, I'm afraid. He's obviously got caught up in some important decision making and I suspect he won't be able to make it at all now. Such a success that man. So clever."

Until now, Maisie Holbein had remained inconspicuous. She had known Miriam long enough to know never to pronounce to the general gathering if Miriam was holding forth. But the mention of Stephen Tiehurst's name was too much temptation and she threw caution to the wind.

"Oh what a shame, Miriam. I do love it when Stephen can attend our little soirées. He makes them so worthwhile."

No one seemed to notice Maisie's apparent slight, not even Miriam, who was so concerned to claim the soirées as *her* soirées she failed to notice Maisie's suggestion that not even Miriam might be worthwhile company.

"My soirées I think you mean Maisie dear. Yes, he does enhance our community, doesn't he? When he first came I told him so. 'Stephen,' I remember saying to him, 'It is such a pleasure to have someone of your calibre arrive at Glade Heights.'

"Not one person of any moment had moved in for years. We were quite beginning to despair."

"But Miriam, I think you'll find we moved in only a few months or so before Stephen," Maisie exclaimed, grasping too late the flaw in her remark and shrinking as far into the background as the taut grandmother chair she sat on would allow.

"Ah, so you did indeed, Maisie." Miriam glanced with dark and previously-discussed understanding at her husband before reclaiming the conversation.

"Now, getting back to my dear friend, Stephen," she continued, "I hear his company is doing extraordinarily well. Such a clever man. So very successful."

As Miriam held court, Carrie relaxed a little, pleased to be no longer the focus of attention. She even felt at ease enough to express an interest in the conversation. "Who's this you are talking about?" she asked.

"Good heavens, Carrie. Surely you know his name?" Miriam gave a lilting laugh. The others, too, looked at Carrie with surprise.

"Although, come to think of it, your circles probably wouldn't cross, would they?" Miriam continued. "Stephen is our neighbour and friend. Stephen Tiehurst. Owner and chairman (need I say it, ha-ha!) of Tiehurst Industries."

"Oh," was all Carrie offered.

Miriam rattled on with an ill-concealed smirk.

"It will be a pity if you don't get to meet him, Carrie. But then, perhaps you might feel a little awkward. He's not intimidating, you understand, but meeting someone of his standing can be a little overwhelming, can't it?"

Carrie glanced at the others, wondering if they too

thought Miriam didn't seem entirely balanced. But they appeared unphased. And as Miriam harped on, Carrie felt herself slipping into some sort of echo chamber.

She listened to the conversation, but felt removed, not able to take part. Everyone was so concentrated on Miriam. What was it about her? She exercised some odd control over these people, yet she was so thin on pleasantries and compliments. With the exception, perhaps, of her remarks about Stephen Tiehurst, all anyone ever seemed to receive was a stark or, if they were lucky, neatly camouflaged tongue lashing. What rewards could they possibly receive from attending her functions if this was how they panned out?

It reminded her again of her own entrapment by Craig. He had held sway in a similar fashion. He beguiled her into marriage, not letting her see his bitterness until she was cornered. Only a mother's keen instinct to help her children survive allowed her finally to break free. Like Carrie in her marriage, these too doey-eyed guests looked hopelessly locked into their relationship with Miriam.

The evening began to suffocate her. She was keen to make friends, but if it meant she was to be interrogated and made to conform to this obtrusive potluck formula, she was better to keep her distance – starting then and there. Suddenly, she just wanted to leave; to rush down Miriam's stairs, out the door, and be gone. And with the possible arrival of the celebrated neighbour, her desire to leave was made even more urgent.

Carried waited until she felt she had eaten sufficient to avoid appearing rude, and after a studied glance at her watch, she rose.

"Help. Is that the time? I'm so sorry Mrs... I mean, Miriam. I've not been able to get my usual babysitter tonight so I'll need to go back and rescue the young girl who's looking after my sons. You'll have to excuse me."

"But you've only just arrived," Miriam told her. "We can't have you leave now."

"I'm so sorry," Carrie apologised again. "It isn't very easy with young children. I'm sure you are all aware."

"One last drink, perhaps?" Angus offered.

"Thanks, Angus, no. But thank you both very much for asking me to meet everyone."

The group watched Carrie with critical eyes and muttered their cued goodbyes.

"Please don't worry about coming to the door, Miriam. I can see myself out."

Miriam was handing Carrie her plate.

"Oh good heavens, dear. That would not do at all."

As Miriam turned with Carrie to go downstairs, the calm was rent by the McGregors' cacophonous doorbell chiming the arrival of the famous last guest.

"Stephen!" the women all chorused.

"Carrie, you cannot go now, surely?" Maisie asked, her face alight with anticipation.

But Carrie simply smiled her determination and followed her hostess down the stairs.

Miriam opened the door, throwing her arms out in a welcome of large embrace. There on the doorstep standing tall, dark, and unquestionably handsome was a man of about 40. It was inevitable he would be looking at least a little attractive, Carrie thought as she stole a glance at him.

He was wearing well-tailored suit trousers, and while the suit jacket had been discarded in favour of a more casual sweater, his dress still looked crisp and assured. His air of confidence was only a little dented by the packet of Sara Lee apple crumble he was carrying.

Carrie felt a moment of regret that she was leaving. He looked so normal. What, she wondered, was he doing at an event like this? How would he cope with that lot upstairs?

"Stephen!" Miriam strode across Carrie's reflections. "How simply wonderful you could make it. I'm afraid our guest of honour is leaving just as you arrive. Can't be helped. One of those little things. Not organised enough, Carrie dear, were you? Carrie Thompson, mother of two little ones and a much older other, this is Stephen Tiehurst, chairman of Tiehurst Industries, second largest plastics company in the country, ha-ha!"

Carrie thanked her hostess once more, averted her eyes as she garbled hello and goodbye, and, giving him no opportunity to respond, slipped past the bemused man on the doorstep. As she did so, Miriam grabbed Stephen by the elbow and bustled him inside. Carrie could still make out his puzzled question as they started up the stairs.

"Who did you say that was, Miriam?"

"The new woman. Carrie Thompson. Honestly Stephen, not worth throwing a potluck dinner for. Very odd girl. And she has two small children and no husband. And she has an older child. Waster I would say. Drain on the community. Bit of a surprise."

"A surprise indeed," was the last she heard before Stephen was swallowed up by Miriam's sugared biddings.

"You fool," Carrie chastised herself as she fled down the McGregors' path. "What did I let myself into that for. Oh – Miriam is awful. I must have been mad not to see that lot coming."

She slipped her shoes off and ran without stopping until at last the sight of her home brought her up short. She paused to collect herself. Here was her house, the one she had rented for herself and her sons. And here it was sitting quiet and undisturbed, its lights beckoning with a warm glow.

Breathing deeply, she let her anger spend itself. The sight of her sons would restore her sanity. Her boys. Slowly Carrie's pragmatism asserted itself. What did people like Miriam McGregor matter? She'd been kind enough to invite her to meet the 'gang', but they were not her types. She would take little notice of Miriam in future. But fancy Stephen Tiehurst turning up. He must have thought she was mad taking off like that. What would she do if he got in touch?

"Tackle it if it comes, Carrie," she advised herself out loud. "He may not have even recognised you. After all, it's been years."

She let herself into the house, calling out to her babysitter as she did so.

"Gosh. You gave me a fright Mrs T. You're home early."

"Yes, Tracey. More 'last' than 'potluck' was that supper. Didn't think I should hang around for the betrayal."

Back chez McGregor a purposeful hum vibrated about the kitchen. Miriam was producing coffee for her guests. She placed her special sweets platter on the kitchen table. The evening was a triumph and she would reward her guests.

First she opened the 'good' cupboard and, having extricated the matching creamer and sugar bowl, she filled the bowl with multi-coloured sugar crystals. Next she opened a cupboard above the bench and chose a packet of liqueur chocolates that had been set aside for an important occasion. These she tipped into a dish. She considered the dashing match of the dish with the sugar crystals, then took out the coffee pot. Her hand hovered for a moment above the jar of her best coffee grounds, then reached instead for the jar of instant coffee.

"There's a limit, after all," she muttered.

Miriam was satisfied her guests found Carrie odd. Didn't understand their code or what was proper behaviour for one of her 'Dos'. And yet, without Carrie the evening would not have proved a success.

If Carrie had been wondering what gave her neighbours pleasure from these gatherings, here was her answer. It was the opportunity to disapprove, to indulge in some good old-fashioned bitchiness. Apart from Maria Holworthy, who had been in a state of happy oblivion all evening, Miriam's guests were suitably intrigued. Carrie departing early was a decided lapse in etiquette, but at the same time they had been impatient for her to leave so they would get to hear Miriam's summary of the new arrival.

This was the reason they attended these dinners. The reward they got for enduring Miriam's potluck productions and her sharp tongue was the gossip. Gossip was food for the soul.

Once they had their coffee in hand, those left of the party were able to summarise the earlier part of the evening to the satisfaction of everyone present. Angus was inclined to be generous towards Carrie. New, young, in an unfamiliar environment. Miriam was censorious.

"You need to read the signs, Angus. The girl is not really the right type for this neighbourhood. She could prove a bit of a menace."

"The word *menace* is very definite, Miriam. Is that quite what you mean?" Stephen Tiehurst asked with a tolerant smile.

"Oh, dear Stephen." Miriam flashed a rich liqueur-chocolate smile back at him. " You're such a dear, you would be kind. But you haven't met her. It's a woman thing. I don't think you'll understand."

Maisie Holbein added her wholehearted agreement. "And I thought she was rather rude, don't you think? Not wanting to share anything about herself. Not normal."

Despite his late arrival, Stephen, too, soon excused himself, Miriam sympathising with his need to attend to important business issues before bed. The others exhibited less willingness to abandon the gossip, but in time all curiosity was satisfied and the McGregors were at last free to conduct their own more intimate dissections.

Angus closed the door on the last guest and went back up the stairs to the kitchen. He found his wife at the sink, scrubbing hard at the final dish. She was on the attack.

"What's happening to you, Angus," she led straight in, spraying him with suds as she thrust the dish mop in his direction. "You're losing your grip."

"I thought the girl was all right."

"Look. We simply cannot allow any chinks in our armour. Let that girl stay in our district and the next thing we'll have a whole lot of beneficiaries and lay-abouts moving in."

"How do you know she's a beneficiary? You're not normally quite so fierce about newcomers, Miriam."

"Look at her, for goodness sake. Three children, no husband, probably different fathers. No job. You and I are paying for that woman to sit about the place, Angus. Those sort of people ought to be out earning a living instead of having child after child. It's not good enough."

"She might have a job," he ventured.

Miriam just snorted her disbelief.

Then her eyes caught fire. "This is a marvellous situation. Can't you see it? We have these two massage parlour women behind us. Need to get on with that by the way. Have the Council out. Need for *Itemizations*. Cars started arriving this week."

She stopped for a quick breath.

"Then we have this Thompson girl. Full scale battle on our flank. I'm telling you, Angus, this is marvellous. We're going to be able to fight the war on two fronts. Two fronts. It's the ultimate."

# CHAPTER EIGHT

# GATED

The next day cracked another Glade corker. Restorative. Embracing. Carrie put the unfortunate events of the previous night behind her. There were much more important things in her life than worrying about the braying Miriam McGregor. This was the kind of positive day the garden deserved, and to show just how deserved, she rummaged about in her still-unpacked boxes to find her rusty old gardening fork.

With her boys in tow, she went outside to rid the garden of its weeds. This was a favourite therapy. Turning the soil was good for the soul. It aerated the mind. Released a little of the anxiety that tied her in knots for so many of her waking hours.

Jake and Tom played boisterous games in the yard behind her. An occasional shriek interrupted her industry, and she extricated one or the other from their momentary agony before returning to kneel amongst the weeds. It was surrender to the mundane and it felt wonderful.

Sometimes she longed for a release from her motherly

duty. Not that she didn't accept the responsibility. She was passionate about her sons. But the unrelenting pressure of solo-motherhood was something she was very familiar with. It was like a weight placed on cheese – designed to reduce and squash; drain and age.

She thought of Astra. Lovely, lithe, mysterious Astra. Carrie had so much more energy when her daughter was born. A young mother full of idealism, she coped so much better. Carrie had never asked for support from Astra's father. She had done it all, the caring, determined her own father would not be proven right about her shattered prospects. And Astra had grown into a beautiful young woman. Carrie should have left it at that – Astra and Carrie. No more children. But her fierce independence made for loneliness, isolation, and Craig had been so appealing when he first turned up, so much the caring father figure.

She dug deep around a dock, diverted by how satisfying it was to prise its deep-seated root free from the soil. Craig was a good businessman – they were good at business together. She had been provided with the kind of life she had not been able to afford until then. And the work was rewarding, building the business, learning so many new skills herself. She did not regret any of that. Now her sons were her lifeline.

She could not bear to think of how her marriage had deteriorated. Craig morphed from the level and pleasant man she married into someone violent and out of control. She didn't lay blame on him, because she didn't think he was capable of helping himself. She just didn't want to be pummelled any longer.

How well Carrie knew what it was to be battered. For so long she was trapped in an emotional prison, the violence only a small portion of the problem. For a number of years she thought herself in love with Craig, couldn't do without him. But as time went by the violence eroded the love. Should she stay; should she go? In the end she realised it was going to be execution whichever choice she made, so what difference would it make if she did leave? The hurt would be as great with or without him.

Recognising how much harm was being done to Tom and Jake finally released her. Now, as she knelt stabbing at her garden she considered herself lucky. So many women never find the exit from that kind of control. The potluck dinner flashed through her mind. So many people never find the exit.

Carrie stared at the garden. Some celine had become hopelessly entangled with clover and grass. She couldn't bear to dig the weeds out for fear of losing the flower's dainty presence, and she sat back on her haunches, considering the complications life tended to weave.

Her lawyer's letter worried her. "...communication from your husband's lawyer. They are justified in wishing to establish contact with your sons. You may have to press charges for assault if you are wanting to convince the courts he is a threat to you all."

Carrie knew she couldn't put off instructing him any longer. The situation was not going to disappear, it would have to be faced. She would suggest they buy just a little more time. The previous night's dinner at the McGregors had delivered a surprising result. The fear that her neighbours might somehow facilitate Craig finding out where she lived energised her to want resolve the problem of her marriage peacefully. Perhaps Craig would be reasonable in the end and they could manage a half-respectable divorce. She would rather not have him charged with assault. Not that. He needed help, not threats of that kind.

She dropped a celine flower into her hand and studied it. The tickle on her skin turned her thoughts to Stephen Tiehurst. She had been thinking about him in the delicious half-sleep of first waking. Imagining what it would be like to wake up and have him there beside her. Her hand tipped to let the flower float down to the garden, then she dug her nails into the earth; felt a flush of satisfaction as a long runner of clover gave up its ground without a fight. She tossed it on the pile of rubbish she was creating. He's not lost his appeal, she smiled to herself. How sad life is such opportunities are lost. Probably he would find her haggard and undesirable these days – if, of course, he even recognised her.

They had been so young, but so in love. A gorgeous union of rich prospects and easy friendship. She had even thought they would marry, but life took a different turn when he went to university. Look at how his career had blossomed. She was glad he had gone on to his big things, but not even time, nor the unmitigated pain of her recent flight from Craig could block her memory of the feelings Stephen had stirred all those years before.

The bright sparkling morning was having the desired effect. Carrie made a few more ineffectual stabs in the earth, dislodging far more of the celine than the clover. What did it matter? They were both going to grow back thicker and more tangled than before. The hopelessness of her efforts made her laugh. She breathed the outside in, deep; closed her eyes to revel in the mix of quiet warmth and her sons' merry noises.

A little up the road, however, the day was not quite so calm. Miriam was making her way on foot down the road towards Carrie's house, stirring the air into invisible eddies of discontent as she went. She was on a mission. She walked with pace and purpose. She hadn't let Angus in on her strategy yet, as he didn't seem reliable enough at the moment to be able to offer safe harbour to a secret.

"Male so-called menopause. No other explanation for it."

So she left him with a note book and instructions to list all the vehicle activity up the driveway to the house behind them.

"We must know exactly who is drawn into the Naysmiths' house. Guns on the ready, Angus. Needs must. On the ready."

As Miriam walked down the hill she sought to justify what she was about to do. Carrie's behaviour the night before had annoyed her. Miriam was very determined once set on a course, and she expected Carrie to be willing enough to become part of their pleasant little group and perhaps even allow herself to be set on a path of self-improvement. Unfortunately, she had shown herself to be the rebellious type. A leftie, no doubt.

In the 12 or so hours since Carrie first stepped over the McGregors' doorstep, Miriam's opinion had made a quantum leap. No longer a slight blemish on the otherwise spotless surface of Glade Heights, Carrie was now a blot on the whole of society. Something deep in Miriam's psyche would have revealed why she felt such antipathy towards Carrie. But they were depths Miriam found dark and frighteningly unfathomable. She never dared swim down to them. For if she did so, she would drown.

So she provided herself with a more convenient and

prosaic rationale for her loathing. She had seen enough of Carrie's goings on to note what sort of life she led. Unkempt children, unmarried mother, a beneficiary living in an exclusive estate. There was nothing else for it, they were not wanted at Glade Heights and it was clearly up to Miriam to see to it they left. She rounded the last corner fast and strident, like a motorcyclist on a centrifugal lean. On reaching Carrie's fence, she drew herself up and summoned Carrie from across the garden.

"Carrie. Carrie, a word, dear, please."

Carrie turned and cursed. She did not want her peaceful morning interrupted, but she could hardly ignore the woman. She tried to be short as she called back. Polite but dismissive.

"Mrs McGregor. Thanks for last night. Good of you to ask me. Sorry I couldn't stay longer."

"Oh, do call me Miriam," the older woman began, giving Carrie a wide patronising smile. "Look. I've been thinking about you down here with your children. It's no wonder you find it so difficult to keep abreast of all the housework."

"I'm not sure what you are talking about?"

"I mean, dear, it can't be easy keeping the boys in the garden and out of harm's way. And keeping the front yard free of toys and tidy for the other neighbours."

This is a bit rich, Carrie thought. The mental anguish of recent weeks had made her brittle. This time her response was uncharacteristically sharp.

"And you're the keeper of Glade Heights are you,

Mrs McGregor?" She realised immediately how rude that sounded. It just slipped out.

"Don't get the wrong idea, Carrie." The small laugh Miriam gave carried no hint of humour. "I'm coming with the best of intentions. It's just that we are used to higher standards around here. And I don't think it's fair on everyone else if you lower those standards. I'm sure you understand. If nothing else, you're an intelligent enough girl."

Carrie swallowed hard. Wasn't she, after all, the conciliator? Everyone listened to and happy. All opinions intact. On this occasion, however, Miriam had riled her, a mark had been stepped over, and Carrie had to clench the gardening fork to steady herself. No one had the right to tell her how she should behave, in particular, not this bombastic neighbour.

Miriam moved towards Carrie and stood over her, a solid block in front of the sun. Carrie rose. She wiped the hair from her forehead with the back of her hand and stood square on to Miriam.

"It's as I say, Carrie dear," Miriam continued.

Rather than calming Miriam, Carrie's silence was stirring her up.

"We try to keep a tidy house at Glade Heights. This is an exclusive estate. That's why the gates at the entrance to the Heights are there, to keep the riff raff out. These toys strewn all over the place from morning to night – and, might I add, overnight at times, my dear – well, it just does the neighbourhood no credit."

Carrie could smell stale garlic exuding from Miriam's open mouth. It reminded her of the previous night's interrogation.

"I think you had better leave, Miriam," she said in a

low voice.

Miriam looked startled. "I beg your pardon, young lady?"

"Go." Carrie's voice stayed quiet and measured but she was shaking inside. "Please get out of my garden and out of my life."

With that, Carrie corralled her unwelcome visitor in the direction of the gate. Miriam was speechless, caught off balance, wrong footed, and as Carrie followed her and closed the gate a little too quickly behind her, the older woman stumbled.

Miriam grabbed at the letterbox and somehow flung herself face about. She narrowed her eyes, tossed her head and levelled her words. They were cold and undisguised. "You've made a big mistake, to cross me, Carrie Thompson. You'll see."

And she turned heel. And was gone.

Without warning, tears flooded Carrie's eyes. It was all too much; brutal husbands, nosy neighbours, responsibility – everything. What on earth had she done to warrant such impossible behaviour? She hardly knew Miriam. What could Miriam possibly know about Carrie? How could she know what went on in Carrie's garden when she didn't even live nearby?

At that moment Carrie cast her swimming gaze up the hill, and there in the distance she saw the McGregor sitting room window with its full and sweeping views across the length and breadth of Glade Heights. It leered at her, then lunged, hitting her square in her stomach.

"Oh God," she wailed, the reality of her situation dawning on her.

Anxious not to let the boys see her unhappiness, she quickly wiped her tears, and making sure Tom and Jake were playing safely – God knows, Miriam would be back checking up on them in a minute – went inside with urgent purpose to compose the overdue letter to her lawyer. She needed another month, that was all. Time to sort out some practical deals in her own mind and to work out how best to persuade Craig separation was necessary.

Another month. That would have her robust enough to tackle the problem of her husband. But tackle it she must, before that interfering old bat up the road created real difficulties.

# CHAPTER NINE

## BALANCE II

Sunny days are meant for the lifting and carrying of the spirit. That Miriam had used the elements to advance her intrusive tendencies was unfortunate, but the day itself took no offence. It was quite happy to shine with opportunity on anyone inclined to a more positive disposition.

Mary Naysmith was one such positive, sunny person. She stood taking in the warm healing rays before closing the door on her latest client. How satisfying. She and Judith had been in business less than a week and already their reputation was growing. They were good at what they did. It was the combination. A good solid old-fashioned nurse-training with its ample opportunity to observe the vagaries of human anatomy, together with that wonderful course they both did. Two long years of flake and alternative – brilliant.

"Judith is softer than me," Mary thought. "More spiritual; less obvious. Funnily enough, will probably be more successful with the sceptics and have them thinking inner health in less time than it takes to unravel an alter ego."

There were a few precious minutes for coffee before the next set of aching muscles would stretch themselves out for repair on her massage table, and as she made her way into the kitchen, Judith came in behind her.

"Phew! What an exhausting day already," her sister said. "If it keeps up like this, Mares, the business will be a roaring success."

"Good, huh? Coffee?"

"Thanks. By the way, did you notice how early Carrie Thompson left the Dragon's house last night."

"Can't say I was looking. Had she been torched by the Dragon's fiery breath?"

"Don't be stupid. Actually, she did look a little flustered. I'm like you, it's the last thing I'd want to do – accept one of those heinous potluck invitations. But I'd love to be a fly on the wall to see what goes on."

Mary scowled. "To be honest, if I were a fly I wouldn't even want to blow her meat. Better to keep a very low profile with that woman. Something doesn't ring quite right with her. Word is she has her nose into everybody's business round here. I don't like people who feel the need to control everyone else."

"Oh look, you're probably right. Probably be poisoned meat. I do feel sorry for that husband of hers though."

Mary eyed her sister for a moment.

"You're far too nice, Judith. The man has chosen whom he wants to live with," she told her sister with pedantic emphasis. "Bet your bottom dollar he's complicit in her doings. Doesn't necessarily poison the meat but enjoys wielding a bit of fly spray."

"Oh, curse the flies." Judith was laughing. "I'd better

get back, I've got someone arriving in about five minutes."

"Me too, young Judith. But it's my last for the morning. Let's take our walk a little later. What do you reckon?"

"Yeah. 12:30-ish?"

While the sisters organised massage tables and towels for their next clients, Angus McGregor sat at his sitting room window, proverbial fly spray in hand, watching the comings and goings of his New Age-ish neighbours. The oppression of the last few days lifted a little. His wife knew how to push the right buttons. He had done her bidding for so long now, a resurgence of the old gossip-induced excitement was inevitable once he had clear instructions and a new project under way.

A vehicle arrived next door and he eased a spyhole in the net curtain. There appeared to be a pattern to these arrivals. The cars were not driven up the driveway as Miriam had supposed they would be. They parked on the roadside instead. Miriam would not like that. It meant cars parked down the length of the McGregors' property. He made a note, detailed the type of car, *Peugeot*, and number of occupants. *One*. No, Miriam would find the constant presence of cars along their fence line an invasion of her privacy. What if she had guests? Where could they park?

Tired of sitting, Angus yawned and decided it was time for coffee. A solid morning's work must have earned some rewards.

However, Angus had no sooner formulated this pleasant diversion when another car pulled up. Now here was excitement. A veritable traffic jam. Angus knew his responsibility, work before play, and he stayed put to jot down all the details.

*Honda, white. Registration No PH 3629. Parked along McGregor boundary. Occupant: one, male.*

No sooner had Angus completed this *Itemization* than Miriam herself came striding up their path in a red-faced pant. His heart sank when he saw her, knowing his peace was about to be shattered. Where on earth had she been with her heaving bosom and blotchy cheeks? She stopped for a moment by the salvia, one hand propping up her diaphragm.

"Good Lord. What's she doing now?" he wondered. "Seems to be having a conversation with the plants."

He watched her pause a little longer then turn and, setting her face, march towards the house. Before long he heard her making her way up the stairs and he coughed a couple of times to call her attention.

"Here's the latest report, Mir..." he began, but he was not given the opportunity to finish.

"This time, Angus, we have a true mission." Miriam burst into the room and having snatched up the binoculars, crossed to the window to examine the scene below.

"There is no question but that girl is trouble. Do you know – she told me to leave. Me!"

"Who told you?"

"To think of all the things I've done for this community. All the people I've helped. And she thinks she can come in here, a nobody from nowhere, and talk to me like that."

"Who, Miriam?"

"Untidy, ungrateful wretch. All I was doing was offering some sensible, mature advice. Look at that. Look at those children now, running around free in that garden.

No supervision. She's a blot on the landscape. Mark my words, Angus. Blot!"

"Who Miriam? Just tell me – who?"

Infected by his wife's agitation, Angus had raised his voice. He was beginning to wonder if his wife had taken leave of her senses, and as if to confirm his fears, Miriam turned a wild look on her husband.

"Carrie-take-what-she-can-Thompson. That's who. Where's the phone book?"

"You're not going to ring her?"

"Not her, you dolt. The CPS."

"The CPS?"

"Children's Protection Service." She stopped and stared at him with indignant intensity. "What's wrong with you, Angus, you're such a fool."

"I do know what CPS stands for Miriam," her husband was defensive. "I'm just wondering what you could possibly be wanting with them."

"Anyone who can talk to me the way Carrie Thompson did isn't fit to be a mother. Needs must, I'm afraid. The CPS ought to be investigating, and I intend to be the one to alert them."

Angus stood wide-eyed. He'd seen his wife on the warpath before, but this time her reaction defied belief.

"Don't be ridiculous, Miriam. You might not like the way she lives, but getting the CPS involved is completely over the top. They'll think you're mad if you ring them. What's got into you? Why let this girl get to you so much?" He could see she was struggling with herself.

"I haven't put in all the effort over the years, Angus," Miriam told him, her voice etched away by emotion, "to have my neighbourhood sullied in this way. If the girl won't listen and change her ways, we don't want her here."

Suddenly Angus felt repelled by his wife. What unhappiness must suppurate in her heart. What was it all about, this war Miriam had decided to wage? Was it in truth about Cynthia?

He had tried so many times to talk to Miriam about how their daughter's death had affected him, to ask how it affected her. But she would never engage. Instead, she would turn her back on him and throw herself into her latest social project. Well, a little innocent interference here and there was one thing. He enjoyed discussing the scandalous details over a cup of tea. But what was she thinking of – attempting to interfere in this young woman's life? Angus shook his head and turned away. He no longer had the stomach for it.

It was a reflection of his own pain that Angus had been too numb to consider how much destruction Miriam's earlier campaigns might have wrought. It was his particular safety net. His lack of insight had enabled him to co-exist with his divisive wife without experiencing too much further hurt. On this occasion, however, it seemed his pain threshold had been reached and a degree of real comprehension was at last percolating through to his consciousness.

All the joy of the morning's more manageable mission evaporated. Angus's shoulders weighed heavy. Miriam, however, was impervious to his sighings and slumpings. She was intent on her phone call and he stole outside to *The Hidey-hole* unnoticed, pipe in hand. Perhaps she would vent her annoyance and then let the whole matter drop. He was hopeful, but the coarse scrape of a tui calling high above him from the campanulata cherry did nothing to dispel his sense of doom.

"No prelude to symphony this time, old bird," he told

it. "Thought I'd better get away from that spider before I am devoured. You'd be advised to do the same."

Back in her War Room, Miriam found the number she was looking for and dialled. From his distant sanctuary, Angus could hear her snorts as she stabbed her way through a series of recorded instructions until at last a human answered.

"I have a complaint to make ... What do you mean you don't take complaints? Honestly what politically correct nonsense ... That may be but,"

Miriam cleared her throat, altered her tone, and let it drip. "If you like – I would like to make a report. Local woman. Have been wa...noticing her for some time now and it is such a worry about those children. They're on their own such a lot. Only toddlers. And so dirty. Didn't even have a proper babysitter when she went out last night...Under-age...And they are so young. I wouldn't wonder if..."

Angus drew on his pipe, aware only of an ebb and flow of temper in the background; a low growling; an occasional raised voice – "Drugs, I wouldn't be in the least bit surprised..."; followed by a higher, oilier register, indicating flattery was being employed to ensure the CPS placed credence on Miriam McGregor's advice. Drip, drip, drip. How plausible she was. She flattered people until they were more than happy to oblige. But he had been watching her over the years become more and more intent on getting her own way. It was making her obsessive – like this conversation she was having now. He was thankful most of it was inaudible, and he began to feel drugged himself. Drowsy.

Ten minutes later Miriam put the phone down. She flared her nostrils in self-appreciation and breathed in deep satisfaction.

"There. I've only done what any responsible neighbour would do," she told the phone.

She sat back, exhausted but cleansed. Miriam would not be named, didn't have to be further involved. Setting the ball rolling towards Carrie Thompson was all it required.

CHAPTER TEN
# LIKE A DOG AT A BONE

Angus dosed off for a time, lulled to sleep by the distant chainsawing of his wife's voice. The sun moved and was full on him by the time the tui's call plucked the air and woke him from his escape. He stretched out his legs and with his eyes still shut, turned his face to take full advantage of its warm caress.

"Miriam's like a terrier," he thought. "And her bone chewing is becoming more frantic as the years go by."

He was reminded of the Holbein Jack Russell business. He called it *Bart's Tale*. Odd that Miriam should have taken the side of a dog, even if she did exhibit a bit of the canine, herself. There was nothing, however, like a common enemy to unite.

The Holbeins' dog had been under siege. An ankle biter from way back, Bart had graduated from feline to human and the dog control people had been called in, putting Bart on notice. The complainant had been one of Miriam's arch-enemies. Angus could not remember why Miriam had telephoned the Holbeins, but in the course of the conversation Maisie said she had received a call from the dog control people who advised her, if another complaint was received about her dog it would be classified as dangerous.

"Not that the man was unreasonable, mind," Maisie told Miriam. "It's just that the person who complained is Rosemary Pettigrew, and she's not going to leave it at this, I just know it."

"Rrr-osemary Pettigrew?" Miriam snorted. " Oh, you poor dear, Maisie. That woman is a simply appalling. Had the audacity to object to my application to Council for funds for the Glade Heights Arts and Crafts Exhibition and Auction."

The more Maisie and Miriam talked, the more irate Miriam became, and no matter how hard Maisie insisted the matter was perhaps best left alone, Miriam insisted even harder Maisie should, "Leave this to me. I am very conversant with all the Council rules and regulations. This woman has exaggerated the issue. I will contact the dog control people for you and sort it all out."

Even if Miriam had talked to the dog control people and left it at that, matters might still have been all right, but she decided Rosemary Pettigrew needed a lecture.

She rang to deliver it one morning soon after. Quite a sharp woman, Rosemary Pettigrew, Angus recalled. Tall and shrewish, but not unintelligent. Distinctive grey stripe across the front of her otherwise dark hair. Told Miriam to "de-sticky" her beak or she'd report Miriam for biting her ankle, too.

"That woman is so provoking, Angus. But she won't get the better of me. Mark my words. Not me."

To prove she was made of sterner stuff, though what possessed his wife on this occasion Angus had never been able to figure out, Miriam organised to look after Bart for the weekend while the Holbeins were away. She took him for a walk – extraordinary detour – past the Pettigrews' gate, and he had just flown, deaf to command, straight for the Pettigrew ankle. Got declared dangerous after that and made to wear a muzzle. Miriam could not believe it. She had even written Bart a character reference in support – but to no avail.

"You mustn't just lie down and roll over, Maisie," Miriam had instructed. "We should appeal to the courts over this. Yes, yes. I know it's your dog, but there is a greater principle at stake."

In the end poor Maisie almost cracked under the strain and in desperation she and John gave their lively pet to a relative who lived on a farm. It turned out Bart had a penchant for sheep ankles too, and in the end he was shot by the farmer. Pity, Angus thought. He was a feisty little chap.

Of course, Miriam had not seen the outcome as the disaster Angus had seen it to be. She turned the event into a victory. The martyrdom of Bart. Man's Best Friend, no longer muzzled by Rosemary Pettigrew and gone to live in dog heaven.

These musings of Angus's roused him from his earlier reverie. The thought of the gun shot did it. He went inside to find his wife. If Miriam likes to take control so much, he thought, she can take control of the traffic movements next door. It might take her mind off Carrie Thompson.

He found her in a much calmer mood, sitting at the

kitchen table with the tools of her trade spread out in front of her: *Itemization* pad; pen; cup of tea; ginger and pear muffin. She was already working on the notes Angus had made that morning.

"Not a bad morning's work, Angus. A distinct pattern is building here, don't you think? We can't have these awful people parking outside our house. I can't imagine what goes on in those corrupt minds of theirs, and I won't feel safe gardening if this continues."

Although Miriam was happy enough and back concentrating on the relatively pedestrian subject of massage parlours and council regulation, Angus was still not feeling terribly receptive. To avoid replying, he walked over to the bench from where the teapot beckoned. He liked his brew thin and milky. Miriam preferred hers dark and tar-like.

"I'll want you to continue this work, Angus," she prompted him again. "It will bring rewards, I'm sure."

"Don't you think you should be involved more with this matter, Miriam? You're the one who wants to find out what's going on."

"And you, don't?"

"I'm not sure I do. No."

Her lighter mood changed in a flash. "Look, Angus, I've got far too much on my plate as it is. What's wrong with you? Are you not feeling very well, these days? You should see your doctor, you know. Probably prostate problems."

"I'm feeling fine." He was, in fact. He was finding a voice that had been lost for many years. "I'm just not sure I can tolerate this sort of thing any more. And those girls up the drive, we'll probably find their business is fine. Why can't we just leave all these people alone?"

"You're problem is lack of imagination," his wife

scolded him. "We let our guard down for one minute and the Heights will be overrun with undesirables."

She paused to quaff some tea and devour a large chunk of buttered muffin. Refuelled, she continued.

"It cannot be left to me to wage the war on my own, you know. Not cricket, you do know that."

"I'm not sure I see it as you do, any more. I'm tired, Miriam. This business of the Thompson girl. That's serious stuff, contacting the authorities about her children."

Miriam exploded. "Of course it's serious. Do you think I take these things lightly?" And she proceeded to harangue him, honing her tongue into a sharp point with her talk.

Angus watched but did not listen. He had become increasingly deaf to Miriam's increasingly insistent complaints. It was as if she reckoned her world would collapse if she eased off. The outside world was trespassing on her territory and the only effective bulwark against such a threat was a barricade from where she could fortify then fight. Her behaviour wasn't balanced but his gentle protestations were never going to be an effective way to get through to her.

Angus was regretting a pleasant life lost. His wife had shut herself away from the things in life that truly mattered. A successful fight was what now stimulated her, but it didn't make her happy. And if she couldn't be happy herself, apparently no one else was to be happy either. She nourished herself by sapping contentment from others. Oh, there were brief moments when she appeared to experience normal pleasure: holding meetings that put her in the limelight; attending certain functions she identified in the Glade social calendar as being worthwhile – there was one coming up that apparently excited her; and more than anything, the thrill of associating with Stephen Tiehurst.

But it was the grit of life she now seemed to rely on to produce the pearls of her limited existence. Angus appreciated this summing up of his wife was an awful indictment, but what worried him more than anything was the fact he was beginning not to care.

The scolding of Angus ran its course. Miriam vilified, magnified, qualified and finally rectified the world and its doings. She had said all she needed to say.

"So that's the way it has to be Angus. Needs must. I will have my hands very busy. You must play your part."

The ringing of the phone interrupted. Angus picked it up, glad of the respite from Miriam's ear bashing. His relief, however, was short lived. He made no attempt to hand the phone over. He just dropped it on the table.

"Some woman from the CPS for you," he told his wife in a flat monotone.

Miriam snatched up the phone. After a short conversation, she slapped it back down on its stand and fired a look of triumph.

"Bingo! They're sending someone round to see young Mizz Thompson."

Angus had no more tolerance for his wife's presence and went to remove himself. Miriam downed the last of her tea, and as she made her way about her fastidious kitchen, rearranging its contents into strict disciplined rows, she began her ominous warble.

# CHAPTER ELEVEN
## PARLOURS

The morning's activities had worn Miriam out. In the past she would have handled such intense activity with vigour. However, she was getting older, and even she allowed for the sapping effect of age. Subconsciously, she also wanted a diversion from the Carrie Thompson problem, which had unsettled her more than she permitted herself to think.

Having finished whipping her kitchen into shape, she decided she would retire to the sitting room to energise herself. She was not one to rest by rest alone, however. She had no intention of taking 40 winks. Forty winks was what Angus did, now he was over the hill. No, she would retire to consider the dubious activities taking place next door and what should be done about them. Once finished, she would send her observations off in letter form to the Glade District Council. A good wholesome complaint to Council would restore her energy levels nicely.

Miriam chose to sit at her escritoire, which she had bought mostly because she thought its name represented refinement. This straitjacket piece of furniture obliged her sit ram rod, and thus added to the air of authority she regarded as necessary in these exercises. She fussed about to ensure everything was arranged as it should be. Then placing her half-frame glasses on the end of her nose she picked up Angus's *Itemizations* once more and subjected them to a fine scrutiny.

She was looking for evidence of incriminating activity. As much as she disapproved of the cars and how they might crowd her out, she accepted the parking issue would not qualify. Nor was there any adverse noise she could insist the Council abate. The traffic volume would not raise official eyebrows, either. Even Miriam considered it light.

Distracted, she took off her glasses and gazed for a moment at the lake. Unwittingly, she found herself thinking about Carrie Thompson again. The morning's confrontation had done more than affront Miriam. The sharp pain it had sent through to her short-circuited emotions had taken her breath away. An image of Cynthia flared up in front of her face then faded, and in its place came a surge of nausea. Miriam blinked to refocus on the view outside her window. Was she beginning to lose her touch? The job at hand – she must concentrate. Concentrate.

With an effort she made herself look at the Naysmiths' driveway. A contentious angle, that was what she needed. It was proving difficult to find, and she would unquestionably need one in order to make an official complaint. However, experience told Miriam some actionable morsel would eventually present itself. It always did. And with renewed heart and an exaggerated flourish she replaced her glasses – and just like that, there it was. The morsel she had been looking for. According to Angus's notes, there was only ever one occupant in these cars. She summoned him.

"Angus. Tell me. How many people came in each of these cars. You have here, for instance:

*'Nissan, comma, Blue, stop. Occupant, colon, One, comma, Male, full stop'.*"

Angus put his head round the door. "Precisely. Always one occupant only. That particular one was an athletic looking chap."

"Many women?"

"I didn't notice any, today."

"That's it then. That's our lever in."

"What? Don't be ridiculous, Miriam. It hardly constitutes an illegal gathering. If you insist on pursuing these girls, wouldn't it be better to tackle the parking problem?"

She peered at him from over the top of her spectacles.

"I've thought about that. No. I don't think it would work. I know, I know," and she waved her hand in the air. "It is completely unreasonable to have cars constantly parked along side our property. But I have a much better idea. Those licentious young hussies won't need to have their clients parking if they have no business for their clients to go to. I'll make sure their business gets shut down. It only takes a few suggestions. Do you remember Franklin Mitchell, at all, Angus? Perhaps not. But take it from me, if dirt is hurled with enough water, there'll be mud to stick."

She outlined her plan. She would send off a letter to the Council, expressing her fear that a massage *parlour* had opened up right next door. There were children about and so on. If the Council chose not to pursue the matter, Angus was to continue with detailed *Itemizations* of every male visitor who came alone to the Naysmiths' house.

"And make sure you take down a physical description of them each time," she instructed. The assembled details would then be forwarded to the police. "Yes, Angus. Needs must. The police. I won't be wasting too much precious time with that ineffectual Council. All the police will need is an idea of what times particular men arrive – they'll do the rest. We just have to continue calling it a 'massage parlour'. And if that doesn't stop this sordid activity, I'll write to the paper. Mark my words. One simply needs to say it's a disgrace to have massage parlours in such marvellous hide-a-ways as Glade Heights, where retirees stroll and children frolic. No mention of a specific address. No risk of defamation, I'm sure."

"I thought 'one' wasn't mad about frolicking children at Glade Heights, Miriam?" Angus interrupted, then moved to the other side of the room when his wife's contemptuous snorting refused to let up.

Angus may not have looked thrilled with the continuation of this particular battle, but at least a plan had been laid out.

Miriam busied herself composing her letter to Council while he returned to his own post at the window.

"I can see them coming up the road now. Fairly healthy pace they're making. Fit pair, those two," Angus told her with a degree of relish. "There is always a chance, I suppose, you're right about their business. Perhaps it is a front for prostitution. There's a way for me to find out, of course Miriam, though I don't suspect for a minute you would approve."

And she only needed to discharge one of her looks for him to have his answer.

The air of Glade Heights was saturated with social strategising, and even clean and green Mary and Judith Naysmith discussed the intrigues of neighbourhoods as they had walked around their own. How, they wondered, did seemingly sensible people become so immersed in the affairs of relative strangers? Curiosity, perhaps? Or was it more? Anxiety about their own status? Or worry that others might be better, or bigger, or richer; or get the upper hand in some way? Was it by interfering with others these busybodies felt they could control the situation to their own advantage? Neither sister could admit to being sure. But whatever it was, Mary and Judith agreed such behaviour was unhealthy.

"Mrs McGregor is our version of the ultimate busybody, isn't she?" Judith prompted her sister. "You heard what Sally Brimsmead said about her. Apparently she just needs the bare sniff of non-conformity in someone and she's down on them like a ton of bricks. Sally thinks the only reason why she's not been targeted with more than simple dislike is because her husband's a lawyer."

"You mean the Dragon is actually worried she'll be sued or something?"

"No. No, apparently she's taken on several people in the courts, so she's not afraid of a legal argument. No, it's because she sees lawyers as having sufficient status to exempt them from harassment. Gosh, Mares. I hate to think what she thinks of us. She could make trouble, couldn't she?"

Mary said nothing for a while. They were nearing their driveway and she kept her head well down so as to avoid any eye contact with the McGregors, whose house was by now in full view. She pondered the question of how to handle nosy neighbours. What was the best way to avoid confrontation with them? Ignore them? Disarm them with humour? Mary had no idea what Miriam was really like, although she suspected she was a bully. She hoped she would never have to deal with her. It was such a waste of time dealing with people you had no desire to deal with, answering argument that had no substance. It was all too easy to get drawn in and start behaving the way they did – illogically and spitefully.

Mary didn't trust herself to remain calm under fire. Judith was different. She took her time with problems. Weighed them up. Considered them. Mary reacted. She would keep cool in most situations, but if pushed over the edge, she was likely to explode. For now, though, she didn't see their neighbour as a particular problem and it was not constructive to predict the consequences of something that had not even happened.

"Oh look, Judith," she said to her sister at last. "We're no doubt going to get some complaints about the business. This is a residential neighbourhood, and some people will see us as running our business in their territory. But the reality is we're not in their territory. It's our house. We've done everything by the book. I don't think she'll have anything justifiable to complain about. Truly."

"But Sally has said to be careful. She reckons we're prime candidates for an attack."

"Well, if the Dragon tries, I'll be waiting." And Mary flicked her head up towards the McGregors' window in a direct challenge.

At that moment it seemed as if a breeze had caught the McGregors' sitting room net curtains, though they disclosed no secrets.

"If the McGregors think massage therapy is bad," Mary added as they walked in through their front door, "I think those curtains are far worse. If anything suggests prurience it's net curtains, not massage. I'm telling you."

# CHAPTER TWELVE

# REUNIONS

Thus did a mischievous breeze whisper its way around the corners of Glade Heights as the sunny morning moved on. By the time people's lunches had been eaten and their late lattes drunk, Carrie had agonised and written all she needed. She had recovered sufficiently from Miriam's unwelcome visit to label it nothing more than a minor irritation. She had a greater worry – formalising a safe separation from Craig. With the email sent to her lawyer there was nothing else she could do about it for the moment, and Carrie was quite capable of stepping into the rest of the day on a positive note. She gathered up her irrepressible sons and got them into the car.

"Time for a treat," she told them.

She loved watching Jake and Tom together. Tom was beginning to talk and encouraged his older brother into conspiracies – usually to do with the consumption of forbidden foods. He giggled as she strapped him into the car seat, flinging himself forward to shield himself from her tickling and allowing her to bestow a flurry of loud kisses into the soft nape of his neck.

"Chewing," Tom prompted.

"Can we get chewing gum, Mum?" Jake had taken Tom's cue.

And Carrie laughed. "Tom, you're too little for chewing gum. One day, special treat, I promise. But not today."

She got into the car and they set off for town. This was a time of contentment. The boys always entertained each other in the back. With laughter or argument, it didn't matter, Carrie was able to ignore whatever noises issued forth behind her. This was her thinking time.

The Glade Heights Estate was not far from the town of Glade. Just around the lake a little, skirting one or two bays, and down the straight. Often day-trippers came out for a ride, causing Carrie to brake to 30kph, slow enough to remind her of the days long ago when apart from the joys of the water, there was little to do around Glade but make sight-seeing trips in the old family Chev. She had gone on holidays to the lake with her own parents many years before. The safe years: lovely lethargic Sunday-drive trips out past the black-stained houses and around the shore; the huge ice creams in a cone at the end of a sticky summer outing; bumpy, rutted, unsealed roads with pumice dust lighting on every surface; the scent of gum trees made sweet in the late summer heat. These were the memories she had held on to when she fled Milltown and her embattled marriage. Glade had never been home before, but it was familiar, felt secure. Nor was there any reason for Craig to think of it as her place of refuge. He would be more likely to imagine her in Auckland, hidden deep in the city.

She wasn't sorry to be gone from the soulless streets of Milltown. She and Craig had perhaps made a mistake moving there, where there was no family support and few friends. It was true, it worked for the business. There was good labour and much cheaper premises for their factory. But there was no emotional support for either of them.

The business – Carrie knew she couldn't hide away much longer. Quite apart from sorting her marriage out, she had responsibilities to the business and all the people who relied on her and Craig for work.

She refocussed on her surroundings. The same dusty route that had carried her as a little girl out to the lake's distant bays was now refined by tar seal and lined by an architectural muddle of mis-inspired houses. Some boasted wrought iron balustrades that skirted mock-Tudor batons; others sat vibrant and turquoise as a backdrop to pseudo-rock walls. Glade was not so very different from Milltown, perhaps, but it was brought to life by the sparkle of water. Anyway, some of these houses she liked and she begrudged none of them their declaration of independence.

The discordant architecture brought Carrie back to thoughts of disagreeable neighbours. The image of Miriam McGregor haunted her in a way she found most disconcerting. She thought she'd managed to rationalise Miriam's conduct and dismiss it as passing loopiness, yet here it was creeping back into her conscious thoughts, niggling at her.

They reached town before she knew it and she shook the feeling off. The boys fell silent as the increased traffic, particularly the trucks, demanded their critical appraisal. Carrie cheered up. The morning's resolutions were in truth quite cathartic and she was ready for more positive activity.

She checked for mail at the Post Office and suggested to the boys they get an ice cream and some bread to feed the ducks. The afternoon was hot and, once they had fed the ducks, they paddled in and out of the water. Carrie stripped Tom's clothes off. She helped him splotch after the ducks and delighted in his belly chortle as he and Jake attempted to catch the darting cockabullies that fed just below the surface of the water. Finally she sat down near the water's edge and let the boys dig moats for flooding while her own toes dug through the warm, gravelly sand and felt the cool water seep up to tickle the skin between them.

"Hello, Carrie."

Carrie's heart missed a beat. She turned in response to the warm male voice behind her.

"Stephen."

He was smiling. "I saw you down here. Noticed the boys first, then saw you. I couldn't resist coming to say hello. I hope you don't mind."

"Of course I don't mind." Carrie gave a slightly guilty grin. "Why would I?"

"Oh, it's just you seemed in such a hurry to be off last night, and I wondered if... well, you know. I wondered if I was the reason for that."

Carrie blushed. "No. No, it wasn't you. I didn't even know it was you who was coming until I was on my way out. To be honest I was late for the babysitter," she fibbed. "And I truly didn't think you'd recognised me. I wasn't sure you'd want to recognise me."

"Goodness. Why would you think that, you funny old thing? You're looking just the same, Carrie. Perhaps rather more gorgeous, and certainly not changed enough to disguise yourself."

She grinned again, then lowered her head hoping he wouldn't see her confusion. Stephen had lost none of his familiarity. That pleased her. She looked up again and indicated her sons.

"These are my boys, Stephen. Tom and Jake."

"You're married, then? Carrie Thompson?"

"Yes. I did get married. I've recently separated, though and I've not been in this area long. What about you? Are you married?"

Stephen had sat down by Carrie and was sieving the sand through his fingers. He paused to throw a stone in the water.

"Oh. I was in a relationship for many years." He sounded reticent. "We broke up not so very long ago. No children. Unlikely to go down that track now."

She glanced at him. It was the same capable strong face she remembered from long ago.

"Why not?" she asked. "You're hardly over the hill. Look at me with two young boys. You guys don't need to worry about getting older and having children."

"The right partner matters, though. Oh, and it's a work thing – I'm so often away around the country, overseas. I'd not be there to help particularly, and what sort of a dad would I be if I was never around."

Carrie was amused. "Gosh. You really have thought about this, haven't you? Perhaps I should have thought about it more too. Don't get me wrong, my boys are my life. But sometimes you get into these situations without any real thought, or long term planning." She paused. "I have another child, you know."

"Ah yes. I gleaned that much last night, too."

Carrie thought it tactful to let the picture of Miriam in full flight slip from her mind without comment. It was disconcerting to think Stephen associated with such an awful woman. She wiped the sand from the palms of her hands, rubbing them where the tiny coarse pebbles had left their itchy indentations, and conjured up a picture of her daughter instead.

"Astra. She's the boys' half-sister. She's at Uni, and when she's home she's the one to sort me out."

"You moved away when I went off to university." Stephen sounded hurt. "I never did find out where you'd gone. Your parents said you had gone to try your luck in Australia but they wouldn't say where. They never did approve of me, did they? I felt so awful because I didn't expect you to leave. I guess I just assumed you loved me enough to be there when I got back."

"I know. Actually, I did love you, Stephen but we were so young, weren't we? And you were away. Mum and Dad thought I was mucking around too much and encouraged me to think I might get some kind of useful training, so I went to Oz. Not much training took place, of course, once I found Astra was coming along."

She turned to smile at him. "You look great. This corporate lark suits you. I always knew you'd have gone done well."

His eyes twinkled. "In that way life's been pretty good to me. I enjoy it, always have." He hesitated for a moment, then murmured, "You were to have been part of it, you know."

He had turned away from her and was staring at the sand in his hands. She kept her eyes on her sons, afraid to reply. All her teenage agonies flooded back. What a fool she'd been. She had so wanted to be part of that life, too.

"You needed the space, Stephen. I'm sure you did. Just think how young we were. I wish we'd had the chance to catch up again sooner, but by the time it seemed the right time to call you, Astra was growing up and I heard you were in Europe. I had no money and came back to New Zealand. What was the point in trying to track you down? I'd have been an unwelcome distraction."

Tom came waddling up the beach and sat his wet bottom down on Carrie's knee. As she dried him off with his tee shirt, he snuggled into her, giving Stephen a possessive stare.

Stephen took a moment to reply. "Well, that's the past, isn't it?" He gave her a deep inviting smile. "I'm very glad to see you now. Look, I'd better get off – I've got a plane to catch in a couple of hours – but I'll be back Sunday. Why don't we catch up properly?"

"I'd love that," Carrie managed to say, though she felt perilously close to melting away.

Stephen got up while Carrie rummaged in her bag for her phone. Tom rummaged, too, determined not to let go of his mother while this man was demanding so much of her attention. Stephen gave her his number so she could text hers back and they smiled their goodbyes. She watched him climb the bank. Wave his way over the top. Then she was left.

Here was the man she had always been crazy about, had not seen for so many years, and suddenly it was as if he had never been away. Foolish, she reprimanded herself. Don't think you can pick up again after all these years. A lovely familiar feeling stirred inside her, however. When had she last felt like this? She shook away her thoughts and called for Jake to come. There was no way she'd be able to sit still now and she was anxious to get home.

Carrie found it hard to concentrate as she made her way back to Glade Heights. For once, the lively banter from her sons set her on edge. Meeting with Stephen again should have made her heady with happiness. Yet, far from a flow of joy, her thoughts were all worry and abrasion.

Look where her impetuous decisions had got her. Yes, she had Astra, and she had Jake and Tom who were divine – when they weren't quite so noisy. But did the good things always have to come so weighted down with hardship? No partner to support her with Astra. A partner who hacked and hacked and hacked away at her until she had no supports left at all with her sons.

She stopped the car briefly before turning left for the road for home. Suddenly, she punched the steering wheel with her fists. Dammit – she was a good person. A kind person. It all seemed so unfair.

She realised the boys had gone silent and could see Jake's worried face in her rear vision mirror.

"What's wrong, Mummy?"

She turned and gave him a smile of reassurance. "Don't worry, Jake. Sometimes grown ups remember something they should have done but forgot to do. I was just remembering. Home soon."

She put the car in gear and pulled on to the road again.

Carrie knew she would have to stop feeling sorry for herself and start fighting. That was the real Carrie, not this cowering woman. Resolve, that's what she needed, a greater sense of resolve. The real Carrie was no roll-over pussy-cat. She was competent and affectionate. She was.

"And you never know," she whispered to the ether, "if I play my cards right, I might even have my old friend back in my life."

# CHAPTER THIRTEEN

# CHARGED BATTERIES

The warmth cast by sweet memories of teenage romance was quite absent back at the McGregor household. Miriam finished her correspondence and continued to catalogue her latest *Itemizations*. Angus was not able to exhibit the same degree of zealotry. Having got over the momentary thrill of being sprung as he spied through the net curtain on the Naysmith sisters, he lost interest and wandered off, intent on pottering in his garden hide-a-way until dinner called him in again.

He knew what Miriam thought of his lack of commitment. At first she berated him at length, then spent the rest of the day subjecting him to her icy cold shoulder, which was not so bad, given it meant she remained relatively quiet; apart, that is, from the odd, "Why must I always carry these burdens alone, Angus?" and "Am I the only one able to grasp the full magnitude of life's iniquities?" and "Could not a little help come from somewhere else?" But this was relative quiet where Miriam was concerned.

Miriam's shoulder was chilly but it did not slump. As dusk fell she rallied, buoyed he supposed by the huge dose of self-vindication she had been injecting all afternoon.

"Solo-mothers, massage parlours – the Heights does not need them, Angus. I know just how to get rid of them. All we have to do is massage the truth a little."

"More massage?" Angus ventured with a hopeless smile.

"Be serious, Angus, please. With the right kind of tactics it is possible to mould innuendo into hard fact. Using such an offensive makes people unsure about where falsehood ends and truth begins."

Angus thought of recent US elections and knew she was right. Miriam's trick had always been to remain vigilant. Like a snake. In that way, at the very moment her victim's vision became blurred she was ready to strike.

"They had dare not even blink at the moment," the brighter Miriam advised her husband at the dinner table. "One must be on the qui vive. Qui vive! Oh Angus, I've not felt so vitalized for years."

Angus shuddered at the idea of a vitalized Miriam. He felt safer taking a good gulp of wine and hiding behind the pleasant mist that wafted into his head. From within this protective miasma he could cope with his wife prattling on.

"There is much to do. I'll need some others on outpost duty as well, you know. Truly, the Heights is the most scintillating place one could possibly live in. There is so much to look forward to, Angus. Not the least of which, don't forget, is the Mayor's Gala for the Visitors From France. They arrive Saturday."

As he continued to fuel his contented oblivion with alcohol, Angus told himself none of these matters were of any concern to him. Why should he worry? He had done no wrong. And the Gala? Angus took in his stride the news that the festive day was upon them.

Had he known, however, just what the occasion would deliver, he might not have been quite so sanguine.

# CHAPTER FOURTEEN

# ENCOUNTERS

The Mayor's Gala had been long awaited by many of Glade's inhabitants and by Miriam McGregor in particular. Her previous week had proven hugely exciting. Now she was in the Glade Domain celebrating a Grand Civic Event.

A breeze darted off the lake and played briefly with her hair. She fingered a loose strand back into place and looked across the gathered throng. A satisfactory milling of notables and 'little people' – Miriam counted herself squarely in the former group – spread out in front of her and she looked around for familiar faces.

Amongst the crowd she noticed a rather rotund woman standing some distance away and protruding above the hats, making her presence known. Miriam frowned – she knew most of the people in town, knew who they were, more precisely – then her face brightened. This was someone new. Could she be associated with the Visitors From France, perhaps?

Miriam's nose twitched. She had expected to be included in the official welcoming party, and it irked her to think this woman might have something to do with the Visitors from France. Then Miriam's confidence reasserted itself and she relaxed.

"No, on second thoughts," she mused, "that woman couldn't be associated with anything so sophisticated. She looks far too nothing to be anything connected with something."

Miriam lifted her shoulders back into a fitting air of authority and looked about until she spied Angus. Seeing him talking with Mayor Whyte, she hastened over to bask in the civic presence.

"Mrs McGregor." The Mayor's greeting was polite but guarded.

"What a thrilling occasion Your Worship," Miriam replied and bestowed a generous smile. "When are the Visitors From France to arrive? I do so want them to understand what a welcoming nation we are. Glade, particularly so."

"Of course, Mrs McGregor. Though let's not overwhelm them, eh?"

"Oh no. Definitely not, but you know, we are to have a potluck dinner out at Glade Heights later this weekend and if you were taking them out on the lake what better way to show them the lie of the water, so to speak. Ha-ha! Bring them along. I am sure we could cater for the extras. We have such a marvellous place you know, with such interesting views."

"I'm sure you do. But please excuse me, I think this may be them coming now." And the Mayor moved off, making little attempt to disguise his relief.

The Visitors From France were arriving on a bus. A small elevated podium had been erected for the Mayor and other local luminaries to stand on. Near the podium was the GladeFM radio car from which the local radio station was broadcasting information about this dazzling event.

"This is quite an occasion for Glade, Dave," the on-location DJ enthused into his microphone. Dave was apparently back in the studio. "It's not everyday you get to see the twinning of two towns as twinnable as these."

He fell silent for a moment while Dave added the kind of amorphous substance to the broadcast only radio DJs can add.

"Yep. That sure is right, Dave. And I have to say – *Dave* – things have truly come up a...um-ah... a notch. We've also got the Glade Brass Band here today. They sound real mighty. Must be pretty hot in that get-up though – *Dave.*"

On cue the Glade Brass Band burst into song – an enthusiastic *La Marseillaise* delivered slightly off-key. The Mayor and Mayoress, various portly councillors and, for some inexplicable reason, the local fire chief jostled into position to welcome the Visitors. Right beside the podium, staking her claim by way of her relationship to Counsellor Johannsen, stood Mrs Johannsen, solid and self-important, the overly-decorative flowers on her hat quivering at each turn of her head.

The Visitors From France looked a little overwhelmed as they stepped off their bus. They stood mute at the end of the red carpet, attempting to gather their purpose but not succeeding at much beyond looking out of place.

Someone yelled out from the back of the crowd, "Where did you leave your rubber inflatable?" and the ripple of laughter that followed caused the Mayor to look embarrassed in apology at this tired old reference to the bombing of the *Rainbow Warrior* decades before.

Out of the corner of his eye, the poor man could spot Miriam McGregor edging her way ever closer to the podium. The Visitors From France began to inch their way across the carpet only to have their guide motion them to wait for a troupe of young Māori dancers who had started to call and sway.

"We're getting ready for a haka I reckon, Dave." The DJ's voice boomed out across the crowd just as the dancing finished and the noise dropped, provoking a flurry of applause.

Miriam had edged right up to the Visitors From France by this stage. She tilted her head and offered them one of her most enticing expressions. Her benevolence, however, was lost on the Visitors. The Māori kapa haka boys stamped forward, beating their arms, swirling their eyes. Then, right at the very moment of their challenge when their passionate cries were scheduled to start a slow curdling of French blood, the ever obliging Glade Brass Band chose once more to imprint its own stamp with a rousing blast of *The British Grenadiers*.

Miriam McGregor, GladeFM Radio, and the Glade Brass Band all looked to be causing the unfortunate Mayor considerable mortification. Yet somehow the formalities were dealt with. The Visitors From France reclaimed their *équilibre*, thanking their hosts in a most effusive and Gallic fashion for the welcome. And at last for those more worldly souls who had remained on embarrassed tenterhooks during the proceedings, the towns were duly twinned and there came relief.

The crowd began to relax and mill, circulating in its current odd and inadequate snatches of French and good-humoured gesticulations. Miriam continued to hover around the podium looking for an introduction to the luminaries should the opportunity arise. The Mayor, in return, showed an enviable talent for tactical withdrawal, managing to avoid her at the very moment she seemed about to secure an introduction and leaving her no time to attempt a double parry.

It began to get late and with no introduction forthcoming, Miriam became restive.

"It is about time I was acknowledged as a key part of this community," she thought and glared across at the Mayor. But he continued to ignore her.

Out of the corner of her eye she saw her husband approaching. Angus would be wanting to go home and she was not yet ready to abandon her social quest. She inclined her head to signify to anyone who might be looking all was well, and she measured her step in the opposite direction.

"Can't secure an audience eh, Miriam?" Angus puffed when he finally caught up to her.

She strode on, making him jog to keep pace.

"Don't be stupid, Angus. These little French people, they're quite delightful I'm sure, but they are not as important as our own people. I'm not worrying one way or another about them."

At that moment their attention was caught by a voice cutting swathes through the throng. Miriam had to stretch in order to see who was so imposing. It was the same woman she had seen before the ceremony. And what's more, she was talking to one of the Visitors From France.

"Carpe Diem, Angus," Miriam cried. She grasped her

husband by his sleeve and yanked him over to the voice, where, without warning, she shoved him off balance and straight into the large woman's embrace. Angus could do little but watch aghast as her overripe knees buckled and she stumbled to the ground.

"Miriam. For God's sake, look what you're doing," he protested.

"What? Oh I am sorry," she gushed at the woman with feigned surprise, and helped to heave her up.

"Miriam McGregor. How do you do. You must be visiting these parts.

"And you are from France perhaps?" she smirched, turning to the startled Visitor From France who had somehow managed to avoid being toppled.

"*Comment?*"

"I said," and Miriam repeated herself, shouting with deliberation, "you...must...be...from...France. How divine," she prattled on. "Perhaps you would care to join our little potluck dinner we are giving later this weekend?"

"*Pardon?*"

"Potluck din-ner," she yelled. "And are you staying long Mrs...?"

"Ah - um - Gumphry. Leyla Gumphry. Goodness. That gave me such a fright. Actually I live in Glade. My husband and I have recently moved here."

She readjusted her broad brimmed hat and dusted herself down. "I was just telling this gentleman in my broken French that this is a charming part of the world. Isn't it," and she too upped the decibels "*miss-su-er?*"

"*Comment? Mais oui. Certainment. Charmant.*"

"Quite. Quite." Miriam said, dismissing the Visitor in a sudden change of tactic.

Miriam never missed an opportunity to establish herself

with new Glade residents. French he may well have been, but the Visitor was now of lesser consequence. She turned to concentrate on Leyla Gumphry, instead.

"Then you and your husband must come and visit our modest little harbour of green," she condescended. "We live in a delightful area called Glade Heights Estate. Quite the place. You've probably not had the opportunity to get out our way, ha-ha!"

Leyla lifted her shoulders and tilted her head back. "As it happens, that's exactly where we have moved to."

Miriam eyed Leyla up and down. This was unexpected. These must be the new arrivals she'd seen unpacking. In fact, she was so distracted by this interesting development, the original reason for launching herself at Leyla had slipped her mind and she failed to notice the Visitor From France had taken the opportunity to escape.

Nothing, however, was escaping Angus. He stood back and considered the two women as they began to conduct a mutual sizing up.

"They look about as intense as each other," he thought. "How's Miriam going to handle this situation? Looks like the other one is a bit of a match. Even seems to have perfected the body language. And a Glade Heights resident to boot." His eyebrows lifted in silent wonder. "There's hardly room for two of them."

He gave Leyla his careful consideration. She was overall a very big woman. She had big length, big width, and a big nose that seemed to pierce the air with a formidable flaying action as she talked. And marching with purpose in front of her, Angus could not help but notice, was a very big bosom to carry it all off. They were not your average, simply over-large boobs – as he had just discovered. Big bosoms of this nature, he believed, were uncontrollable and better never to be grappled with – unless you were married to them. Not that he would choose to be married to them. If it were possible, Leyla looked to be a woman even less likely to tolerate nonsense than Miriam.

Leyla was with her husband. Angus gave him a narrow smile of acknowledgement, and they introduced themselves. Hubert Gumphry stretched in opposite complement to his wife. He was a long man. A long man with a wide wife. And it seemed to Angus he was about as thin in body as he was in conversation, offering little beyond an initial pleasantry. Being talkative appeared to be Leyla's preserve.

She was also, Angus realised, big on words.

"Angus," Miriam pulled him back into the conversation. "I've invited the Gumphrys to dinner Tuesday night. Pity they missed the last potluck dinner. You'd have found it riveting. Truly," she told Leyla, turning her most welcoming smile on her new acquaintance. They were already on the best of terms. "On this occasion, however, I think we might be able to stretch to a leee-tle soirée – our treat, just the four of us."

And Leyla Gumphry oozed with approval. "Sounds quite delightful, doesn't Hubert. I do look forward to hearing all the local comings and goings. Yes, quite delightful."

Having settled the arrangement the two couples said their farewells. Miriam was now happy to grab Angus by the arm and depart for home. There was an energy about Leyla that excited her and she had already decided to persuade the newcomer to join in her latest Glade Heights crusades.

# CHAPTER FIFTEEN

## STRIKING HOT IRONS

Miriam had been unable to wait until the appointed dinner date with the Gumphrys before making contact with Leyla again. Stirred by the promise of friendly conspiracy, she had woken early on the morning after the Gala. She had matters of utmost importance to discuss with Leyla prior to their Tuesday night soirée. Away from Angus who, she decided, would complicate discussions.

She chose not to walk down to their house. She didn't have quite the sense of stridency that had sent her on foot to visit Carrie. No, she would drive. Park right outside the Gumphrys' house in full view. Just let that Thompson girl see her walking in.

She set off, hoping Leyla's husband, Hubert, would be out for the morning. That Leyla would tune in to what was needed in the neighbourhood Miriam was already quite certain, but she hadn't had the chance to develop the same confidence in the husband.

"Better he's not present for our first true confab," she thought.

So it was with a degree of irritation she noticed two cars in the garage when she drew up.

Miriam got out of her car, locked the door, and with her hand still poised with the key, turned her head with melodramatic import over her shoulder to stare through narrowed eyes at Carrie's house across the road. Whether the girl was looking or not was irrelevant. Someone would be looking. Someone was always looking, and they would know Miriam meant business. She then walked up the path and knocked on the Gumphrys' front door. Whatever Leyla's husband was like, Miriam wanted to make this relationship work for the sake of the Heights.

As it happened, it was Hubert who opened the door.

"Oh hello. It's Miriam, isn't it? Come in, why don't you?" He let her in and led her through to the kitchen.

"Well, I was just passing, and well, you know how it is? I was quite delighted to meet you both yesterday and I thought...well... I would bring the local newsletter in for you to see. Doesn't go to everyone of course, ha-ha! Only the *chosen few*. So I suppose that means you and your dear wife. Ha-ha!"

Leyla was busy taking a tray of rock cakes out of the oven. Her cheeks bulged with the piping-hot sample she had just popped into her mouth, and they reddened considerably at the sight of Miriam. Unable to speak for a moment, she held her hand over her mouth while she swallowed her embarrassment and removed the evidence. She still managed a deep nod of welcome, clearly gratified her new acquaintance had chosen to visit.

"How good of you to call," she spluttered. "What a delightful surprise. Perhaps you could make us all a good cup of tea, Hubert? Then we can get to know each other better, and sort out the world, eh? Hubert has an excellent brain, Miriam, I'm sure you'll find."

Miriam sat down at the kitchen table, her critical gaze following Hubert across to the kettle. She was surprised Leyla expected her husband to stay. It was always so much easier for two women to cut to the social chase unimpeded by a male presence. And this male didn't look like the sort who could contribute much. All the same, she was gracious.

"Oh I'm sure you have an excellent brain, Hubert."

"He should have been a lawyer, you know," Leyla chatted on. "He is such a logical thinker, a brilliant advocate. And his letter writing skills; well, I've not ever known anyone quite like it, even if I do say so about my own husband. Show Miriam that letter you wrote to the Council about parking down at the beach, dear.

"Can you believe it, Miriam? They have *No Parking* signs all the way along that road. How can one use the beach with ease, I ask you? Do they expect us to walk down?"

Miriam, although intrigued, remained sceptical. What sort of a letter could Hubert possibly have written? She chose not to reveal she was the one who had beaten the Council into submission over the parking. She would put the pair of them right, because there was no way they would succeed in getting the parking reinstated, but first she would see what the man was capable of.

Hubert was not shy. Having served the tea, he retrieved the letter from his study and handed it to Miriam. It was an impressive length. That, she had to concede. Four pages long. Paragraph headings and meticulous indented sub-headings. And the final paragraph, while not exactly pithy, was written by a man who clearly had campaigning in his heart.

*Furthermore,*

Hubert Gumphry's letter concluded,

*should the said Council choose not to consider the lawful and strategic parking alongside the hereinbefore mentioned lakeside recreation area duly and in the course of its Glade District Council proceedings (hereinafter referred to as the Glade District Council proceedings, unless otherwise stated herein), the author will be forced to commence legal proceedings in a due Court of Law to obtain recompense and compensation for the unfortunate damage that this inconvenience causes.*

*I am the undersigned*

[and Hubert had signed with an inspired flourish]

*Hubert M Gumphry esq.*

"I can see why your wife says you have missed your vocation as a lawyer, Hubert. This is most impressive. Have they replied?"

"As a matter of fact they have. But a most unsatisfactory response. Phoned Friday afternoon to let me know they'd given more than due consideration to the matter of parking over the years and they would not be sending a formal reply.

"I tell you, I will be taking the matter to court. They inform me a majority of the owners out here at the Heights have no wish for parking along the esplanade as it causes traffic jams. It's absurd."

"Ah Hubert, dear Hubert," Miriam carolled. "The idea of traffic jams at Glade Heights is absurd, indeed. Our little nook is far too peaceful and unique for such a common inconvenience. But I have a leee-tle confession to make."

And here she paused for dramatic effect.

"I am the one responsible for the *No Parking* signs."

The Gumphrys lowered their tea cups and stared at her, mouths agape.

"Yes. I organised it," Miriam continued. "I know. I know." And she held her hand up to prevent any sort of reply. "Don't look so alarmed. We had to devise some sort of system for keeping the riff-raff out. Needs must. It was clear, if they can't park by the beach, they don't come to swim there and plague us with their presence. Don't you see?"

Leyla's plump hand wobbled. Her cup rattled against the saucer. "But I'd like to take the odd stroll along the shore. And really, I don't think my health is up to walking all the way down there first. Was this a sensible thing? No parking at all?"

Miriam did not appreciate being challenged. It had been a brilliant idea of hers, one she was extremely proud of. And who were these people coming new to the neighbourhood and within a week of their arrival writing off letters to Council, trying to alter the established processes and other highly satisfactory states of affair? She glanced at Leyla across the table. She was a pitiful weight, poor thing. Perhaps Miriam should be kind.

"I quite see your point, dear Leyla. Quite see it. I do think it is critical we keep non-residents out of the area – if they don't live here what right have they to be near the place, after all. But perhaps we can think of some compromise."

And having consoled her, Miriam then began to consider what this might be.

"I'm not sure there can be one," Leyla whined. "I quite take your point about riff-raff. We're the last to want riff-raff, aren't we, Hubert? However, one pays for one's comfort and…"

"Ah, say no more, dear Leyla," Miriam interrupted. "I've just had a brilliant idea. What we'll do is go for *residents only* parking. We'll find some sort of an argument to get around the traffic jam thing (that was just a clever ploy of mine, to get rid of the general public). You can write to Council, Hubert – I must say you do have a real talent – and I shall sign my name to the letter also. They know me in the Council. They will know what to do."

The Gumphrys conceded this was a great suggestion. It would mean Leyla could drive to the lake to park and still have the energy for a stroll along the shoreline. And Miriam? She realised she ought to make allowances for these new-comers. They were her type of people – Hubert, as it turned out, included.

And so it was, in no time at all these three had found something of great moral significance they could agree on, a plan in which they could collude. As they sat back to sip on their tea, they gazed at each other with the sort of pleasure only an unhealthy conspiracy can arouse. They had discovered in each other the same mean and fixated sense of purpose. That morning at Glade Heights, the three indignant souls made their connection, and surreptitiously, insidiously sealed their fate and seeded what was to become Carrie Thompson's storm of storms.

# CHAPTER SIXTEEN
## HEARTS

No looming tempest but rather the flutter of love had Stephen Tiehurst in a whirl.

True to his promise, as soon as he was back from his business trip he rang Carrie. They agreed to dinner the next evening, at her house. He put the phone down and glanced towards the lake. He couldn't see Carrie's house from his place, but he knew which one it was and he could picture her just a few streets away. The arrangement pleased him. He was intrigued to know what had happened to her in the intervening years. At her place they could meet away from small-town eyes; enjoy the reunion in private, uninterrupted, unhurried.

Stephen had not stopped thinking about Carrie since they had sat together beside the lake. In fact, he had thought of her many times over the years. Being a sociable man, he enjoyed the company of many people, always taking the trouble to keep in touch with them all. But neither their presence nor his demanding work load had been enough to block Carrie from his thoughts completely.

Not even Rebecca had blocked Carrie from his thoughts. Poor Rebecca. He blamed himself for the failure of their relationship.

"You're totally inadequate, shallow," she'd yelled at him after one particular argument.

And perhaps he was – at least, with her. She had so wanted a family. To marry him and formalise their nine years together. He had cared for her, but found he could not love her as she wanted. In time he came to realise it would be kinder to cut clean, not to let the relationship continue a meandering that offered only adequate comfort but no deep joy.

Rebecca had not thought it kinder. "I don't mind it how it is, Stephen. Truly. We should try to make this work. All this time we've put in. And I love you. You know that."

"Becca, I know you want more. And I just can't give you more. I really care about you, and I don't want to split. But is this the answer – for either of us?"

In the end, she had been the one to pack up and depart. That had hurt him. Wasn't it strange he had felt so wounded despite it being his suggestion to separate? Perhaps he was not only shallow but hypercritical, too.

Rebecca's tears of sorrow had disappeared by the time she turned her car into the street and drove off. Instead, her eyes swam with injustice. And he had been surprised how he ached for her. His friends found it unfathomable he'd let her go. Even now, showing the right degree of contrition, he might have been able to retrieve their relationship. They had appeared such a successful couple. Handsome, well-off in every material sense. Happy.

But the perception frustrated Stephen. To his friends he must now appear feckless, but how could a grown man explain? Although he was daily being held lovingly by an attractive woman, inside he carried the pain of love lost for another.

He chose to live with their reproach and keep his other love a secret. Only Rebecca had an inkling his heart was held elsewhere.

Throughout his relationship with Rebecca, Stephen knew he was not being true to himself. The compromises he exercised in order to make things work between them had gone against his nature. So yes, he loved her on one level, but at the same time he felt misunderstood. It was impossible to live the lie to oneself forever. It became too exhausting. Perhaps it would have been kinder to have lied, to have told Rebecca he no longer cared for her, that she was no longer attractive to him. But he couldn't bear to do that to a woman who was kind and affectionate – just not the right woman for him. Consequently, his honesty in telling her he could not marry her despite caring for her hurt her all the more, because she kept hoping his affection would overcome their problems and lead to happy resolution.

And suddenly she was gone. There was a vacuum, sadness. But there was also relief. More and more so as the weeks went by. He found he had time to think clearly, a luxury his fraught relationship had not allowed him. He began to run through the what-ifs of his life, and recently he had become stuck on the ones he longed to put to rest but that seemed to have no answer. What if he had been able to track Carrie down? What if she still loved him? He was sure he still loved her, and as long as he felt that way it was better to be on his own than to play the wrong tune with someone else's heart strings.

Now he had found her – after all this time. Carrie. His first love, whose light natural ways had knitted so sweetly with his own affable nature. Was it ridiculous to be still so captivated by a woman he had not seen for many years? He prayed it wasn't too late. What if the two of them could recapture the wonderful feeling they'd once had for each other?

He felt a sudden pang of guilt about Rebecca. The transition from emptiness to overflowing was so rapid. All the same, it was impossible not to smile and embrace the pleasant warmth he had felt at the sound of Carrie's voice. He stirred and went to change into his running gear. He could indulge all he wished when he saw her the following night.

Stephen loved tracking round the streets at twilight, though he pounded them with less energy than he used to. This particular evening had a special quality. The setting sun stroked the sky into soft turquoise as it slipped behind the hills. In a few minutes it would throw its arms out wide and in a brief farewell, light up the horizon and the mountains with its chosen palate for the day. The lake's reply was always orchestrated by the mood of the wind. Stephen kept turning his head, not wanting to miss the magic. He never ceased to be amazed at how this same composition could empathise with such diverse emotions. The same hills could become as much suffused with joy as with sadness, or the sky beckon with friendship or tell of loneliness. This particular evening imbued him with hope.

His jog took him up the hill. He hadn't noticed the pavement passing under his feet and was surprised to find, when roused by a loud greeting from above, how far he had gone.

"Dear Stephen. Out gracing the streets, I see. Aren't you marvellous?" Miriam was in her garden watering her marigolds in the dusk.

"You're great the way you get out to the garden, Miriam," he puffed. "How are you?"

"Never better. Met the most marvellous couple who have moved in down below. You must come and meet them soon, Stephen. They would love to know you, I'm sure."

Stephen continued to jog on the spot, not wanting to appear rude but keen to get on his way.

"Yes," she continued, with a note of sensation creeping into her voice. "They're right across the road from that frightful young woman. Can keep an eye on her, thank heavens."

"What frightful young woman is this, Miriam?" He was amused.

"*Mizz* Thompson. You met her the other night."

Stephen stopped jogging. "Oh come on, Miriam, what's so frightful?" he asked, trying not to sound too interested.

"It's as we thought the other night, Stephen. She *must* be a solo mother, and bound to be on social welfare. We are paying for that young taker to stay in this wonderful place of ours. Live in luxury – on us. The cheek of it." Then she tilted her head. "You'd be paying a higher proportion than most of course, Stephen, dear."

Stephen decided it was better to give these comments little weight. Surely Carrie wouldn't be ripping off the system. Would she? He thought it better not to continue the conversation. With a wave he started off again and gave her a non-committal reply. "These things always sort themselves out, Mrs M."

Miriam leant well over to admire his athletic figure as it

receded up the road. Her hose leant too, sending a fountain of water over her.

"Watch you don't fall foul of the massage parlour next door, by the way," she spluttered as he disappeared.

But his reply was lost to the gathering night.

Jake and Tom were less evasive with Stephen when he came to dinner the next evening. Once the boys discovered he was prepared to be a springboard, they were won over and Carrie quite clearly was, also.

"I suspect you're rather relieved to see them get to bed," she laughed once they were asleep.

He sat at her kitchen bench, wine glass in hand, while Carrie organised their meal. He grinned. "They're lovely, Carrie. Full on, though, isn't it?"

He noticed the ease with which she moved about her kitchen, full of interested conversation, constructing a delicious meal with a casual toss of the hand, her open smiling face often turned to him. He wondered how on earth she could find space to create the next dish, the bench was in such chaos. Dishes and toys. Mail waiting to be dealt with. More toys. Handbag. Her jacket. The boys hats. Everything overlaid by toys.

She saw him taking it all in. "You're right – it's full on. At least I know it gets easier, eventually."

"Previous experience, eh?" he smiled.

"With Astra? Yes. Although, as I may have said to you, she's pretty good at keeping me organised. She's wonderful, Stephen. I'd love you to meet her. Very honest sort of a girl is my Astra."

He was curious to know what she was studying.

"A double degree. Science and commerce. Done really well, as it happens. She sure doesn't get it from me. I was in another world whenever science was on the menu at school. Do you remember? You used to come over and help me with my homework."

And as Carrie composed the meal, they reminisced: summer evenings staying out under the stars; obliged to head home on frosty nights to beat the cold and sneak a cuddle on her parents' sofa; the call from the top of the stairs to hurry him on his way.

"I never thought things would change," Stephen told her. "It was as if we would go on like that for always. I shouldn't have gone rushing off to university without making sure you'd be there when I got back."

"Yes, you should have. Look at what's happened for you. Think how frustrated you'd have been if you'd always been thinking about me. You'd never have got your business under way."

"But that's just it, Carrie," he was serious for a moment. "I've done just that. Got my business under way, and built, and still been always thinking of you."

She moved round the bench and put her hand on his arm. He felt the warmth melt into him. Placed his hand over hers and held her gaze.

"I've thought no small amount about you, too," she whispered, then broke off with a gay laugh.

"Dinner. Come on, you must be starved."

They moved to the table and Carrie watched in expectation as Stephen tucked into her food.

"Oh this is delicious, Carrie. When did you learn to cook like this?"

"Not sure. Just happened. It's what my husband –

my ex-husband – and I did. We started a restaurant in Auckland and that grew into two, then three. Then we started marketing frozen meals into supermarkets. It's mostly local sales, but some national and quite a big business now."

Stephen was intrigued, and impressed. He had heard about the business – and the restaurants. He had dined out in one of them a number of times. How had they not run into each other?

Carrie elaborated on the business side, how she had gravitated to the kitchen and menu planning, and how Craig had run much of the day to day business. The fun they had building it up.

"So what went wrong with the marriage?" Stephen asked.

Carrie sighed. "Until now no one but my solicitor – and Astra – have had any idea of how difficult things have been. It's great to have someone else to talk to, to be honest.

"It's hard to describe it. He was a lovely guy in many ways – once. It's why I married him, of course. But I couldn't see the whole picture. It took me such a long time to figure out why I was unhappy, get our relationship into perspective."

She paused, Stephen silent and watching her.

"It was subtle at first. The abuse. He'd prod me, verbally, goad me 'til I reacted, and then laugh. You know, making fun of me. Then the irritation set in and the yelling started. I still hoped everything would be manageable, 'cause of course Jake had been born. I wanted the marriage to work. Then I found I was pregnant with Tom."

She shook her head sadly. "It seemed to turn Craig when he found out. Perhaps it was the thought of extra noise, extra pressure. His lashing out became so physical. Just brutal. Astra has never been able to stand Craig. Understandable in lots of ways, of course. He interfered in her relationship with me simply by his being there. But it was more than that, even in the beginning. She saw instinctively what I refused to notice about him.

"She's amazing, Stephen. So intuitive. And she quietly worked on me over time. Gave me the strength I needed to leave him. She gives me the strength to hang in there now, to sort things out."

"Does he still cause you any trouble?" Stephen was frowning.

Carrie gave a helpless laugh. "He doesn't even know where I am. I've... run away. I know. With his children. Not exactly straightforward, is it? Still very new, which is why you find me in quite such chaos."

She lightened up a little. "Actually, I'm always a bit chaotic," she grinned. "But seriously, I'm only now working out how to go on from here, and I have to be honest, I'm still very frightened. I don't think he's entirely sane."

They discussed her letter to the solicitor and what her opportunities were for some sort of resolution. Carrie cleared the table when they had eaten, then sat back down to finish her wine.

"It's a funny thing, you know. I wouldn't have had the energy to do anything about getting back in touch with him even now if it hadn't been for Miriam McGregor. She's a bit odd, isn't she? I mean, I don't want to be rude about your friend, but she's rather manipulative, I think."

Stephen thought back to his run the previous evening.

"What's happened there, Carrie? I don't know Miriam all that well, but she's OK. She's a bit gushy, of course, a bit of a snob. But she does lots around the neighbourhood, and I don't think she'd mean any harm."

"You are a dear. You're so polite and honest yourself, I don't think you'd know a bad egg if you broke one into the pan. Probably she's just a bit of a busybody, no more. Though I'm not betting on it."

As she related what happened when Miriam had marched into her garden with her ultimatum, she realised how farcical it all sounded. She stopped and her eyes sparkled.

"See. It's not just myself who sees me as chaotic," she giggled.

It was getting late. The two old friends, the two once-young lovers, were happy. They'd re-established the bond, both were sure of that. Stephen felt he should leave, though he could not have been more reluctant. They stood at the door for a moment. His hand reached out to her face. With the back of it brushing her flushed cheek, he drew it down to her lips. Held it there. She gave him such a look, the woman ripened from the girl. The thought of her mellowed body sent a thrill through his own. Still, her smile didn't beckon any further. It caressed his hand in return but it continued to protect. With a terror he had not known since he first reached out for her hand years before, all he could do was whisper his hope.

"Can I see you again, Carrie?"

"Yes," she said, and she bid him a final good night.

Stephen was walking home, making his way up the street, no glance back at the lake this time, no thought of

Miriam's intrusive caution. He meted out a silent chant.

"Let this work," he repeated in time to his step. "Don't let her slip away. Let this work."

# CHAPTER SEVENTEEN

## SPADES

The meeting of Miriam and the Gumphrys might have appeared innocuous enough. Angus, however, could already see the two women and, as it turned out, Hubert, were an alarming combination. They seemed to share an inordinate interest in morality. Or rather, they all thrilled to the slur of immorality in others. And far from having little consequence, he feared their introduction was to have the most unfortunate repercussions.

He sat in *The Hidey-hole* as the sun peeped over the horizon, having an early morning puff on his pipe. Deep in his Miriam-befuddled brain he worked it out. When scandalized personalities like this met, they spawned an emotional maelstrom.

"What a terrible resentment those three carry," he told himself between puffs. "Think the world owes them something."

If they continued with their alliance, he feared it would mutate into such animosity it would be under no one's control. And once uncontrolled it was capable of whipping

the world around it into a frenzy, leaving all in its path
torn and battered – himself included.

The tui croaked in the cherry tree above him.

"Quite," Angus told it. "But even worse than out-of-
control animosity, old bird, there is this cursed dinner I
have to put up with tonight."

And he blew out an especially large puff of smoke.

A rogue draft caught the door and slammed it shut,
waking Miriam from her guiltless dreams. Tuesday, and
the day of her intimate soirée had arrived. As far as she
was concerned, this day dawned with the sole purpose of
hurrying through to dusk and her dinner-for-four.

It was unusual for Miriam to be quite so enchanted by
others and it didn't occur to her to question what attracted
her to the Gumphrys. She did have, however, a burning
need to inform them of how undesirable Carrie Thompson
was, and she had decided on this occasion to go to some
lengths to impress. Leyla and Hubert's firm opinions had
not escaped her notice. Neither looked as if they would be
easy to relegate to sub-lieutenant. If Miriam was to remain
in charge, she must overawe them.

She climbed quickly out of bed and busied her way
through her morning routine, eager to prepare for the
evening.

Miriam tackled cooking the way she tackled life.

Without any real understanding of what constituted good taste, she had an unwavering conviction – whatever she did was correct.

"We will start with gazpacho. Redolent of the Iberian Peninsular," she reported to Angus as he stood later in the morning watching her ready her kitchen. "Followed by a delicate salad of rocket with a lemon dressing."

"Rather too American, don't you think?" her husband asked. "Having the salad before the mains."

"Precisely."

The main course, he discovered, was to be chicken masala with rice, and spinach dressed in a garlic yoghurt sauce, followed by a dessert of zabaglione. Masala followed by Marsala. Angus's stomach groaned. A Miriam culinary masterpiece marinated in geographical sophistry.

He watched with churning stomach as she went through the overstated steps of zabaglione making. It was a recipe Miriam always pulled out for these occasions. Part of the sophistication she talked about. She had eaten it once in some fancy Italian restaurant and had produced it at every single-handed dinner party she'd had since. Made not a jot of difference when he told her it made him queasy it was so rich.

She pulled out the double boiler.

"Huh. That's apt," he thought.

And as the cracked eggs were dribbled from shell to shell to extract the waxy yellow yolk; and as the sugar, an awful lot of it, was folded into the eggs, Angus's stomach turned in time to the whisk. He could never understand why she persisted with this recipe. She would make it too early and then let it sit, causing the custard to separate from the Marsala. That did make it manageable in one respect, at least. The alcohol could always be reached by a judicious manipulation of the spoon, and thus the custard avoided. If only he could have consumed the Marsala and left the rest, but Miriam would insist – in front of the guests, what's more – he eat the lot. It exasperated him, being treated like some school boy. The top was so sickly it would set the nerves around his temples on edge leaving him no option but to excuse himself and make a bee line for the bathroom.

The finished zabaglione was caressed into Miriam's tall crystal best, some chocolate hail flaked in misconceived decoration on the top. She took off her apron and wiped her hands with satisfaction.

By evening Miriam had everything organised, and as per the normal order of things, Angus had the responsibility of distributing nibbles. As he carried the tray through to the sitting room he was suddenly struck by an urge to vary the routine, add a little spice to his evening. Instead of allocating each item to its set position, he left them all arranged on the tray, which he placed on the coffee table. He took some precise little steps back to admire the result. Modern. Attractive. Perhaps this was what he should do more; assert himself, put his own stamp about the house for a change. Why not? What was the worst that could happen?

Within milliseconds of Miriam entering the room her wilting reaction showed him precisely what would happen. She was not at all impressed by his perfidious act.

"How can you do this to me, Angus? These are strangers coming. We must not loosen the standards."

He was to follow the set game plan. There was to be no breaking ranks. The peanuts would take the side table. The crystallized ginger, the mantelpiece. The pâté could stay on the coffee table, but under no circumstances was it to remain on a tray.

"Guests do not cast their eyes upon trays, Angus."

It was no use. Of course Angus knew that. The only chance at independence he would ever get now would be if he made a final getaway through that front door of theirs. Never to return. His thin shoulders made to lift in protest then retracted in a dispirited slump. This was the second time in as many weeks he had thought of putting distance between himself and his wife. It made him nervous.

He turned without further protest and rearranged the nibbles before taking the tray back to the kitchen, and at a bare minute past the appointed hour the sound of the doorbell jangled up the stairs.

"I'll go, Angus, thank you. You stay here."

Angus could hear Miriam's enthusiastic welcome and he waited with a degree of trepidation as she climbed back up the stairs with her guests. While he was not sure about these two, he could tell – even at this distance – his wife was far from disappointed with them.

Hubert strode into the room and shook Angus's hand. "Confident enough," Angus thought, "but a bit of an odd one."

Hubert was carelessly attired. His long legs pushed his ankles down below the cuffs of his dark green slacks to display brown shoes and cream socks. The purple knit shirt was a little tight. Short-sleeved, as Angus found out when Hubert removed his tweed jacket. There was a gold chain around his neck but apart from that, no obvious sign he had thought of anything tonight other than hurrying over to the McGregors to discuss the world and deal with its encroachments. Miriam would consider this man's look indicated he was keen but presented no threat to her social superiority.

He had a chance to sum Leyla up as he got their drinks. She had at least attempted to dress for dinner, but with a lack of taste Angus knew would gratify his wife. Her generous figure was squeezed into a black crocheted dress. The shoes were flat and utilitarian, with chunky soles Angus had heard squeak as she had crossed the tiles downstairs. He watched Miriam glance down at her own gown with a look he recognised. There would be no difficulty keeping these two in their place, that's what she would be thinking.

He sighed. Nothing about the evening gave Angus to believe he would relax, but despite his misgivings, the meal proceeded without a hitch and the Gumphrys obliged with effusive appreciation for Miriam's cooking. Hubert, in particular, enjoyed the zabaglione.

"Thank you Hubert. Just a little something I've not made much before. I must make it again for you some time soon."

Angus took refuge in the wine, pouring liberal top-ups for their guests at the same time. Leyla became more and more voluble, causing him to think she might be doing her chips by out-talking his wife. Miriam, however, was all grace and patience and waited until coffee before she attempted to outline her plan. By that time the Gumphrys were sufficiently pickled to be content just to sit and stare, all smiles.

Miriam took the floor. She was purring. She edged forward on her chair and gave the newcomers an exhaustive briefing on everything that mattered concerning Glade Heights. Street numbers were assigned owners, whose attitudes and suitability were detailed. Past episodes of misbehaviour by particular residents were discussed and Miriam's general tactics in each matter outlined.

The Gumphrys in turn revealed their own curriculum vitae. Successes and a few honest failures in their previous neighbourhoods were disclosed with a candidness Miriam declared most agreeable. There was a procession of loud exclamation and confirmation. In fact there was so much mutual congratulation, at one point Angus, who had long before confirmed his spectator's role for the night, thought the relationship might collapse in on itself, neutralised by the pervading spirit of self-approval. Instead, as the murmurs grew warmer they began to generate an electricity that before long arced and cracked from one to the other, leaving only Angus untouched by its thrill. And of all the issues covered that night, the most galvanizing was the discussion about Carrie Thompson.

"To be honest, Miriam," Leyla told her, "we haven't noticed her yet. But how ghastly. It's a scandal such a person is living at the Heights, let alone right across the road from us."

Angus was amazed they accepted Miriam's analysis without question. They were so enchanted by their hostess, they took it as read Carrie must be someone whom they should dislike and distrust.

"I can't tell you how grateful we are with indebtedness, Miriam," said Hubert with a creased brow, "for drawing this most unfortunate matter to our attention. We will now be juxtaposed in an advantageous position to observe her with an informed eye, from close range, and with an interest of fervent urgency."

"I agree, Hubert, dear," his wife added. "It is absolutely disgraceful these people are allowed to get away with it. How can we help more directly, do you think, Miriam?"

"Well, of course, I have the matter very much in hand.

But any back-up would add weight. Those children. They are the first priority. Heaven knows what might happen to them if they are left to free range in the manner they are. I've already contacted the CPS and they are sending someone around to investigate the matter. But you know what these government agencies are. Never do their job properly. No concept of taking advice from those of us truly in the know."

"Miriam, you don't actually kn..." Angus attempted, but was flagged down by an irritated hand.

"And..." She continued, looking daggers at him. "And, as I was saying...I do think if you were to send off one of those marvellous letters of yours, Hubert, it might have even more impact. We'll wait though, until the CPS have made their first move."

Hubert beamed. "That would give us more time to consider the formulation of the correct tenor for the letter with respect to its general tone. I find with these matters it is important to draft, draft, and draft again. People are rather impressed with the way in which I can cut through all the unnecessary material and get to the nitty gritty of the matter."

His chest rose as he outlined the magnitude of his own competence.

"It is also important to impress with one's language. The layman is little able to appreciate the subtleties of the substance which one wishes to implicate in the body of any complaint that one might wish to present to the uninitiated."

Angus blinked. Perhaps he had downed too much wine. Hubert may well be right, but for the life of him he hadn't a clue what the man was talking about. He was impressed Miriam appeared to be more on the ball.

"Quite," she concurred. "One must advise others, Hubert, for they simply have no idea themselves."

The soirée ran its course and the Gumphrys departed with sincere farewells. Miriam returned to the kitchen where Angus was pouring himself a final tipple for the evening. He waited for her rebuke, but it didn't come. Instead, as she glided back and forth across the room organising its contents into their latest compartments, she had on her face a look of beatitude. And she sang as she floated. In a voice that wobbled as it hit the higher register. Somehow disturbing, so it arrived a semitone too discordant in Angus's ears.

He raised his eyebrows at her. "This is an unusual conclusion to one of your dinner parties," he suggested.

She stopped trilling and spun around. "The Gumphrys were meant to arrive at this time, Angus. Fate. It could not be better. They are the ones we've been waiting for to help knock this place into shape. They understand how imperative it is we get rid of that girl. You may not have the wit to see it. But I do and they do. They are so motivated. And that spurs me on."

And she burst forth once more, sending Angus scampering off to bed, hounded by her piercing renditions.

*"The hills are alive with the sound of music…"*

# CHAPTER EIGHTEEN

# BLINKERED

No one sees us quite as we see ourselves. When we look in a mirror, the image that looks back at us is quite different from the image we present to everyone else. It is not just because the image is reversed. The perspective is altered in every respect. Therefore, no one who was not Leyla nor Hubert Gumphry could view them in quite the same way as they viewed themselves.

When someone first met the Gumphrys, they generally came to the conclusion this was a couple not without merit. It was true, her voice was a distinct disadvantage for her, and his tendency to pontificate was a decided lack of advantage for him. But who was counting?

These were their first impressions.

It never took long, however, unless the person was imbued with the same single-minded compulsion as Miriam McGregor, before their belief in the Gumphrys' merits faded. And it was generally agreed by those with experience and a level head, an acquaintance with the Gumphrys was not something you wanted to hold on to.

This picture, which outsiders gleaned of Glade Heights' newest residents, did not, however, tally at all with how they saw themselves. Where others saw Leyla as strident, she saw herself as one of life's leaders – alongside her husband. She conceded this meant she dealt with things in a direct manner, but by no means did she see herself as loud or over-bearing.

Others clearly did.

While she also saw herself as confident, it was an ill-based confidence, delivered without logic. Leyla could not be considered bright. Any real intelligence she might have been born with was negated by an entrenched conservatism that shackled her judgement. It was not surprising the one person she was prepared to defer to was Hubert, who had developed obfuscation (for such he would have termed it) into an art form. She never really understood his convoluted speeches but he was of the same ilk, shared the same irreproachable morals, and whatever he said was unquestionably correct.

Red neck blind faith might have summed Leyla up.

Her foil-for-life, Hubert, was just as ensconced in the far right wing of opinion, but his driving force was different. He was seen by others as slightly unbalanced. This was their charitable view, when they were not the current target of his attention. If, however, they did become the poor harassed soul upon whom Hubert was fixated, they saw him as more than just a little unhinged. And he had driven many a normal person to question whether it was worth continuing to struggle through the tangled web that is life if it meant Hubert was on their case.

This manic image was not how Hubert viewed himself, of course. Even as a young boy he believed himself blessed with the capacity to grasp the intricacies of complicated issues far beyond the reach of normal men. He was barely into his teens when he had set about analysing these issues. In detail. He did this, he felt, for the benefit of less fortunates who would have no hope of ever understanding them otherwise. He saw himself as an incomparable philanthropist, offering society the benefit of his intellect for free. Laying the path for a better world for all. To his tired opponents he was vacuous and obtuse. To himself, he was simply showing others how best things might be run. He knew, he could tell you, and you would be best to concede, it wasn't better done your way but rather done his way.

Thus, both Gumphry husband and Gumphry wife were instilled with an overstated confidence in their own opinion.

This remarkable couple moved in perfect harmony, always lending unquestioned support to each other. They were not like Miriam who was ever on the look out for crusadable issues, pursuing them in order to control and survive. Argument in itself was not what the Gumphrys needed for sustenance. Once they caught the aroma of a brewing issue, however, their appetite was insatiable. Their hunger for gossip and social resolution was fuelled further by the fact neither worked any more. Hubert in particular had quivered with frustration since he had retired. Simply, if they were not hard out campaigning they were bored, which was why they had found dinner with the McGregors so mouth-watering.

The Gumphrys spent an intense few days following

the soirée salivating over the fruits of scandal Miriam had supplied.

"It's not just the parking problem, Leyla," Hubert stated at breakfast some days later. "We have an enormous lot of work to do regarding these prostitutes up the hill, let alone the research required on this welfare-fraud neighbour of ours."

These were inflammatory labels Hubert was assigning, but keeping things in perspective was not one of Hubert's strong points.

"I'm going to need to be extremely organised to get through the work load," he added with a sigh.

"You can count on my support as always, Hubert."

His wife filled her lungs to the brim, then bit by bit she released her view of the situation.

"You'll need to do the paper work of course. You're so good at that. Really you *should* have been a lawyer. But I'm very happy to observe and feed in information, and of course, I shall delight in being a go-between with Miriam. How rare it is to meet someone with such sound sense."

"I couldn't agree more. Now, Miriam tells us she is very familiar with Council regulations regarding businesses being run from home. And while I'm quite sure she has an excellent grasp of things, she could benefit from my assessment. It's quite appalling there are prostitutes practising in our midst. If the authorities can't work this out for themselves I will need to work it out for them. I think this calls for a morning on the internet. I should be able to download all the necessary legislation. It should be possible to produce an opinion before lunch. Then I'll call in on Council with it and see if I can't get some sense out of them. What will you do with your day, Leyla?"

"Me? I'm best to keep an eye on that Carrie woman

across the road, don't you think? Tell you what, I'll get out and do some gardening in the front of the house. That way I'll see who comes and goes. Better make sure the CPS people turn up. If I'm in the right place at the right time, I might even be able to have a word. And I'd like to get back up to the McGregors at some point. It would be good to run through these problems with Miriam again."

And so it was the Gumphrys began to weave their outlandish pattern into the fabric of Glade Heights society.

A little after midday, Leyla left the garden and went inside to prepare lunch. The Gumphry lunch was always formal, a set meal with table cloth produced and tea pot readied for later. Leyla enjoyed any meal time, in particular if Hubert was working on a project. He would run through his findings and they would discuss the merits of different approaches.

Hubert's morning had been very productive and he came to the table in an affable hum.

"The best way to impart this latest information, Leyla, is to have you read it. Perhaps you'd be good enough to read it out loud so I can think about refinements as you go along."

"With pleasure," Leyla beamed. She took his notes, a veritable ream of paper, on top of which sat a letter. "Oh Hubert. What a lot of work. You have done so much. You could so easily have been doing this professionally you know."

"Ah well. I'm quite happy to give others the benefit of my insight *pro bono*. If it helps, you know."

She cleared her throat in order to read his letter out loud.

" '*Sir.*' Who are you addressing this to, Hubert?"

Hubert assumed a very clipped, business like manner. "Recipient uncertain as yet. Need to liaise with fellow complainants to ascertain the certainty of their veritable view, you know."

"I do," she smiled, dazzled by his grasp of language. She continued to read. " '*It is with considerable alarm that the aforementioned matter…*' "

"I've yet to append the matter in question," he pre-empted.

Leyla continued. " '*… has come to our attention. In seeming contravention of the laws both of the locale and the nation, two women have commenced a lewd and wanton business in the precincts of this quiet suburban neighbourhood about which the resident residents…*'

"Do they need to be resident residents, do you think dear?" Leyla trod carefully, not wishing to be seen to be editing such a brilliant piece.

"Point taken. But no, Leyla, I must remain firm on this point. One must distinguish between the temporary resident and the resident resident, as the former would not be empowered to the extent of the latter notwithstanding the encompassment of any lease that the former might thereinbefore have entered into that would not need to have been entered into by the latter."

Leyla was impressed. But persistent.

"Well, could you put that in then, what you've just said? In order to be more precise?"

"Good point again, Leyla. Write that down then, do you mind? And I'll type it up later."

Thus lunch continued until the pair was replete with

both food and information. With the dishes done and the house tidy Leyla decided to pay a visit to Miriam. She would be able to discuss Hubert's sublime appraisal of the prostitute situation, having no doubt her husband's kudos would rub off on herself. She slipped a little coral-coloured lipstick on her thinning lips and went to get the car out.

She was already in high spirits. By the time she had reached the McGregor house, her heart was soaring. Just as she had driven her car out of her driveway, she noticed a small white car pulling up outside Carrie's house. There was no mistaking it, or the woman driving. Both positively reeked government-departmental – the Children's Protection Service had come to call.

# CHAPTER NINETEEN

## PROTECTED

Carrie stood at her kitchen bench, arms folded. The noise of Tom and Jake rushing around the living room furniture barely penetrated her thoughts. Being protected, being cared for – Carrie had forgotten what it felt like to be secure and nurtured. Her mother had looked after her when she was young. Certainly she was always loved by her. She did wonder, though, if either of her parents had ever truly understood what made their daughter tick.

When she became pregnant with Astra all the sense of security she had grown up with was snatched away, and not just because her parents berated and criticised when she had told them the news. "How could you have been so casual in a relationship?" they had asked. "Surely not the girl we raised with sound family – married family – values."

She had waited until Astra was about to be born before telling them. By that time she felt so on her own she chose not to confide in them further. Their lack of understanding had not helped. They had not asked about Astra's father, asked if Carrie needed help. Isolated in Australia, Carrie steeled herself to care alone for her child, and while, over the years, she took Astra to see her parents, the barriers of suspicion between them were too concrete to break down. She never did share her secrets with them or let them know of her needs. They continued to love her but not to wish to help her.

Neither of her parents survived to see her married and with sons. Would it have healed their hurt? Carrie was not sure. They would never have understood violence in a marriage, nor her leaving Craig.

Her marriage – she had hoped Craig would protect her, hadn't she? That his family might welcome her and offer support. But in time she found out Craig was not close to them. There had never been any day-to-day or encompassing connection that might have met his emotional needs or helped their relationship survive. It was only now she realised someone as needy as Craig was incapable of offering protection. And now she needed protection against him.

Placing a reliance on Stephen had its dangers, too. What she longed to do was find a balance – to be capable of embracing independence without at the same time fighting it for fear it might scare off the caring she yearned for.

The whoops and calls of her sons continued around her, but not until the doorbell rang, and she saw what greeted her on her doorstep, was she finally roused from her reflections.

"Hello." Standing at the door was a round short woman, be-suited in a pair of navy trousers, with a navy jacket pulled tightly over a white shirt. The whole package Carrie decided, was in need of an iron.

"Are you Miss Thompson?"

"Who are you?"

"Marilyn Philps. CPS. Just a routine call Miss Thompson, to make sure everything's all right."

Carrie's face rushed with blood. "What are you on about?" This, she had not expected. She folded her arms defensively.

Marilyn Philps from the CPS seemed unperturbed. She poked her head around Carrie to look into the house.

"Ah…just as I said. A routine call. You have children, I see?"

"CPS? That's the Children's Protection Service isn't it? Well – what on earth are you doing here?" Carrie persisted.

"Two boys, is it? They sound happy."

Despite herself, Carrie answered the question. "My sons are fine. Yes, very happy. Now if you'll excuse me, I'm very busy and I don't want to continue this conversation any further."

Marilyn Philps gave Carrie a fleeting, tolerant smile.

"I understand," she said. "I'm sorry to trouble you, only sometimes people need help when they're on their own, but they don't know how to ask for it. And we're here to help. Any time. You seem sorted enough, though, so I'll be on my way. Here's my card if you ever want to call me."

"I won't."

With a firm click, Carrie shut Marilyn Philps out. She leant back for a minute and digested the strange encounter. An unsettling concern seeped in. Why on earth would the CPS people be calling on her? Was Craig behind this? But the woman had called her Miss Thompson. Craig would have told them they were married. Couldn't be him, then, surely? Then she groaned, remembering the threat she had received.

"Oh my God…Miriam McGregor. Who else could it be? What on earth have I let myself into?"

Rattled by this odd turn of events, Carrie decided to do something she didn't often do. She needed consolation. She went straight to her phone to call the one person she could be certain really cared.

"Hello? Mum?"

"Hello, darling."

"What are you doing calling me at this hour? Where are you? Are you all right?"

Despite a giggle, Carrie couldn't disguise her nervousness. "I'm fine. Just had a rather strange visit from the child protection people and I thought I needed to hear something sane for a minute or two."

Carrie explained to Astra what had happened. She tried not to make too much out of it, not wanting to worry her daughter. What she did want was to hear the quiet confident voice, and Astra obliged. After talking the facts through, Astra dismissed the visit as just one of those silly, irritating things. Not something to worry about. Before long they were laughing together about some of the odd neighbours they had lived near in the past. They agreed, Miriam seemed positively tame in comparison to some, and Carrie began to feel real once more.

Then Astra became serious with her mother. "You have been in touch with the lawyer, though, haven't you, Mum? You need to clear up this thing with Craig. It's going to eat away at you otherwise. You need to get your life back to normal."

"I know, and yes I have been in touch. I think he's trying to organise a meeting with Craig's lawyer. Craig's obviously pretty agitated about what's happened. My

lawyer's advised me to take out a protection order – oh
help, there's that word again – but I don't want to inflame
things more."

"Be careful. Won't you? Look, I've got no more lectures
from the end of next week. I might come home for some
study leave. Would that be OK?"

"Oh that would be wonderful, Astra. The boys would
be thrilled. I'd be thrilled." She paused for a second. "Um.
There's someone I'd like you to meet, too."

"Who?" Astra sounded wary. "Mum? What have you
been doing?"

Carrie laughed. "It's OK. He's an old friend. I'm not
getting into any more trouble, promise. It's just that apart
from you kids it's the one bright spark in my life right now.
I'm sure you two would get on."

She quickly steered Astra on to talk about the boys, and
university, and summer, and having organised when she
would come home, they said goodbye.

The call had worked. Just talking to Astra helped put
things into perspective. She must not get sucked in by the
lunatic behaviour of one unbalanced neighbour. She called
to Jake and Tom and together they walked down to the
letterbox. Carrie lifted Tom up so he could put his chubby
arm into the box and pull out the mail, then she set him
down, and as he squealed with delight, she and Jake chased
him back to the house where she finally caught him and
secured her letters.

The boys raced back to their games while Carrie sat
down to digest the day's mail. She picked up the fattest
envelope first and examined it. It was from her lawyer.
"That's quick," she thought. She tore it open, apprehensive
about what he might have arranged. But inside was another
unopened envelope. The handwriting made her heart

stop. It was Craig's. For a moment Carrie froze. Then, swallowing hard and mustering all her courage, she ripped the envelope open.

The stark message that unfolded snatched at her breath. "Bitch!" The words spat out at her. "You can't hide. I'll find you and when I do – Bitch – you'll regret you ever lived."

# CHAPTER TWENTY
## VULTURES

Up the hill and around the bend, Angus was letting a breathless Leyla into Miriam's eyrie. He offered her the barest lifting at the edges of his mouth. He was tired from the intense conversations that had taken place, first at the dinner party, and subsequently during the many phone calls and flurried visits of the previous few days.

Leyla was not offended. She did not appear even to notice. It was those same discussions that propelled Leyla past Angus and straight up the stairs to her new friend. Angus dragged himself up behind her and plopped down in the large armchair at the far corner of the sitting room. Not to be seen. Not to be heard.

From this safe haven Angus could hear the gushes and hushes of Miriam and Leyla's latest exchange. First one would lift to impart an important item of information, to which the other would suck up a lengthy breath, then after a further and dramatic pause, let out a more breathy and scandalised, "Nooooo!" or "Re-a-lly!"

"They're like pistons in an engine," he thought as he

watched them. Rocking to and fro in unison. As one spoke forward the other would listen back. Then they would reverse roles. Back and forth. Forth and back. He was mesmerised. He had never seen anyone quite so equal to his wife's rhythmic harping. He tried to listen but as he found himself dosing off, he could only just register Leyla's shrill voice, like a creaking door rocked by the wind.

Angus surrendered to the press on his eyelids, and in no time at all he was dreaming, deeply. He was caught in an eddy on the river, whirled downstream, the eddies moving not just round and round, but in deep green sweeps ever further down and away from the river's source. Down towards the falls. It wasn't cold, but it felt ominous and threatening, out of control. Leyla sprang up at the river's edge and she was pulling him out. At first he felt only relief. But soon she began to berate him.

"Why didn't you protect Miriam from the pain of Cynthia's death?" she demanded. "Didn't you owe it to your wife to carry the burden and not let her be drawn down so over all these years?"

Struggling to warm himself in the misty sunlight, the dream Angus shivered at her accusation. "What business is it of yours?" he shouted back.

But Leyla persisted. "It is up to you to control these things. Don't you know your own job? Her face came closer, her voice grew louder. "You're the husband. It's your job to open the floodgates and let out her grief," she reproached him.

He tried to explain. He had tried to soothe her all these

years, to talk to her. He had wept. Why hadn't Miriam wept? How could he force her to weep? He had his own pain to deal with that was just as deep as Miriam's. She didn't have the monopoly on heartbreak.

But on and on Leyla went. Angus gasped for breath. He was back in the eddy. Knew it. An inexorable drowning rush towards the falls – except, he wasn't back in the river at all. It was Leyla. He was going to drown in the woman's flood of words.

"Everything is out of balance," she was telling him. "Do something about it. Do something about it."

"Leave me alone," he lashed out.

"Angus? Are you all right?" His wife's voice this time. Annoyed. Distant. "Angus!"

He opened his eyes, wiped his clammy hands on his trousers. From the other end of the room the two women were leaning forward on their chairs, staring at him.

"You've interrupted our train of thought here. Do go off and leave us to organise things, will you."

"And as I was telling you, Miriam..." Leyla was not diverted for long. Angus was in the end a small distraction from the women's greater purpose.

He got up from his chair, and as he stretched, he remembered his dream. In that instant he saw the correlation between the river and Leyla's barely-drawn breath. She was telling Miriam she would attempt to befriend Carrie Thompson in order to find out more about her. Then they would be able to strike with sound effect.

"She's more devious than I first thought," he muttered to himself as he left the room.

Leyla returned home full of virtue, her communion with Miriam having consolidated their spiritual direction. The peace that had settled on her, however, was short lived, for she noticed with surprise the white car had already gone from outside Carrie's house. She hastened inside to tell Hubert.

"Can't have been there very long, Hubert. I'm going to give Miriam a call. She can follow it up."

"What did she think of my submission on the prostitute problem?" he called to her as she hurried to the phone.

"Brilliant of course. You must get that off tomorrow and..." But Leyla already had Miriam on the line.

"Miriam? Hello, Leyla," she gasped. "Listen, that CPS woman can't have done a proper assessment. Long gone, I'd say, by the time I arrived back... Right...yes...no... oh, right ho. Yes, goodbye then."

Leyla found Hubert again. "She's furious. Going to give the authorities a call. I'm not sure, though, Hubert. How effective she'll be, I mean. I have a feeling this is going to require your expertise in the end."

Hubert looked at his wife and sighed. "Ah well. It's as I always say, Leyla. Leave it to those who know."

Leyla's head tipped to one side as she looked with loving appreciation at her husband. A wonderful man whose talents were so wasted.

## CHAPTER TWENTY-ONE
## OFF-SPRING

The sun enfolded Angus in a generous blanket. And with his eyes closed and his head turned skyward, he conducted a happy daydream about cruising the streets in a red open-topped sports car. "Or should it be racing green?" he wondered.

But as he dreamed, a cloud sauntered across the sun and he felt suddenly colder.

When he opened his eyes, he found the shadow had come not from a cloud but from Miriam. She had taken the unprecedented step of going to find Angus in *The Hidey-hole* and she was standing over him. The incongruity of her rigid presence within the honest earthy reach of its ferns and bobbing dionellas did not escape him. He winced as she opened her mouth.

"Can you believe it, Angus?"

"Probably." His tone was sarcastic but she did not react.

"Leyla is absolutely correct. The CPS woman could not

possibly get an accurate picture of what was happening at Carrie's house unless she had spent time there. Talked to the children. Had a look about the back yard. That agency has blown the whole thing. It seems to me no matter how authoritative one is, it makes no difference. One might just as well talk to the moon."

Angus fidgeted. The discomfort he was beginning to experience over his wife's quest for dominance was awkward enough without her bringing her venom into his normally untainted private space.

He tried to dismiss her. "This probably just confirms there's no problem with Carrie in the first place. I'd let it drop, Miriam. Turn your mind to something more fruitful."

"I will not." Her mouth was tight. "Where there is smoke there is fire, you mark my words."

"And you've got the bellows."

Miriam's fury shot out. "I will not have you talking to me that way, Angus. If you can't help, and you're obviously not going to, I shall enlist the help of our neighbours. Needs must. Hubert will be able to get the CPS to take the matter further."

The thought of the Gumphrys emboldened Angus.

"You've anticipated a problem where there isn't one, Miriam. A flying flag doesn't necessarily signify a battle standard."

His wife let forth an infuriated explosion of air and stormed off, leaving Angus sitting there, annoyed his haven had been contaminated by her noisome presence.

It's ridiculous, he thought once he was on his own again. It reminded him of an absurd business over some balloons, *The Balloon Tale*, begun because Miriam resented a family renting a house up the hill when they quite clearly didn't have the money to buy property at the Heights in their own right.

Perhaps Carrie presented the same type of irritation – had got under his wife's skin because she had not earned her way into the estate. Or had she? Anyway, what did it matter?

And what was the name of that family? Abbotts. That was it. Had quite a few children, which was another minus from Miriam's point of view.

Angus hadn't seen it coming, though he had seen the balloons – hanging in merry salute off the tree near the Abbotts' house.

Miriam had marched into the kitchen in a huge lather. "Angus, that family are having a party. The rowdiness, the noise. I simply will not tolerate it. And do you know what?"

Angus had expressed genuine interest, for he had absolutely no idea what.

"They've put up balloons. Balloons, for heaven's sake. What is this neighbourhood coming to?"

Before he could work out what she was doing Miriam had rung the Council. But after an agitated conversation, she had come away from the phone in disgust. Council, she had been told, could only do something about a noise problem when and if it started.

"If, Angus. What do they mean if? Needs must, I'm afraid. I'll have to deal with the matter myself."

Immediately she rang the Abbotts.

Keen to listen in, Angus had quietly picked up the other

phone as Tim Abbott answered. He told Miriam it was none of her bloody business what they got up to in their own house but since she had asked, they were having a Pop Luck Dinner for his elderly mother.

"You see, we've drawn your face on each one of the balloons. And what that means, you interfering old bat, is every guest gets a chance to pop your balloon."

Angus could have sworn he heard repressed laughter in the Abbott background. It certainly hadn't come from his wife.

"I think he may have been making fun of me Angus. How could they, after all the work I've done on the Residents Committee?"

It didn't seem to matter no noise ever ensued from the party. Tim Abbott had gone beyond Miriam's bounds of decency. From that point, every time she heard even the smallest utterance of good cheer coming from the Abbott house she got on to the noise abatement officer at the Council.

"I shall wear them down, Angus. Mark my words."

A few months later Angus noticed a removal van being loaded with the Abbotts' household bits and pieces. Had Miriam finally pushed them out of her patch? Angus could not be sure.

Miriam clearly thought she had.

"Another job well done, Angus, and good riddance to those appalling children," was all she bothered to say.

It was a tortured business, Miriam's attitude to children. The McGregors' surviving child, Malcolm, was an unfortunate mix of his parents. He had inherited Miriam's piercing voice and outlook on life and his father's apologetic appearance and indifferent operational capabilities. Those who knew him were rather startled such a mousey looking person was capable of voicing such sarcasm. He was in constant conflict with himself.

Angus decided Miriam's fondness for Malcolm was purely superficial, did not stem from any deep maternal feeling. She had locked up any maternal warmth after Cynthia died and assigned Angus the emotional responsibility for their son. As a consequence, Malcolm and Miriam's relationship was devoid of any obvious affection.

Once he left school Malcolm had buried himself in a career communing with computers and had become quite successful. That, at least, Miriam was able to express pride in.

Angus found it safer not to think too much about how he viewed his son. He felt an attachment when the boy had been small, but Angus found it difficult to relate to the awkward adolescent, and with Miriam not encouraging open warmth, he had little in common with the adult son. Malcolm was there – not inviting particularly pleasurable contact, but his child all the same.

Angus did not mind children as a group, unlike Miriam who had some years after Cynthia's death told Angus bitterly they held little value beyond their use in guaranteeing the perpetuation of the human race. Perhaps all tenderness had been expended on Cynthia so now, in her later years, she had no love to give to any child. And perhaps if Carrie had not had two young sons bouncing with joy in the garden below, and thus within focus of Miriam's binoculars, she might not have presented such a threat.

While Angus was contemplating the vagaries of his wife's character, Miriam, herself, retreated to the sitting room and made the necessary call to the CPS. But she did not find it fruitful. So she called Leyla, and between them they organised the next manoeuvre.

"Then Hubert will fire the next salvo, Leyla? Excellent. Honestly, I rang the CPS and asked for an explanation. Do you know what the woman said? They will not discuss particular cases. I ask you. Even when one has exercised one's civic duty and reported abuse, one cannot then find out what is going to be done about it."

"Oh it is a disgrace, Miriam. But I'll go to see the girl over the next few days. I'll think of some pretext. We'll find out how the visit went and Hubert will know how to take it from there. Excellent debating skills, my husband. He could have been called to the bar, you know.

"Incidentally, Hubert has finished the opinion about the massage parlour next door to you. He'll call in at Council tomorrow, and I think you'll find there is a prompt response."

As she was about to hang up, Miriam surprised herself by voicing her appreciation.

"Thank you so much for all your support, Leyla. Up until now it's been very lonely at the top, I can assure you."

It was a pensive Miriam who came away from the telephone. As she walked past her sofa, she took up each cushion in turn and plumped it into precise fat squares before replacing it in its pre-arranged spot.

"They are a pro-active pair, these Gumphrys," she thought, punching the last cushion into submission.

To date she had controlled Glade Heights' comings and

goings. And since she was not about to relinquish control, her wish to involve the Gumphrys in this way was a puzzle. They were on her side, of course. Very gratifying. But they seemed to want to approach all the neighbourhood issues head on. Her preference was to dig a careful circle around a problem then take up the proverbial spade, and shovel the problem on the compost heap slowly and with consideration.

"I suppose having them so keen must do some good for the moral health of the Heights. Needs must. But one must stay alert."

It was the perfect moment for an *Itemization* to get everything into perspective. She sat down to make notes.

*Thompson campaign in full swing.*

*Hubert and Leyla to support call for children to be taken into care. Leyla to visit. Hubert to write Letter.*

*Massage parlour: sniper fire effective. Hubert to handle matter with Council*

The scribbling paused for a minute. There was a lot of Hubert to do this and Leyla to do that. Was this too much delegation? Would it mean a loss of control? This hands-off approach did have its merits. It would protect her from seeming to be implicated. But it also required clever forward thinking. She must pull the strings. They were quick to take up suggestions, the Gumphrys. Miriam needed to make sure they received the right ones.

She nodded a smile of calculation back on her lips and turned back to her pad:

*Scatter seed of massage 'parlour' further afield. Advise Glade Herald of Gumphrys' disapproval. A Glade Tidings column should prove useful.*

## CHAPTER TWENTY TWO
## CRACKS

Carrie was to have a brief respite before she was to face Leyla's inquisition. For the moment she could remain in ignorance and focus on Stephen.

He had asked her out for dinner, and she was counting the hours until she could see him again. She had not mentioned Craig's letter to him. Her husband's vicious words had terrorised her into silence. Instead, she blocked the menacing picture of Craig with thoughts of Stephen.

The settled shadows of the evening revealed no threat as Stephen drove up to Carrie's house. The warm glow of welcome drew him up the path to her door. Inside, Tracey was obliging the boys by swinging them around by their arms. Tom exhibited a little less exuberance than Jake, which his mother was thankful for.

"Perhaps just two more whirls, Jake, then that's enough. Tom should have been in bed already, Tracey, but he wanted to say hello to Stephen."

She picked Tom up and gave him a long hug. "Weren't you, you rascal. Time for bed now, though."

Tracey was able to take him without any fuss.

"You two go off and have a lovely evening," she told Carrie and Stephen, rolling up the sleeves on her amply tattooed arms. "The boys and I are going to cuddle down for a book."

"What a remarkable looking young girl, that one is," Stephen said with amusement when they were in the car.

Carrie grinned. "I know. Wonderful hair, isn't it. But you know, she's awfully capable. It's such a relief to leave the boys with someone I can trust."

"How old is she?"

"Oh, maybe eighteen still. Perhaps nineteen."

"Going on thirty,"

They laughed. Carrie hadn't felt so free for ages. All the oppression of the last few weeks – the last few years – lifted, taking the furrow from her brow, leaving her feather-like, a little intoxicated. She nestled into the soft leather of the car seat, relishing the certain way in which it wrapped around her. It wasn't the car itself, of course, that lent such a secure envelope to the moment. It was having Stephen sitting beside her, his chat, his strong normal presence.

As they talked over dinner, Carrie marvelled at how intimate she and Stephen seemed despite such a long separation. It had been true affection, then, the two of them had shared way back. She was far from ready to take the relationship further – she needed to keep a physical distance from this man while she wrestled with her separation from Craig. But she felt more confident about the future than she had in years.

Distracted for a minute by the pleasure she felt in Stephen's company, she smiled an absent smile at him before concentrating on what he was saying.

"You must have felt something for Craig," he said, his face carrying the trace of a frown. He quickly took a sip of wine.

"Of course I did. I hope I'm not heartless. He's an attractive guy. And incredibly good at what he does in the business. But I stopped loving him ages ago."

She reached over and touched Stephen's hand.

"I'll not disappear on you again, you know. Not on Craig's account. You know, Craig might be far from ideal as a father, but Jake and Tom's father he is. I have to try to make things work out peacefully for the boys' sake."

She paused, trying to deflect the threat of Craig's letter. She wanted to change the subject.

"By the way, I had the most extraordinary visit yesterday, from the Child Protection people," she stated.

Stephen was surprised. "Really? What on earth did Child Protection want?"

"I assume they were checking up on the children. They'll do that on a report, of course. And do you know who I think is behind this?"

"Craig? It's got to be Craig."

"No. No I don't think so. No, I think it was old goggle eyes up the hill. Miriam McGregor."

The minute Carrie spoke she regretted it. She should not have mentioned Miriam's name to Stephen, not in disparaging terms, anyway. She remembered how tolerant he was of people, and how loyal. The last thing she wanted was for him to see her as catty. His response made her heart sink.

"Oh Carrie, don't be mad, not Miriam. Why would she report you to the authorities? Even if she is a bit bossy at times, she's not nasty, I'm sure."

Carrie cursed silently. "Oh, you're probably right," she

conceded – reluctantly. "It's just that she did seem very irritated with me the other day when I ushered her off the property. And who else would do such a thing?"

"It was probably Craig," Stephen persisted.

He wants it to be Craig, Carrie fretted. But she knew it wasn't – not this time. She wilted a little, knowing there was little point in carrying the conversation further. Forcing herself to rise above the cloud that had suddenly been cast, she changed the subject again.

"I'll tell you what is happening," she said, sounding more cheerful. "Astra's coming home for study leave at the end of next week. I'd love you to meet her. I'm sure you would both get on."

"Great. Why don't we all go somewhere together? Jake and Tom, too."

Her face lightened. That's better. Don't be too hasty, she thought. Carrie looked at her watch and saw she needed to rescue Tracey.

She stood up, her good spirits restored. One other couple remained in the restaurant, finishing off their coffee at a corner table. While Stephen paid their bill, Carrie could not help but notice them staring.

"Did you see that older couple in there?" she asked him, once they were outside.

"Can't say I did. Couldn't help hearing her," he laughed, "but I don't think I recognise the voice at all."

"Vaguely familiar. Bit strange the way they were staring."

"Carrie Thompson, for goodness sake," he teased her. "You're getting paranoid."

He put his arm around her shoulder and drew her close as they walked to the car. Carrie laughed, but the voice from the restaurant pursued her, and as they drove off she could see the same couple standing in the shadow of the restaurant doorway, staring after Stephen's departing car.

# CHAPTER TWENTY THREE

## BALANCE III

Mary Naysmith woke thinking it must still be quite early. She could hear rain pounding on the roof, hard enough to justify burrowing beneath her duvet. A luminescent light filtered through the curtains. Heightened colours, yet somehow subdued. Vivid and muted in one. She stretched her legs, then her feet, as far down the bed as she could wiggle her toes, and hugged the duvet closer. Mornings were her favourite time of the day. Time was less pressing – always so much to look forward to.

She made a mental note of all the things that needed doing. It was Monday and she had a busy appointments schedule, she remembered that. And some book work to do. She groaned at the thought of accounts, and the rain sympathised, hitting a little harder above her. In unison her alarm clock clattered into life, chasing her peace away. Mary was surprised. It was later than she thought.

She climbed out of bed and opened her curtains. No wonder it seemed early. Thunder-dark clouds hovered above. Out to the east enough fine slivers of sun peeped through, making the western sky even blacker. The lake mirrored the heavens and churned itself over and over as white horses galloped past on their way to town.

Mary could hear Judith up already. She grabbed her dressing gown and, wrapping it around herself, followed her sister into the kitchen. "Good morning. What a wonderful sky. Have you seen?"

"Morning, Mares. Divine, isn't it? Coffee?"

"Thanks."

They sat together to enjoy their breakfast – another item on Mary's list of favourite things. Domestic ease; a satisfying day of work in store; they were quite the picture.

By the time their first clients arrived at 9:00am, each was scrubbed rosy in the cheeks and bursting with good health and bonhomie, and as the sisters parted to start their work Mary could not help but remark on the pleasant status quo to Judith. To do so, of course, was a terrible error in judgement, the worst possible thing to do, since, as everyone knows, the minute it is acknowledged life could not be better, a problem is sure to be waiting just around the corner.

In Judith and Mary's case, the problem took about 27 minutes, and it came in the shape of a ring on the doorbell. It was Mary's day to interrupt her appointments to attend to such intrusions but she ignored it, hoping whoever it was would disappear. The bell sounded again, however, interfering with her concentration, so she excused herself and went to answer the door.

"Good morning. Are you Miss Naysmith?"

"Why?" Mary asked, evading the question.

The man on her doorstep took that as an affirmative.

He continued. "John Goodall from Glade District

Council, Miss Naysmith. Look I'm sorry to interrupt. It's just that we've had our - ah - attention drawn to the business you run from this house and we are obliged to follow up and ensure there's nothing – um – ah – untoward going on."

Mary stood at a loss for something to say.

"Presumably, you are complying with the permit you got from Council. Just one client at a time, and – er – therapeutic massage only," he continued, clearly embarrassed. "No, you know, additional therapy."

"Yes. And no. In that order." Mary was blunt.

"Great. Yes, yes. That's great." John Goodall grinned with open relief. "Right ho. Yes, yes. Great. Sorry to trouble you. As I said, obliged to follow up."

He turned and scuttled off down the Naysmiths' drive.

"How odd," Mary said to the air. She returned to her waiting client and continued the non-additional therapy for the rest of the appointment without interruption.

Being the dismissive sort, Mary did not at first think too much about this visit. Just a routine call the Council conducted for all businesses. Didn't they? But as the morning wore on she began to remember Judith's conversation with Sally Brimsmead.

"Judith," she queried while the sisters were having a coffee break, "what do you think 'additional therapies' means?" With a nonchalant flick, she tossed the last of her blueberry muffin into her mouth, then closed her eyes to extract maximum enjoyment while she ate it.

"No idea." Judith said.

"Only, this guy from the Council came round this morning saying he was doing a routine check. And he asked if we were doing any additional therapies. I was just wondering what he could have meant."

"Guy from the Council? What routine check?"

"Well, maybe what he said was, they'd had a comment about our business or something. Apparently they have to follow up with a visit. I wouldn't worry about it. Probably just someone a bit curious about what we're doing. Won't amount to anything."

"You think it's OK, then? How did he react when you spoke to him?"

"Seemed mostly a little awkward to be honest."

"I don't like it Mares. I think we should try to find out who's behind this and sort it out."

"Nah. My advice is ignore it. Look, the Council guy was clearly cool about everything. That's all that matters, and that's the end of it."

She gave her sister a quick smile and swept the remaining crumbs from her hands in a business-like dismissal. She could tell Judith wasn't convinced. And if she were honest, her instinct was telling her it definitely was a problem, and one best nipped in the bud. But how?

She found it hard to concentrate on getting ready for the next client. It was most unfair, she sighed. She would be stuck thinking about the problem all day long, her lovely, stretched out day now ruined.

# CHAPTER TWENTY FOUR

## STORM CLOUDS

How synchronistic things were becoming at Glade Heights. Carrie was about to have her day ruined, too. Leyla had woken to the wet morning feeling the time had come for her to visit Carrie Thompson. Over breakfast she and Hubert planned the best approach.

"I really do think my strength is in the female intuition department, Hubert. I should be the one to go over and chat to the girl," Leyla suggested. "You're the analytical one. You will be able to exercise your mind with the information I glean.

"Ah," she continued, shaking her head. "It truly is a travesty you don't get to demonstrate your advocacy skills in the court room."

Hubert didn't agree he was lacking in the female intuition department, but he was flattered enough about courtrooms to say nothing to diminish his wife's chance to shine. "If that is what you wish, my dear," he deigned to concede.

The principal purpose of Leyla's foray into Carrie's

house was to establish the length of time the CPS had spent investigating her circumstances. The secondary purpose was to glean as much other useful information as possible about Carrie so the Team – which was how Leyla now thought of Miriam, Hubert, and herself – had plenty of material with which to solve the problem of their 'bludging, layabout' neighbour.

Leyla waited to have her morning tea and chocolate cake first. She then collected her handbag – Leyla felt stripped and naked without her handbag – took her coat from the front door rack and grabbed an umbrella. The rain had given way to showers but these were heavy enough to saturate her carefully constructed hairdo should she get caught in one. Thus equipped, she made her way across the road and knocked on Carrie's door.

Jake opened the door wide.

"Good morning young man. Is your Mummy in?"

Jake's expression remained impassive. He waited without a word, staring up at Leyla. Soon Carrie appeared, wiping her hands on a tea towel.

"Good morning. It's Carrie isn't it? I'm Leyla Gumphry from across the way."

"Hello," Carrie said. She'd seen this woman about, but couldn't decide where.

"I thought I should come across and introduce myself. My husband and I moved in only a couple of weeks ago. May I come in?"

Carrie never welcomed an interruption in the middle of her morning routine, but she didn't want to seem churlish.

"Um. Look I'm quite busy, but I'd be happy to make you a quick cuppa, if you'd like."

"Delightful," Leyla gushed. In this she was genuine, for cuppas implied morsels.

They went through to Carrie's chaotic kitchen just as the sun came out. Jake had joined Tom on the floor near the window where they were busy building Lego towers.

Leyla greeted them with loud, high pitched, adult condescension. "What lovely boys. You are good to be playing like that, eh?"

The boys stared silently back and Carrie hurried to put the kettle on in an attempt to gloss over their less than friendly response. She invited Leyla to sit on the stool she hastily cleared at the breakfast bench.

"Sorry about the shambles, Leyla. There's such a lot to get through with two children, of course."

"I suppose you could do with some help? You must be awfully busy. You're on your own then?"

"Yes, I am. Oh I get through it all in the end. You have to remain positive and not worry about a little mess."

"I couldn't agree more. I thought you must have someone in to help. I was out in the garden the other day and noticed a woman turn up. I had hoped, having realised you must be on your own, you know...I had hoped that perhaps you had a cleaner. I could always do with help myself, you see. Not as young as I was, of course. Trouble was she'd gone when I thought to come over and ask."

"Tea or coffee, Leyla?"

"Oh, tea thanks. Strong if you don't mind, with a little milk. No sugar. Too fattening, of course." She was silent while Carrie made the drinks. Then she tried again. "So you can't suggest anyone? That wasn't a cleaner, I don't suppose?"

"No," was all Carrie said.

"No. But of course it might be very difficult for you. To afford help, I mean. It's all very well for my husband and I. He's been an excellent worker over the years. Rather a wasted mind as it happens. Could have been a leading attorney. We'd not struggle to get domestic help. You young are in a different situation."

The boys let one of the towers crash with a great din of collapsing plastic and shouts of glee. Leyla winced.

"Well, I'm quite fit enough to do the house work myself," Carrie told her, not a little bemused. "Do you have children, Leyla?"

"Just two. And of course both grown up. I had help with them, but then, we were able to afford it. The Benefit is not enough to live on half the time, having to spend money on extras, as one does."

"What benefit?"

Leyla was nothing if not determined. "Domestic Purposes. Isn't that what all you solo mothers live on these days," Leyla ventured. "Not that I'm intending to be unkind. Of course you girls need help."

Carrie's mouth fell open. Another huge Lego tower clattered to the deck.

"Ah," she thought. "Now I know where this conversation is leading." There were too many people making too many assumptions about her these days. At least, she supposed, it meant she was becoming well practiced at dealing with them. She would be polite, but direct.

"Mrs Gumphry, I'm not sure what you're getting at, but I don't think my affairs are any of your business."

"So you admit, then, you do need help." Leyla siphoned up a large gulp of tea and ploughed on. "It's perfectly acceptable. There's no need to feel ashamed of it, Carrie. We all quite understand and it doesn't make people feel any differently about you."

The familiar ring to these comments sent shivers through Carrie. Where were all these people coming from? It seemed to her in that moment Glade Heights was saturated with meddling neighbours. She had to get rid of the woman. Quickly.

"I'm sure it doesn't," she snapped. "Look, Mrs Gumphry, you'll have to excuse me, I'm sorry. I really am busy."

"Of course you are."

"I need to get off with the boys into town."

"How lovely for them."

"I hope you don't think me rude, but I'd better get on."

"Oh don't worry about me."

Leyla's backside remained cascaded over the stool, unmoved by Carrie's obvious attempts to have it vacate the spot and leave her house. Carrie sighed. Her voice remained calm, but the extraordinary affront gave her courage.

"You have to leave, Leyla, I'm sorry. I don't like people coming into my house and making accusations about me. I know what you're about, and I don't like it."

She came around to Leyla and placing her hand lightly on the older woman's elbow, nudged her to standing and directed her to the front door.

"Oh, don't you?" Leyla's tone, until now wide and entrapping, narrowed. "Well let me tell you a thing or two, young lady. I think it's not on for the likes of Hubert and myself to be supporting the likes of you. And if you can't even show a little bit of gratitude, I can't answer for what might happen."

Carrie said nothing further. It would do no good, and she was too upset, anyway, to make any sense. Having ushered Leyla to the doorstep, she closed the door and gave the handle an extra yank to ensure she had shut the venom out.

She hurried back to the kitchen to revive her spirits with a last mouthful of coffee and saw to her horror Leyla's frightful clip handbag and her umbrella still lay at the base of the stool.

The sight of these objects incensed her. She snatched them up and ran back to the front door. Leyla was still in sight. Without thinking, Carrie hurled first the umbrella and then the handbag down the path after her.

"One bag for another," she yelled and slammed the door shut. As the rush of anger subsided, she slumped back against the door.

"Oh what have I done?" she groaned. "That was not a good move."

## CHAPTER TWENTY FIVE
## VANITY

Leyla felt fantastic. Admittedly, her pride had suffered a cursory dent as she bent to pick up her scattered belongings. But it was an elated figure who, oblivious to the thunder rolling far off in the distance, managed to skip up her own path and arrive breathless in the kitchen.

Hubert sat expectant while his wife struggled to yank off her coat. His pen was poised above his note paper, ready to précis Leyla's findings. He intended that very afternoon to create the letter to go to the CPS.

Her pink cheeks bulged with information. "Oh Hubert. What a woman. She didn't even offer me so much as a biscuit. Miriam was absolutely right about her."

"I knew it." Hubert waited for more.

"Not that she said anything directly, mind. She didn't have to. It was the CPS woman the other day. Definitely. I'm sure of it. Hardly stayed to gain an insight into her hair colour, let alone the welfare of those children. Oh – and Hubert, those boys," she scandalised her voice to its lowest level. "They're so inexpressive. I hate to think what horrors they must have to put up with."

"How dreadful."

"Absolutely. Anyway, there is no question – she's on the DPB. You should have seen her face when I challenged her. No shame at all. Then she had the cheek to usher me off the premises. Just like our poor Miriam."

"Unbelievable."

"I know. I'd forgotten my handbag. And do you know what that wretched woman did?"

Hubert sat, waiting.

"Hubert – I asked you if you knew what that wretched girl then did."

"What did she do?"

"She hurled my handbag down the pathway at me, spilling all the contents. I think the strap is broken."

"No! You realise you can sue her for damages."

"Exactly. That's what I thought."

"Oh Leyla, what a morning. What an excellent, constructive, actionable morning."

"Very excellent, I'd say. Very constructive and action-a-whatsit. I'm off to call Miriam. You get started on the letter."

Leyla rushed off to call Miriam and repeated the information, with much embellishment. "...not only that, but the little boy left me standing at the front door with it wide open. I could have been anybody, wishing ill-will on the family or anything. What was the foolish girl thinking, leaving him to open the door like that to a stranger?"

And even more gusto.

"The bag was thrown with vengeful hate, right down into the path of an on-coming car. It was only my quick eye that caught it before more contents were ruined. As it is I think the damage is irreparable."

The commiseration Miriam poured down the phone was most gratifying. It made the running of Leyla's morning gauntlet so much more worthwhile. She poured her thanks back, lingering over each detail a second then a third time, describing the letter Hubert planned to write, confirming its content.

"Marvellous *Itemizations*, Leyla. Well done." Miriam cooed.

But the full value of the *Itemizations* had still not been revealed. Leyla had been waiting for just the right moment, one which would deliver the most impact. At last she let her gem drop.

"Miriam," she said with surprising resonance and control. "There is something else I must tell you." She paused. "That girl was out to dinner the other night." Another pause. "With a man. That's right. A man."

Miriam retained her superior silence no longer. "Good Lord – who?"

The surprise in the Miriam's voice delighted Leyla.

"I'm not sure. Tall man, well dressed. Actually quite good looking. Swarthy sort, though I hate to allow her that. But definitely, definitely not the boys' father."

Miriam's curiosity heightened. "What sort of hair?"

"Oh, that's the whole point. It was quite dark. Those boys are blond, aren't they? I mean, the girl's got dark hair so presumably one of the parents has to be fair. So he can't be the father."

Leyla was offered nothing for this brilliant piece of deduction, so she went on.

"He drove a black Audi, we noticed. Sports car thing – 8 something or other. They were parked right outside the restaurant."

A gasp came down the phone from Miriam.

"Stephen. It's Stephen Tiehurst."

"What, Miriam? Who? Tell me all."

"He must have taken leave of his senses. Oh Leyla, I must warn him. Stephen is marvellous. Haven't you heard of him? He owns Tiehurst Industries."

"Not *the* Tiehurst Industries?"

"The same. Most marvellous man. Capable of so much you know. Quite our best friend. At our house quite most of the time."

Miriam had laced her voice to this point with saccharine. Now she let the acid drip in.

"He must have taken leave of his senses getting involved with that awful woman. Let me think about this, would you? I'll call you back."

Miriam hurried to her escritoire. Her head spun. There was no rational reason why this news should have rattled her so much. It was not that she fancied Stephen. He was years her junior and it would never have entered her mind to consider him attractive in a romantic way. Miriam, anyway, was no longer capable of relating to people with affection.

That she was acutely jealous of her relationship with Stephen, however, was unquestionable. It was bad enough when Maisie laid claim to the acquaintance. It was Miriam who had introduced the Holbeins to Stephen. He was *her* friend, the trophy that told of the success of *her* social quests. She could not bear to think of anyone else getting close to him. There was that Rebecca, of course. But

Miriam sensed Stephen's aloofness with Rebecca. He was far too good for Rebecca, and yet, here he was taking out Carrie Thompson. What lies she must have told Stephen to have him turn his head her way.

Miriam sat up. Somehow she must alert Stephen to the danger he was in. Perhaps if she organised another dinner and invited Stephen along – with the Gumphrys to back her up. She was not stupid. She could see Carrie was attractive. Of course Stephen might become infatuated with a pretty girl. It was not enough for Miriam to plough in and hope to convince him to her way of thinking. But with other friends expressing the same opinion she must prevail.

Miriam phoned Leyla back.

"Miriam again, Leyla. Look, this calls for immediate action. Needs must. We will have a dinner. Potluck. Time to rally the troops, and the potluck strategy proves most effective under urgency."

Without drawing more than a moment's additional breath Miriam began to organise the latest potluck dinner with Leyla. Despite this being a first for her new friend she was relieved to find Leyla undaunted by the amount of work involved. The two of them were driven by the same goal and, Miriam felt, by an equal anxiety. Miriam's quite best friend Stephen must have the wool pulled away from his eyes and the truth made clear. Carrie was the worst type of trouble. Both Miriam and Leyla were resolute on that.

Although the sky cleared, the rest of the day remained full of turbulence and bluster. Much driving up and down between the McGregors and the Gumphrys took place as potluck plans were laid and letters drafted. As she drove past, Leyla noticed the washing on Carrie's line being picked up and snapped in the wind. It riled her the girl was getting on with mundane chores when she should be reflecting instead on the full horror of her situation.

Already by late afternoon Miriam had secured a commitment from Stephen to join them for their potluck dinner. He had sounded hesitant, and she did wonder whether it was rather too soon after the previous engagement to be inviting him again. But she overcame his reluctance by reassuring him the dinner could only do Carrie a lot of good.

Now it was important to enlist more support. Peter and Helen Ryan said they could come. As did the Pattersons. Maisie and John were also asked, and having been briefed on the latest transgression in their neighbourhood, Maisie expressed a satisfying concern. Did Miriam mean to say her favourite young man might be being mined by a beneficiary?

"Oh Miriam. How awful. Doesn't he realise she's only after him for his money?"

Maisie also came up with an ingenious suggestion.

"I say, Miriam," she ventured in a small please-don't-rebuff-me voice. "Why not ask Penelope Lewis to the dinner? She has always held some allure for Stephen. Not only might we enlighten Stephen as to Carrie's lack of suitability, but Penelope could probably be enlisted to turn his head away from the girl altogether."

Miriam agreed. "Well done. That is ex-actly what we will do," she told Maisie, who squeaked her delight. "We will arrange things so Stephen falls in love with Penelope Lewis."

# CHAPTER TWENTY SIX

## EPISTLES

Hubert had much too much on his plate to be distracted by dinner planning. It was enough Leyla informed him of this secondary strategy. He would look forward to it, but it was woman's work and for now he needed to get down to meatier stuff. His primary concern was to finish his letter to the CPS. Its content had been agreed. Now he must polish it.

He sat at his imposing desk and began an elaborate ritual. First he stretched his arms out in front and entwined the fingers of both hands. These he then twisted and drew back to his chest. He turned them in once, then back again, then stretched them out once more. Arms length. Click click click. Arms up and down. Fingers twiddled above his computer. He was ready.

He had learned to type so his output would be more efficient. Recently he had also invested in a smart new PC that allowed him to surf the internet at speed. It was the perfect set-up for Hubert. The extra knowledge he gained as he wove his way through the web would serve to enrich the lives of others.

He booted up the program and made a new file box, which he labelled 'DPB Abuses'. This correspondence would grow. Then he formed a new document and saved it as 'Thompson C_CPS Advisory'. He placed his rough paper drafts to the side of his computer and with his brow already quite creased, considered how best to start.

Hubert's labouring took him right through the afternoon. He barely heard the chase of wind through the trees outside. By the time he was finished he was exhausted and the sun was already yawning in sympathy. He stretched, turning to look out the window at some clouds that scudded across the sky. He knew how they felt as they took their urgent business across the world. They had an understanding, the clouds and he, bringing as they did life-sustaining riches.

He roused himself. The printer had churned the letter out and he picked it up to look at the written word.

"For all the marvels of computers," he told himself, "the elucidation derived from reviewing a printed epistolary contribution is supreme. Every time."

Leyla was in the kitchen when she heard Hubert call.

"Finished," he beckoned. "Come and cast your eyes over this if you wouldn't mind."

She hurried to find him, gasping when she saw the sheer scale of Hubert's masterpiece. She shook her head in earnest disbelief. "Oh Hubert, what a sublime effort. How do you do it?"

Hubert stood, stoic, as his wife began to read. The letter

stretched far into the distance. Punctuation was spare. She could see the meticulous planning, the hard spent hours that had gone into it. Was he being too hard on the girl? No – what else could he do? She needed to be taken in hand, and the children, at least, needed proper care. Miriam was right, having a family like that in the neighbourhood lowered its tone. Heaven forbid, it might even lower the property values.

*Dear Director,*

*It is with a heavy heart that I write this letter, for it is not without reluctant due reticence that I the undersigned am inclined to enter into this correspondence herewith.*

*However, as regrettable as it is, it has come to the author's notice within a relevant time span that a young woman in our neighbourhood has not been conducting herself in a manner which would benefit her offspring to the best of their advantages when one considers the common considerations which are due children of any background. Indeed now at this very moment as I write she is behaving in a way which as I have hereinbefore indicated can only be described as harmful to her two boys who are deserving of more than they appear to be receiving now at this particular point in time.*

*As a concerned citizen of Glade, indeed a resident resident of Glade Heights and therefore I might suggest someone on whose information your organisation can place absolute trust, I would ask you to investigate this young woman with a view to rescuing the offspring referred to above. As I appreciate such matters cannot be investigated on some whim of a member of the public it is with respect that I should wish to elucidate the following information for the greater edification of your department.*

*Namely that on Saturday the 11th Inst. at 3:30pm*

*a) The children were left unattended for hours while the mother disappeared during which period:*

*i) the younger boy was heard crying pitifully in the back yard.*

*ii) the older boy appeared to be battering the younger boy to within an inch of his life in the back yard all of which took place without the supervision of the mother which has already been discussed hereinbefore. (see above)*

And so on.

Hubert slid his hand into his back trouser pocket and creased his forehead. His thumb and forefinger stretched to impress themselves on his eyebrows. As Leyla read and glowed, Hubert paced, passing an erudite observation or two about his own creation between steps.

"You'll note the reference and cross-reference to Miriam's *Itemizations*."

And, "The third paragraph from the end is crucial in disclosing to the CPS the true nature of this matter in its most lucid interpretation."

And even, "We may need to reorganise paragraph 7.25 subsection i) f)."

When Leyla had finished reading she looked up, her face pink with ardour. She placed the pages on Hubert's desk, and slapped her hand down on them.

"Hubert Gumphry," she declared. "This is your best ever. I'll deliver these to Miriam so she can glance at them. We'll get them off in the post tonight. You look exhausted. Go and put your feet up for a bit."

"Oh, I'll manage, thank you. Best to keep the campaign active."

Hubert sat back at his desk and turned to his computer, a delirium of self-importance feeding his unfounded contempt for Carrie Thompson who, to this point, he had not even met. His wife, equally fuelled, went to find the keys. She had one more flurry to make up the hill in her car.

Angus was not at all worried the triumvirate was neglecting him during this period of intense activity. The responsibilities assumed so naturally by the Gumphrys meant less pressure on him. His growing sense of freedom coincided with their arrival at the Heights, and he realised they were instrumental in helping to release him from his wife's tendrils.

This realisation did not make him excitable. Rather he felt overtaken by inertia, as if he were encased in a fog. His spirit was exhausted. He had been stirred up and discomposed on so many occasions over the years, he had never had the opportunity to stop and consider what he might want from life. Even visits to *The Hidey-hole* had proven insufficient to recharge his batteries.

At last, however, space was what the Gumphrys were providing. They were drawing off the heat his driven wife hurled at him and channelling it back in their own direction. He noticed how sleepy he became each time they all gathered in his presence. What they thought of him he did not care. He was rather enjoying himself. And he found himself more and more often sinking into reveries and thinking of his youth. Life AM. Ante Miriam.

When Leyla arrived up at their house for the fourth time that day, he no longer bothered to hail her. He did not even proffer a half-hearted wave. She had not acknowledged him beyond the brief greeting made on her first sortie and there was no point in him now becoming bogged down in niceties when it was clear neither party wished for any contact.

Watching his wife talking with Leyla had an hypnotic effect. He automatically headed to the far side of the room and his armchair. From there he let the monotony of their conversation dull his senses. The day's conflicting weather seemed to marry with the social atmosphere. The lids on Angus's eyes lay heavy, blocking out the planning he could hear droning on in the distance.

Finally Leyla's visit was complete and her impending departure was Angus's cue to snap out of his dreaming. Both women were in a heightened state of excitement. Miriam saw him stir and was moved by the positive state of affairs to address him quite pleasantly.

"We have a winning combination here, Angus. Mark my words. I think this calls for a celebratory drink. Why don't we get Hubert up, Leyla?"

Angus did not resist. If he must face redundancy he was quite happy to do so with a drink under his belt.

Thus Leyla drove home to collect her husband. By the time the Gumphrys had driven back to the McGregors' house Angus was several sheets to the wind. By the time they had all sat, imbibed, and been breathless at what had been achieved in such a short space of time, Angus was near to capsizing.

The Gumphrys' were keen observers of social decorum and knew when it was time to leave. They babbled their thanks to Miriam and, having expressed much positive expectation with regards to the potluck dinner planned for the following week, they bid their farewells.

"That's an unusual relationship, Hubert," Leyla commented when they were in the car.

"Which?" Hubert asked.

"The McGregor relationship. I mean, what on earth do you think of him? Of course we like Miriam. Don't we?"

"Miriam? Oh we do. He is unusual, though, isn't he? I'm not sure he is entirely reliable."

"Did you see how much he drank? What a difficult situation for Miriam to live with."

"Yes, poor woman. Marriage should be a union in every respect, I always say. You can be rest assured Leyla, you are lucky in me."

"How observant you are always, Hubert," she replied.

# CHAPTER TWENTY SEVEN

# PERSISTENCE

Carrie had been disconcerted by Leyla Gumphry's visit, but several days had gone by and the distance allowed her anxiety to disperse. She could even look across at the Gumphrys' house without having an overwhelming urge to go and pop all the ripening fuchsia buds that hung over their fence. It was better to ignore her impossible neighbours. Playing them at their own game would only lead to a repeat of what she had just put up with.

Having Stephen now in touch each day was helping. He had been around a number of times since their dinner together. A few weeks ago he had been miles from her thoughts. Now he never left them. She also had Astra's visit to look forward to; sitting at the kitchen bench, chatting like school girls, more like sisters than mother and daughter – a love bound together by fifteen years of just Carrie and Astra.

Still the cloud of Craig hung low. She had received no further communication from him, allowing her to hope his earlier contact might not be repeated and he still did not know where she was living. But she had heard back from her lawyer. Through that source, at least, Craig had agreed to leave her alone for another fortnight, after which she must agree to a meeting.

Two weeks. It was not long. Craig had indicated he was willing to meet in a neutral environment. He had stipulated, however, she must bring Jake and Tom, and from that point on she accepted she must expect him to be granted some sort of regular access. The thought of her sons being alone with their father distressed her more than anything. If their boisterousness tipped him over the edge, if they were alone with him when that happened...it made her head spin. But she was thinking too far ahead.

On this particular morning, she and the boys were out on the back lawn busy at their warm-day routine of cheerful calls and occasional tears when she heard the door bell ring.

"Wait there and behave you two horrors," she called to them. Jake and Tom rushed to ambush her, and she was laughing as she extricated herself.

Her good humour disappeared the instant she opened the door. Marilyn Philps was back.

"Morning Miss Thompson. Sorry to trouble you again. But I think I need to come in and have a chat."

"What about?" Carrie was defensive.

Marilyn sighed. "Look, it's better if we chat inside." She leant back and scanned the immediate neighbourhood. "It will be more comfortable for you."

The release of Carrie's breath was slow and resigned as she stepped aside to let the CPS officer in. "Wait in the kitchen, will you. I'll go and get the boys. Shall I give you a cup of tea?"

While Carrie organised some hot drinks, Marilyn Philps

watched, making the kind of judgement she had refrained from making on her previous visit. They were seated in Carrie's kitchen while the children played on the floor.

Carrie was making her own assessment. It had gone against her grain to let Marilyn in, but she decided it was better to confront this rather surprising development than to try to run away from it. She had nothing to hide.

"What are you wanting to say to me?"

"We do a difficult job, Miss Thompson."

Carrie didn't correct the title nor the preconception Marilyn had of her.

"I'm not here to dictate how you look after your children. I am here to find out simply whether they are OK. Whether they are being looked after adequately. Full Stop. You know what I mean? It's the kids we're interested in. You understand that? May I call you Carrie?"

"Well?" Carrie kept her self-control.

"We may need to consider whether they need taking into care."

"On what grounds?"

"Umm...your general suitability as a mother has been questioned, Carrie."

Relieved to have the facts presented so honestly, they were still a shock.

"Ah. You're here to see how they are, not how I get them to how they are. Is that correct? I'm not a fool. I know you couldn't take them away from me just because I might have an unconventional approach to life. Not that I do. It's that Leyla Gumphry, isn't it? She's behind this. That fog horn of a woman."

"Actually, the complaints don't just come fro..."

"Oh no, I know. They'll have come originally from goggle eyes up the top. Miriam-bloody-McGregor."

Carrie was getting distressed again.

"She's orchestrating this. She thinks she can control it. When you finally get through the shit to the facts you'll feel sorry for yourself for ever having run into any of them."

Carrie threw her arms out then dropped her head into her hands. How was it possible these people could involve her in so much unwarranted hassle?

Suddenly she exploded. "Actually, everyone is full of so much shit, the place is in danger of becoming a cesspool."

"Look, there's no need to have a go at me, Carrie," Marilyn Philps shoved her chair back.

"No need? No need? And don't damned well call me Carrie. You call yourselves the arbiters of sensible approach, right living – and yet I bet you've come here to investigate me before you've so much as tapped on the door of those lunatics. Now get the hell out of my house. You've met the children, you can see they're happy, you can see they're well fed. If you want to take someone into care go retrieve that poor, mauled, breast-obsessed husband up the hill there. He'd probably relish a visit from you – God knows you've got big enough boobs to qualify."

Carrie was on her feet, glaring at Marilyn. Then she caught herself, startled by her own outburst. She let out a shallow laugh and sank back on her chair. Placing her head in her hands, she wept quietly.

"I'm sorry," she murmured at last.

She looked up at Marilyn, and shook her head, reason beginning a quiet flow back into her veins.

"I just can't handle all this interference. Believe me – I am able, financially, in every other way, to look after my kids. Use your stretched resources to sort out some real problems. I'm afraid by wasting time to come and see me you've been used by someone who has an ulterior and much bigger social-climbing motive."

The CPS officer, who had cowered at Carrie's outburst, began to relax a little. They were both silent, transfixed by the boys who sat transfixed by their mother. The next time Marilyn spoke she, too, was more reasoned than she had been, less patronising.

"Look, Miss Thompson, I'm sorry. We're under an obligation to check up on these things. It's obvious to me now there was no need for us to be here. The boys do appear to be well cared for – and happy. You must understand, we do always act on a tip-off, for the safety of the children."

"Sometimes. Perhaps."

Carrie got a clipped response. "We do our best. But look, we're the first to admit we don't always get it right. Perhaps I should have tackled this from a different direction. I mean ... are you OK? Is everything all right for you?"

Carrie's shoulders dropped as she took a sip of tea.

"I'm fine. My boys are fine. I have an older daughter who is grown up and healthy and just about through university and well adjusted. And she's fine. OK? And when I said I can look after them all financially, I mean it.

"I can give you the name of my lawyer if you like and instruct him to give you an account of my affairs. Anything to be left alone and to put this whole thing to bed before it gets out of hand."

Her voice had started to rise again. "I mean, how do you stop this juggernaut? It seems to me, no matter how sensible one tries to be, these idiots are able to knock everything out of orbit. Can't we all step back and behave normally again? I'm not in trouble. My children are not in trouble. I am not Miss Thompson but Mrs Thompson. I am divorcing my husband and between us we can care for our children. The only thing I have done wrong is to come to live in the unhappy shadow cast by that awful woman on the hill. Spend your time looking after children who are real victims. I'm just the target of some vicious, frustrated neighbours who have nothing better to do than to wage a parochial campaign of social terror."

Marilyn Philps looked as exhausted as Carrie. She scanned the shambolic but well-stocked room and turned back to Carrie.

"I'm sure you're right. I agree. I think we've been misled. I'm so sorry. Our problem is we've so often been accused of not checking on children who have in truth been the subject of abuse. Now we tend to err in the other direction.

"I can see you don't deserve all of this and I will make sure you don't get worried by us again."

"Thank you, but I don't share your confidence that it won't happen again."

Marilyn considered Carrie for a minute.

"This letter we got from... from the complainant. I'm not past hurling a few appropriate words back in the direction they came from. So take it from me, as far as we're concerned, this case is closed."

Carrie shut the front door on Marilyn and went to receive a reviving cuddle.

What sort of a hell hole had she been lured to? As she looked across to the lake for an answer, a fantail made a couple of diverting loop-the-loops outside her window before alighting on a branch and flicking her an enigmatic look.

This was where she had uncovered her cherished Stephen. And in between the ogres she was aware of pleasant neighbours. So how had she been caught in such a mesh of unprovoked intrigue? She couldn't seem to get rid of it. It was like a tacky substance adhering to her brain, shaken off for a time but always reappearing, still holding on.

She shuddered. What dreadful women they were, Miriam and Leyla. Sounding like foghorns yet functioning like sirens – there not to warn off but to lure in.

Stephen. She would think of Stephen. Distract herself with dreams of him. He was coming for dinner and she could look forward to that. She thought she had better not mention the visit she had just had, though, or he would think her paranoid again. She shook her head. Perhaps she was paranoid. She hadn't imagined the visits from the CPS, or Miriam, or Leyla Gumphry – she didn't think – but was she placing too much importance on them?

"Oh curses," she muttered, then called to the boys. "Come on you lot. Let's head off to the supermarket. We have dinner to get."

"And 'scream," Tom said.

"Can we have an ice cream, Mum?" Jake asked.

Carrie laughed.

"Maybe an ice cream. And maybe not," she said.

## CHAPTER TWENTY EIGHT
## RESISTANCE

Stephen arrived for dinner precisely on time. Carrie opened the door to find him smiling, handsome – irresistible. He drew her in to him. Melted her with his brown eyes. Stirred her depths with his kiss. The soft night breeze that brushed her bare arms made her nuzzle into his warmth.

"Don't keep the boys waiting," she chided, feeling far too much like the teenager he had kissed years before.

She led him through to the social hub of the house. The boys hooted with delight when they saw him. Watching him with Tom and Jake she could believe it was possible to have a conventional family that functioned normally, happily; a father who was attentive without drama; children expressing emotions without having to brace for the repercussions.

Carrie had fed her sons already and she made her once-daily effort to regain control of the room while Stephen read them a story.

When the noise had been banished by bedtime, Carrie

and Stephen collapsed in an amused heap. They let the transfused over-excitement dissolve into a blessed adult hush and a welcome glass of wine.

They offered each other trifles from the day. Stephen described how entertaining he found the factory floor and the relative lack of pleasure he got sorting out middle-management insecurities. Carrie talked about the boys but she was careful to avoid talk of the CPS visits.

"I guess my day must seem awfully mundane," she suggested. "All children, washing machines and neighbourhood."

"I know you're not mundane. I like the sound of your day. Although I like the part of your day when I'm around, best."

Stephen moved from his chair to where Carrie was lying on the sofa. She let him take her bare feet and place them on his knee as he sat down, smiling at him as he talked and caressed. For no apparent reason she let out a laugh of real amusement.

"What?" he asked, his tone suggesting she might have wounded some serious male intent.

"Nothing."

"What nothing," he persisted.

"Oh, I was just thinking, it's so natural for you to be here, such a short time after we met up, being so sweet, so loving, while you discuss your work day. As if you and I had been married for years and this is our practiced wind-down."

"And that's funny?" he asked.

"Endearing. Loving. I can't tell you why I laughed. You're a boy, I guess."

Stephen bent towards her and held his hand to her face. Dark on her pale cheek. He was so serious. Tender.

"So I am a boy, huh? I'm a man also."

She kept her eyes on his face and let his hand work softly on her body. Strokes which stirred and tingled. She felt such a conflict, knowing that to make love to Stephen at this stage would create more confusion in her already muddled emotional life, but nor was she sure she could resist any longer.

She tried distraction, whispering, "Don't we need more time to readjust?"

"I feel quite readjusted enough."

"More chats? More practice at just being?"

"I'm quite practiced and just being enough."

She laughed. "You need to ask me out more."

"Ah," Stephen was laughing too. He pulled himself to lie beside her, holding her tight so she wouldn't roll off the sofa. "Well," he said with mock seriousness, "why don't I escort you formally to next week's potluck dinner."

"What potluck dinner?" Carrie felt the alarm ring inside her.

"Aren't you coming? Miriam rang the other day and invited me. I was sure she told me you were coming. She said something about it being for you."

"Miriam? Potluck dinner?" Despite all her promises to herself, Carrie was losing her calm again. "Stephen, what are you talking about?"

She struggled to sit up, and looked down at him still lying there. "You're not going to another meal with that dreadful woman. A meal for me. A meal about me don't you mean?"

Stephen looked puzzled. "Don't be silly Carrie, Miriam's not an ogre. I've told you before, she gets far too involved in all the neighbourhood stuff, but she doesn't mean any harm. I've only ever found her friendly.

"Look," he continued, "I can assure you I'm not desperate to go – but I was sure you were invited, too, and I thought it would be a bit of a lark. I think she's just trying to help you 'cause you're new to the neighbourhood. She said it would be good for you. I…"

"I suspect," Carrie cut in, "she'll really have said it was for my own good. And you know what that means?"

Carrie looked at him. The ground was disappearing from under her. Her lack of confidence, so undermined over the years by Craig, made her doubt she would ever be able to overcome misfortune. Here was yet one more disappointment in the offing. She tried to explain what had been happening to her, the effect the interference was having on her. And finally she told him about Marilyn's visit that morning.

"How can you even doubt the woman's got it in for me?" she asked him.

Stephen had listened without interruption. Now he spoke. "You know, Carrie, I don't think you are being realistic about this CPS thing. I really do sympathise, but it won't be Miriam who's set that up. It will be Craig, you know it will."

"Stephen, listen to me," Carrie was getting distressed. "Marilyn Phelps as good as told me it was Miriam."

"Did she actually say so? In so many words?"

"No. But she didn't have to. It was obvious from what she said."

"You have to have proof Carrie. You can't just jump to conclusions like this. No wonder you've got yourself into such a muddle over the years if this is how you react to things."

Carrie let the comment pass. It hurt too much, particularly coming from Stephen. He had a point – in part at least. She changed tack.

"Let's forget about the CPS visit," she suggested. "I just know Miriam is trouble."

But no matter what Carrie said, Stephen remained convinced Miriam was no more than a local gossip who might try too hard to organise things and invite him to too many potluck dinners, but was not a bad sort underneath.

Carrie stood up and moved to another chair. Stephen followed and crouched down beside her.

"Look Carrie," he told her gently, "I think you've got this whole thing completely out of perspective. I actually feel quite sorry for Miriam."

Carrie gasped.

"No, seriously," he said. "She and Angus lost a young daughter many years ago. That's probably made her a bit potty. But someone who's suffered that fate wouldn't want to harm a mother like you, or your children. Anyway, forget about that. You're much more important to me than Miriam and her neighbours. You must see that?"

Carrie understood why Stephen thought she had everything out of proportion. It did sound completely nuts. However, she had seen a nasty calculation in Miriam he had clearly never seen.

"You're not jealous are you?" he asked her suddenly. "That you haven't been invited?"

He was teasing, failing to see her anxiety, not picking up the very real unhappiness his misunderstanding in particular was causing her.

Carrie closed her eyes for a moment, attempting to let go of some of the tension. Then she looked at him with a wistful smile.

"I'm not questioning your loyalty," she told him, "but can't you see, if you go to the dinner, you're agreeing to be part of their mischief."

As Stephen continued to tease her, Carrie persisted until his humour waned and he became irritated with her intractability. Finally, Carrie realised she was getting nowhere. To get through the evening she would have to rally and make light of the situation, but her heart lay lead-heavy. She closed the discussion with a disguising smile and went to serve their meal.

As they ate, Carrie grew more and more taut until she thought she would snap. While he may not have picked up Miriam's undercurrents over the years, it was clear Stephen was aware of Carrie's at that moment.

And at last he said, "Carrie, would you rather I saw a little less of you? Perhaps we are rushing things."

He was misreading her again. This was a shock. Immediately, Carrie locked herself down. She looked at him as impassively as she could.

"If you think that's best," she said.

The evening kept its brittle edge as Carrie willed it to finish. She was desperate; not wanting him to go, needing him to stay, knowing she would lose her equilibrium at any moment unless he left immediately.

Since the morning she had packed herself and the boys up and left Craig, Carrie had shed few tears. Even then her weeping had been mostly for their sons, not for herself.

She shut the door on Stephen and encased herself in her misery. She felt so alone. How could she have been so foolish as to think the love she had shared with Stephen could be reinstated? Too many years had gone by. They had different expectations, viewed life in different ways.

Her head pounded as she cleared the table then dragged herself off towards bed. Even the sight of her sleeping sons did nothing to lift her spirits. Stephen obviously found her petty, unbalanced. He would not want to see her again. Hadn't he said as much?

She cried from her soul, for herself and for Jake and for Tom. "That woman has got her way," she wept. "That's it, then. What's the point in fighting Craig any more? What hope have I got of warding him off now?"

# CHAPTER TWENTY NINE
## POTLUCK II

Slow painful days tortured Carrie through to the following week. But for Angus the days ran at a very different pace.

Already another week, he thought, and here they were at yet another potluck repast. It was hard for him to put his finger on what worried him. Something unpleasant niggled. He didn't quite know what.

However, one thing Angus could put his finger on was the very been-there-done-that experience he was feeling. It was the peanuts. Here he was placing them for the umpteenth time. Like some Glade Heights version of feng shui, if they were not positioned in exactly the right spot they would end up mis-channelling Miriam's latest social energies and bad karma would result. Thus he was once more placing them according to the long held plan.

Unusually, the grande dame was herself busy preparing food. It was the norm for Miriam at the potluck dinners to restrict her own efforts to a few small culinary extras such as the garnish for any potluck contributions she considered not up to scratch. She managed to avoid making any substantial contributions herself by providing the potluck venue each time. That way no one ever seemed to notice she arrived – as it were – empty handed. That is, no one noticed but Angus, and on this particular night he was alert to the change.

"Going to some trouble I see, Miriam."

"Yes. Well. Needs must. You see, Angus, one cannot ask Stephen to contribute too large an item as he is such a busy man. And I did think it was important Penelope's energies were conserved for her main task of the night."

"Oh?" Angus was puzzled.

"Penelope was not asked to bring food this time, Angus. Just herself. We'll get Stephen's head turned well away from that awful Thompson girl, see if we don't."

The potluck inner-circle reported for duty at 7:00pm sharp. For once, Stephen was not far behind them.

Stephen came to the evening with an open mind. Time had distanced him from the discomfort of his argument with Carrie. Torn in his own mind as to what he should do, and believing she wanted space, he hadn't called her since. In any event, work had occupied him and kept him out of town for most of that time.

He was no longer as agitated about their exchange, but he remained unable to dismiss his worry that the trouble with Carrie's marriage might be an imbalance with her and not her husband Craig.

Why, for instance, all those years ago while he was at university, had she left without telling him – so suddenly and with no explanation? He couldn't bear the hurt of re-establishing his relationship with Carrie only to have it collapse again. Perhaps she had left him because she didn't care for him and was capable of doing the same again. Certainly, as he had made his way home the week before, he told himself he was better off on his own rather than risk the pain that could be the end result of loving Carrie.

He decided not to have any preconceptions about this evening. He wasn't sure quite why he did accept these potluck dinner invitations. Miriam's odd gatherings never held any appeal for him. But attend them he did, out of politeness. On this particular occasion, he also had a degree of curiosity.

It happened Stephen had always been spared the worst of Miriam's scandal. She was shrewd enough not to invite him when the topic for an evening was too hot or petty. But she invited him enough to convince the others he was one of her gang. Her special friend. So Stephen could not have anticipated this night would be any different from normal.

As he walked into the McGregors' sitting room, however, he became immediately aware of a more heightened atmosphere than usual. This he put down to Carrie's passionate appeal to him not to attend – making him more self-conscious.

He scanned the room. It appeared there were to be twelve for dinner. Peter Ryan was chatting to the Holbeins. Strange chap, that, Stephen thought. He knew the manager of the bank Peter used to work for. Peter was made redundant because he had a tendency to stockpile client files in the too hard basket. Should have been fired, so the manager had said. Stephen was curious. Why would Miriam be attracted to him?

Maisie Holbein was another odd choice, he realised. A kind woman, but not someone to advance the social heights Miriam seemed to aspire to. She and her husband were rather grey.

And the Pattersons. Good Lord – the only colour the Pattersons brought to a conversation was the blush on Stephen's cheeks as they sought to ingratiate themselves each time they saw him.

He glanced at the other couple. He didn't recognise them, although their attire, he decided, was certainly a point of interest. He cursed under his breath. This was hardly keeping an open mind.

His thoughts were interrupted by Penelope Lewis.

"Stephen. How divine." She gave him a lingering kiss on each cheek.

"Hello Penelope," he said. "How are you?"

She was taller than Stephen, and he took a step back to ease the chat. Penelope was a pole-like individual, though not unattractive, with large dependent eyes. Her silky clothes emphasised her pencil shape as they draped in and out of the shallow depressions of her body. The previous times they had met, he and Rebecca were still an item. He had been entertained by Penelope enough to provoke Rebecca into jealous accusations. Tonight he had no diverting partner and their conversation was easy and animated.

He was surprised, however, to find no one else came across to chat with them before dinner except Angus, who plied them with drink.

After an hour of wine being poured, small talk exchanged and peanuts gulped, Miriam called her guests to their meal. This time she seated everyone at the dining table. It was, after all, a conference she had summoned them to. She sat Penelope next to Stephen who, she was pleased to note, appeared not at all averse to his neighbour's tactile enthusiasm.

As the meal progressed, Miriam threw meaningful glances at Leyla across the table. They were on track. However, the evening needed to be conducted with great skill, and not until she noticed Penelope's hand drop beneath the table in order to emphasise some comment with a strategic stroke of Stephen's thigh, and Stephen's smiling response suggesting the stroke was not unwelcome, did she bring up the subject of the Glade Heights problem.

"How wonderful to have you all here again. It seems an age, although it can only have been a couple of weeks ago when we last gathered. I tried you Penelope, dear," Miriam lied, "but you must have been out of town."

"Quite possibly, Miriam." Penelope smiled. Her eyes remained focused on Stephen and her hand remained beneath the table.

"And of course, our wonderful new neighbours. What a treat to have you both here, dear Leyla and Hubert."

"The pleasure, I'm sure, is entirely theirs," Angus quipped through his alcoholic haze.

"Well, it's my pleasure also," Maisie Holbein ventured. "John and I have been dying to meet you both. You must come round and have a drink some time. Perhaps in…"

"In due course, Maisie." Miriam said, silencing her. "For now we must concentrate on our mission."

At this prompting a number of her guests leant forward at the table.

"What mission is this, Miriam?" Stephen asked.

"Oh Stephen." She cast her most ensnaring look at him. "We have been sorely misled. You realised immediately, of course, how could you not. So astute."

She turned to the table at large. "Our solo mother, young Carrie Thompson, needs help. That is quite apparent. She has absolutely no control over those children and heaven knows how she thinks she can live in our little haven and still have enough money to support herself."

Seeing Stephen blink hard, Miriam continued urgently. "As a community we owe it to those boys to alert the authorities to the travesty which is taking place under our very noses."

"I can second these comments," Leyla's voice broke across the table. "I live opposite and I have been quite appalled at the laxness I have witnessed. Not that I'm going out of my way to look, you understand. It's so obvious. Dreadful."

Stephen put his elbows on the table, rested his chin on his hands, and cast down his eyes down. Miriam shot Leyla a warning glance. It was important to get the mix just right. They wanted to put Stephen off Carrie, not get his back up.

"I gather," Miriam continued, "that the older child, the daughter you know, is rather wayward. Hardly surprising. Different father from the younger ones, obviously. Have you met Carrie, Stephen? Other than briefly at our last leee-tle get together, ha-ha!"

She didn't give him time to answer. "Such a nice girl on the surface, so unassuming and friendly. But what goes on beneath the surface is, I am afraid, alarming. She would be better off living amongst her own sort, I feel." Miriam paused to draw breath.

Hubert, who had been quiet to this point, grabbed the moment. "Without doubt," he pontificated, "one finds with these domestic purpose benefit situations, the circumstances are extenuated by a decided inability to cogitate on the realism of the facts. A need for more exact precision by the authorities is required before events overtake us."

Leyla bestowed a grateful smile. "Thank you for that thoughtful approach, Hubert. The girl doesn't know how lucky she is having all this care lavished on her from afar."

The talk went on in much the same vein, tackled first from this angle then from that angle, with occasional inept interjections from Angus causing Miriam to reflect on her husband's state of mind.

"He has deteriorated over the last few weeks," she had time to think.

She did not think, however, they were in any sense losing direction with the problem at hand. On the contrary, Miriam took Stephen's silence to be agreement, and she became more and more satisfied they had convinced him he would be best to leave the likes of Carrie well alone.

Stephen, however, was struggling. As he listened to his hostess it dawned on him at last and with horror, Carrie had been right all along about her neighbours. Their intentions were obvious. These awful people were trying to persuade him to their adverse point of view, Miriam in particular making her position clear.

As for the Gumphrys. He had not seen the couple at the restaurant about whom Carrie had expressed curiosity, but that voice – it was unmistakable. It must have been the

Gumphrys staring at them in the restaurant.

Carrie was right, it was a conspiracy, she was not off her head, not paranoid. In fact, when he thought about it, she had been remarkably restrained.

He became more and more incensed by the turn of the conversation, and yet he was struck speechless, unable to say anything in her defence; mesmerized, as if he were at some revivalist meeting at which he was required to be born again – as a Carrie opponent.

And to cap it all, he suddenly became aware of Penelope's thin warm hand working its way up his leg to the very top of his thigh.

Stephen shoved his chair back.

"Excuse me a moment," he said, averting his eyes from the other guests.

He made straight for the McGregors' bathroom, turned the lock on the door and leant back with his eyes closed. Eventually, he moved across to the basin and let the cold tap run full before tossing water on his face, hoping to sluice his mind of the poison which was being dispensed from the dining table. His dripping face stared back at him from the mirror as he attempted to regain composure.

"What the hell have I let myself in for?" he asked his reflection.

He patted his face dry and returned to the dining table wondering how he could extricate himself from the evening without being too obvious. He had no intention of giving them further grist for their mill.

Later he was to realise, if he had spoken out in defence of Carrie, things might not have ended in such disaster. But at the time he was so hypnotized by the evening's spell, he didn't know quite what to say or how to escape.

In his absence, Penelope had been drawn further into

the conversation and appraised of the danger Stephen found himself in. She was, however, a rather vacant woman, and only just able to register the gathered company approved of her moving in on Stephen.

But whether she understood much more was doubtful.

Miriam had not noticed Penelope's lack of insight, so fixated was she on her urgent mission. Nor, for the same reason, had she seen the trouble brewing as a result of her husband's attention to hostly detail. Angus had indeed been very attentive. All evening. He had been especially careful not to neglect Penelope's glass.

Thus what little sense Penelope did have, she was quickly losing.

When Stephen returned to the table, Penelope unfolded herself from her chair and threw her long drunken arms around him. The problem was, she had forgotten she was still holding her glass. As her arms swept behind him, Stephen was doused in red wine.

Miriam, Leyla, Maisie of course, and Hubert all dashed to his aid. Penelope didn't. She plopped down in an inebriated heap on her chair.

"Gosh," she hiccuped.

"Please. It's perfectly all right," Stephen protested, resisting the ministrations being forced upon him. "Miriam, I'm sure the best thing is for me to dash home and change."

"Oh but Stephen, you will be back?"

"Of course," he assured her.

He said hurried goodbyes, side stepping Miriam's attempts to delay him, and insisted on seeing himself out. Miriam, of course, could not refuse the creator, owner, and principal shareholder of Tiehurst Industries. Her Stephen. But nor could she disguise her wistful regret as she watched him depart.

Stephen waited until he was well out of sight of the house before heaving a sigh of relief. After a furtive glance behind him, he took off down the hill with the reckless urgency of a lovelorn teenager.

Carrie had spent the evening attempting to distract herself. No phone rang to fill her empty heart, no message came from Stephen to tell her he was sorry. Sorry for what? He must think her mad. This was the night he was going to the McGregors for dinner. She supposed he must have gone.

She heard the hurried footsteps first. Then a loud rapping on her door. At this hour it sounded alarming. Carrie hurried into the hall filled with a mixture of fear and concern. She hesitated. Craig? Surely not. She edged the door open.

"Stephen!"

The jolt of unexpected pleasure at seeing him instantly mingled with worry. "What on earth... what's happened?"

"Oh Carrie." He was catching his breath. "What an idiot I am. I am so, so sorry."

And as she let him in and he folded her in his arms, she knew, before the night was over he would fall – deliciously – into her bed.

Stephen finished relating the events of the evening. He

had shed his wine-soaked jacket and sat close to Carrie on her sofa. She listened, fascinated, her knees drawn up to her chest, coffee mug cupped in her hands.

Suddenly, Stephen sat up. "Oh God – I forgot to ring to say I wasn't coming back."

"Stephen," Carrie clasped his arm. "Surely you don't think you need to... do you?"

"Actually, I think it's more effective if I do. Don't worry. They won't know where I am. We need our own strategy, Carrie. A little deviousness on our part won't go astray, trust me."

With a pensive smile, Carrie released him. She was intrigued by the Stephen who had just come in through her door. He was energised in a way she'd not seen since they were young lovers. The older Stephen had until now been very much more controlled and considered – far more serious. This man was fired up, passionate. He grabbed his phone and made the call. Miriam answered straight away, and from where Carrie sat she could hear her grating voice. She shuddered.

"McGregor residence."

"Miriam. Stephen here. Look, I'm awfully sorry. I won't be able to make it back, unfortunately. Something's come up."

Miriam deferred, understood, expressed deep regret, would be in touch soonest. "We're all agreed," she told him. "A resolution to the problem with that girl is near at hand. Dear dear Stephen. Take care. We will keep you informed of our final discussions."

Stephen finished the call. Away from Miriam's suffocating effect he saw everything in perspective. The evening, those people, the whole thing was mad.

He and Carrie looked briefly at each other and burst

into laughter.

Miriam returned to her remaining guests. Coffee had been served and drunk by this time, and the deflated sense of an evening over was descending.

"Dear Stephen has had some urgent business come up," she confided. "Such an important job, of course. The onerousness of it all must be exhausting. When I speak to him next I will send your respective messages, but I am afraid we shall not have the pleasure of his company again tonight."

Leyla, Hubert, Maisie, John, Helen, Peter, Mike and Patricia – even Angus this time – all sighed their regret.

"Shame," Penelope hiccuped.

## CHAPTER THIRTY
## RECONCILIATION

Stephen chose indulgence over duty the next morning. He had woken in a start, shot to consciousness by two small boys bouncing up and down on the bed. This unfamiliar activity did not seem to perturb him. He turned instead to find Carrie smiling her soft smile at him as she created a barrier with her arms to protect him from the trampolining.

The boys tired of their game and ran off to find other entertainment, leaving Carrie and Stephen to snatch some naked warmth before the day chased them out of bed.

"Can you stay for breakfast?" she asked.

"Do I have to go after that?"

"Not if you don't want to."

He snuggled into her neck. Breathed in her sleepy scent.

"I don't want to," he whispered.

They lay together a while longer, watching each other – not talking, just knowing, until finally Carrie pulled herself away and got out of bed.

"Astra's coming home this morning. Why don't you stay and meet her, at least."

The kitchen reverberated to lively morning noises. Carrie tried not to appear too hyped up with pleasure. She talked too much when she was filled with such happiness, so she made herself busy to thwart the chances of making a fool of herself, and suggested Stephen positioned himself in the strategic safety of the corner seat at the table while she fixed breakfast.

Carrie was just putting the boys' breakfast on the table when she noticed Stephen turn to look outside. A movement in the back garden had caught his eye. She turned to look also. An attractive young woman was making her way up the garden path to the back door; a tall dark girl with a strong open face and an elegant demeanour.

Carrie glanced back at Stephen and saw a flicker of confusion cross his eyes. But it disappeared as Tom and Jake, who had noticed the girl, too, darted towards the door.

"Astra!"

Tom tottered at the top of the steps and leant against the door frame for support, his plump forearm folding over his head as he took in the commotion Jake was creating. Carrie followed Jake and gathered her daughter up in her arms.

As they hugged and laughed, Carrie whispered into her ear, "Darling, Stephen is here. Be nice."

When they came inside, Stephen stood smiling but he

fidgeted, seemingly unsure where to look. Astra, however, was nothing but natural, and as Carrie introduced the two of them she walked across with her hand out to greet him.

"Astra," he stated, relaxing. "You're as lovely as your mother said you were."

Astra laughed. "Thanks," she said. "Mum tells me you two have known each other forever."

"Just about. We hadn't seen each other for years, though. Before we met up again a few weeks ago, I mean. She's just as she was all those years ago. A gorgeous woman, your Mum."

Carrie watched Astra look intently at him for a moment, summing him up. She was still smiling, but there was a protective look in her eye.

"I know," she said at last.

Carrie took Astra's bags to her room and returned, bubbling with small-boy news. Astra scooped Tom up. She carried him to the table and sat him on her lap. Talk, interruptions, laughter, Jake crowding around with his latest toys, more breakfast. Stephen stayed a little longer. Then he announced he ought to get on. He would come back later. Have dinner with them, if that was OK.

"Until then, you two had better catch up with each other."

Stephen had time to think as he walked home. He looked up and saw Miriam's house casting its shadow over the neighbourhood. For the time being he had better make sure she didn't catch sight of him coming and going to Carrie's house, better she remain unaware they were devising their own battle plan.

He smiled. Was this him plotting social strategies? What an eventful twenty-four hours it had been.

He quickly dismissed the unpleasant picture of the previous night's dinner and thought instead of Carrie and Astra. There was no question, Astra had disconcerted him. She was about the age Carrie had been when he had left for university. She so reminded him of that lovely girl he had yearned for. He laughed. He wasn't at all sorry Carrie had grown older. She was just as beautiful, more so, and more mellow than the teenage Carrie had been.

But Astra was not what Stephen had expected. What had he expected? A long-legged blonde teenager – a little bohemian to boot? Someone competent but not quite so much the one in control?

From this first meeting, Astra appeared sophisticated and more astute than he imagined most girls of her age to be. She was obviously bright and ambitious. He pictured her standing there, eyeing him, guarding her mother, clearly not wanting him to walk too far into her mother's life. Yes, it had disconcerted him. He was a trespasser. She was protecting her mother the way a parent might protect a child. Carrie had told him she was like that, hadn't she, so it shouldn't have surprised him. Perhaps the time mother and daughter had lived on their own before Craig appeared on the scene had engendered those tendencies in Astra, followed by the effect of Craig's arrival and aggression. And of course, there was Astra's father.

Stephen hadn't asked Carrie much about Astra's father. He had no idea whether he had lived with them after Astra was born. Or who he was. Or what he was like. Stephen admitted to himself he had been taken aback to see how Māori Astra was. No half-hues. Her skin was a wonderful deep brown and she had sized him up across the kitchen table with obsidian eyes. He had pictured Carrie with a real Ocker, maybe a little rough-cut, uncouth. There was no reason why he should think that.

He just hadn't pictured Astra as Māori.

Astra and Carrie had no truck with reflection after Stephen had left. They lost no time in setting to and solving the world's problems. Not even Tom and Jake's charges into their sister's lap diverted them. The two boys loved her and she in turn showed an easy and affectionate tolerance of her boisterous young brothers.

Stephen was mentioned, of course, Carrie nervous Astra might not approve enough to want to talk about him; Astra guarded about the idea her mother might be getting herself involved in more trouble. She cautioned. Did not make any unfavourable noises about him. Did not pour praise on him either.

Carrie had to content herself. There was time for Stephen and Astra get to know each other better. Instead, she suppressed a girlish desire to chat about love and let Astra talk about university and friends.

They dealt, too, with the subject of Craig.

" I don't like this CPS thing, Mum," Astra said. "What if they get hold of Craig about the boys. You have to settle the matter of separation and custody as quickly as possible. This neighbour business scares me. It's not normal."

Carrie knew not to unnerve her further by mentioning Craig's letter.

"Don't worry, Astra. I'll sort it out. And I have

Stephen's support now too. It does mean a lot, you know."

Astra gave her mother a rueful smile.

"I know Mum. But don't get too involved with him, please. Do you really know this guy? People change with the years."

## CHAPTER THIRTY ONE
## HEEDLESS

Reflection was not something Hubert Gumphry had much truck with, either. He was never one to stop and do a decent evaluation. He did take hours over his interminable correspondence. He definitely did that. He even considered himself capable of deep expression. But his words were dressing. They came later, after a hastily formed opinion.

Hubert was a man spurred into action by his gut, but unfortunately for him, being of a thin and rather wiry disposition, his gut was not as fruitfully intuitive as one that has learnt to feed and better nourish itself. In short, his prejudices meant he was inclined to misread situations.

This knee-jerk tendency came to the fore in response to a phone call that morning. While it was to deliver a precarious outcome for Hubert, it was going to serve to turn the heat away from Carrie – at least for the time being.

The *Glade Herald* reporter was ringing, he told Hubert, in response to a tip-off. An anonymous female caller had suggested Hubert was forming a local action group. He understood the group intended petitioning Council to stop commercial businesses being run from Glade Heights Estate.

"We wondered if you had a comment to make, Mr Gumphry? We would be happy to do a small item in the *Herald Glade Tidings*. It's a great way to reach the wider community with your message. Do you think this is a worthy cause?"

Hubert's gut told him it was. His gut, in fact, told him it could hardly believe its luck. This was an opportunity just wanting Hubert's action in order for it to become golden. He had been so busy researching the social welfare legislation, he had neglected the problem of the massage parlour. Now the heavens were giving him the perfect chance to address that issue, and with minimum effort.

"How did you hear about this, did you say?" he asked.

"A tip-off," the reporter told him. "We get people ringing us all the time about the comings and goings in the community. The *Tidings* lets people have their say about issues that matter to them. The woman who rang told us there's a growing ground swell of opinion at the Heights that the massage business out there shouldn't be allowed to continue. We'd like your comment."

"Well, a-hem," Hubert lifted his chest and cleared his throat. "I have to say, it is time someone stood up to call a halt to the moral decay occurring in our neighbourhoods. It's terrible, isn't it? I mean, this parlour is lowering the Heights. So we've formed..." and here Hubert's brilliant brain worked overtime, coming up in an instant with a name for their group. "...yes, we've formed Victory Against Massage Parlours."

"Eh?" asked the puzzled reporter.

Hubert was not to be diverted. "The whole tone of our

neighbourhood…"

And he was off, delighted to be giving the young man his opinion. The same young man may have regretted the assignment by the time he finally hung up.

Hubert believed he could not have handled the matter better. He wasted no time appraising Leyla of the latest thrilling episode in the crusade to clean up Glade Heights. She in turn, having committed to memory as much of Hubert's statement as she could, wasted no time in ringing Miriam to appraise her, too.

"…and that's precisely what he said. Isn't it wonderful? You didn't tell us you were going to ring the paper, Miriam. Hubert was quite brilliant, I think you'll find, despite being taken by surprise. His advocacy in these matters is second to none. And I'm sure your idea was inspired, also. The surprise will have made his comments so much more meaningful, given as they were, spontaneously. So credit where credit's due, I always say."

"I'm quite delighted for you both," Miriam replied. "However, I cannot claim the inspiration in this case. It must be someone else who rang the paper. I regret to say it hadn't occurred to me to let them know what was going on. Hubert must congratulate himself, I'm sure."

Miriam's artifice, which would have been transparent to anyone not so blinded by their own conceit, slid unnoticed past Leyla's radar.

"Do you know, Hubert," Leyla told her husband when she was off the phone, "I think Miriam might have been just a teensy weensy bit envious that you were the one the reporter phoned."

"But wasn't it Miriam who tipped them off in the first place?"

"No, dear. Isn't it exciting? Obviously, there are others

here at the Heights who feel exactly as we do about this disgraceful boudoir. They knew you'd get something done about it. Now you've put forward an unassailable argument for getting rid of that parlour.

"You're the one who'll get the credit, and quite right."

"Well, as you know, Leyla, someone must provide the necessary intellect to fight these battles. This is just the beginning, but we will overcome."

And with an expression pained by intellectual exertion, Hubert retired to his desk for the rest of the day to formulate further unassailable arguments.

Immediately Miriam got off the phone to Leyla she began some busy formulating of her own. She was confident she remained the one orchestrating the neighbourhood comings and goings, but she must not let her guard down. There was no question, she had got Carrie's wind up.

As for the previous night's dinner. That was an unmitigated success. She had steered Stephen clear and spurred Hubert on with the CPS letter.

Miriam took herself into her sitting room and settled down to review her *Itemizations*. These major campaigns could get complicated.

*"Friday 14th: CPS preliminary visit. Not entirely successful. Hubert to follow up.*

*Monday 17th: Leyla to Thompson household to establish status of children. Reports back. Alarm raised: Stephen seen out with that frightful girl. Potluck dinner organised immediately. Need to spur Hubert on. He obliges with letter to CPS.*

*Note to self: Don't let H get carried away with success. Must keep close control.*

*Thursday 20th: CPS second visit. Have feeling this will have done the trick.*

*Future action: Remember to have Gumphrys on the watch for CPS once court order obtained for uplifting of children.*

*Monday 24th: Might organise for police to visit Thompson household. Add fuel to CPS fire.*

*Herald reporter contacted anonymously. Suggest Hubert has fascinating story on a local massage parlour.*

*Potluck dinner: Huge success.*

Miriam nodded. Her previous entries accorded with her understanding of where matters stood. Now the latest *Itemizations* could be added:

*Tuesday 25th: The bait is taken. Hubert has spread the word about Naysmith girls. Should avoid detection for self.*

*Remember: advise Angus he is losing his grip. Behaviour most alarming lately.*

*V. important: Check Holbeins are aware that rubbish is back on the agenda."*

Satisfied she had dotted all the i's and crossed all the t's Miriam was able to put her notebook down. She folded herself into an envelope of pleasure then reached for the phone.

"Maisie, dear? Miriam. Just a leee-tle matter. The rubbish..."

And thus, and in such a manner, Miriam ensured she kept her grip on the doings of Glade Heights.

# CHAPTER THIRTY TWO

## BALANCE IV

Glade Heights Estate arrived on the map during the optimistic 1960s. It was one of a number of rich slices of cake carved out beside the lake, designed as a gated community to give its residents privacy and security. Initially its sections were laid bare like so many pumice doilies dotted amongst the dark olive-green bush. It puffed its chest out towards the water, trumpeting its lack of environmental sensitivity to sunburnt souls who bobbed up and down in their boats as they marvelled at the advances of Glade in general and of Glade Heights in particular. 'View Glade Heights from the water.' All part of the summer tour.

The first houses seemed nude. Time, however, was kind. After fifteen years the naked structures became clothed in bush. More houses were built and in the nearby suburb the population also grew, until at last a corner dairy could justify itself as the viable provider of essential foodstuffs and neighbourhood gossip to the wider area.

By the early eighties the McGregors had arrived, and

the Glade Flats Dairy soon became the undisputed social centre for all the Glade Heights residents who were excluded from Miriam's potluck inner-circle. Such was its reputation, non-locals were known to direct their Sunday drive to Glade Flats just to pop into the dairy, buy an ice cream and absorb a little gossip.

Into this social hub two mornings after Hubert's press interview Mary Naysmith ventured on her way home from Glade.

She was pleased to see Sally Brimsmead was also in the dairy. Commanding the other side of the counter was current dairy owner Carolyn Smith, who was directing a full verbal onslaught on some heady local subject.

Carolyn was a solid woman, friendly and welcoming, although a little overripe about the cheeks where small broken blood vessels traced an alcoholic history. Those residents with a little common sense dealt with Carolyn at arms length, for fear of having their intimate details disclosed to the public at large. But people liked her.

Mary greeted them. "Morning, Carolyn. How are you? Hi, Sally."

The two women hailed her back. Sally put her wallet in her handbag, then indicated her intention to linger by relaxing her elbow on the counter. Mary found the bread she wanted and was just handing Carolyn some cash when the shop's phone rang. Carolyn excused herself and went to answer it.

"How are you getting on?" Sally asked Mary when Carolyn was out of ear shot.

"Great. Busy. I'm glad to have a bit of a break, to be honest. Good to get out of the house. It's such changeable weather, isn't it? Judith and I had been thinking of doing a hike in the ranges this weekend, but there's a chance of heavy rain, so I'm not sure it's such a good idea."

"No, you're probably sensible. But tell me, how are you faring with that busybody neighbour of yours?"

Mary explained, while things were quiet, Judith didn't share her trust they would be left in peace.

"Some Council chap came round wanting to know what sort of an operation we had."

"Truly? What did you tell him?"

"I can't really remember. I was so nonplussed by the whole thing. Anyway, he seemed relieved to be able to scuttle off without any trouble being apparent. I suspect somebody has just wanted to be sure there's no lurid sex haven being set up in the street."

Mary grinned.

Sally laughed back. "You watch it, though," she advised. "It will be the ghastly Mrs McGregor who called the Council. Trust me."

Carolyn returned and sorted out some change for Mary.

"Gosh!" Her manner was breathless with impending confidence. "Have you heard there's a young solo mother moved into the Heights recently? She's been abusing her children so they say. That was Mrs Holbein on the phone. She tells me she's got a number of children from different fathers. Isn't that frightful? Just imagine."

"Who are you talking about?" Sally asked, making no attempt to hide the censorship in her voice.

Mary's left eyebrow shot up. She was more direct. "I bet I know. You're not talking about Carrie Thompson, are you Mrs S?"

"Oh, is that who they mean? To be honest I wasn't sure. She lives opposite those Gumphry people. Quite a bright man, the husband, apparently. You know – the Gumphry man. From all reports he was destined for the bench but he turned the position down."

As Sally's eyes opened wide in disbelief, Carolyn continued. "The thing is, he's a brilliant barrister, so they say, and they wanted him to be a judge but he decided he could better serve the public by being able to represent them when they needed him. For free. Isn't that amazing? What a wonderful guy. Just imagine."

"Is this what Mrs Holbein told you, Carolyn?" Sally asked.

Mary gave Sally an amused look.

Carolyn was defensive. "Yes. Well, she didn't say that exactly, of course, because I hear it's confidential, but it was easy enough to read between the lines. But he's obviously in the know. What he thinks is as good as the authorities, isn't it? Just imagine."

Carolyn leant forward on the counter, her round forearms splaying outwards, drawing Mary and Sally in with a hungry insistence. Sally stood back and considered her a moment.

"I know a bit about Carrie Thompson," she said at last.

Carolyn was agog.

"She's intelligent, caring, attractive and..." Sally added, becoming indignant, "much nicer than Maisie Holbein."

"And...?"

"And what?"

Carolyn was waiting for a gem. Something she could take from Sally and polish before passing it to the next customer who happened into her shop. Sally, however, seemed to regret mentioning Carrie at all.

"Just that, Mrs S. Don't believe everything you hear. That's all."

Having stood and observed the exchange with interest, Mary thanked Carolyn, picked up a copy of the *Glade Herald*, and made to leave.

"Where's you car, Mary?" Sally asked.

Mary took the hint and waited for Sally to join her.

Carolyn smiled them on their way and turned to serve an older woman who had just come in. Mary caught the beginning of her next session.

"Morning Brenda. How are we? Gosh! Have you met that young mother out at the Heights? You wouldn't credit it. All the education in the world, apparently, and quite a nice person and all that, but she still doesn't know how to look after those children…"

"Oh God," Mary sighed with relief when she and Sally had reached their cars. "Can you believe that?"

"I'll believe anything these days," Sally laughed.

"Do you really know Carrie? She's seems nice. Surely there's no truth in that rumour, is there?"

"It's ridiculous. James acts for her, so I do know she's recently separated. Oh, that's not a secret. I just wouldn't choose to share it with poor old Caro Smith. The next thing you know, the whole of Glade would hear she's suing her husband for adultery or something."

"Where's the husband?"

"Don't know. You know, Carrie's sweet with those boys. They look so happy. I just reckon if I can sow a happier rumour about her it might help."

Mary agreed. "It's awful, Sally. I had begun to hear quite a lot about her over the last week, in one way or another. And you know how it is, you begin to give credit to what you hear, even if you don't want to listen and in your heart you know what you hear isn't true."

Sally nodded. "Carrie rang James at home the other night. I can't talk about the specifics, but I know you're sensible Mary, you won't repeat any of this. She's being harassed by someone in the neighbourhood. It doesn't take a rocket scientist to guess who. She's asked James to look into it."

"Good on her. Poor girl. Judith and I should get her round."

They said their goodbyes, but as Mary reached for her car door, she happened to glance at the front page of the *Glade Herald*. "Oh my goodness."

Sally looked back at her. " What's up?"

Mary's answer was to point to the paper, indicating what was printed: *The Glade Tidings – Have Your Say*

Then the headline: *HEIGHTS' TONE LOWERED*

Mary swallowed hard and read on.

*The Glade Herald has learned that certain residents of Glade Heights are angry Council has permitted a massage business to be started in their district.*

*Spokesperson for the residents group, Mr Hubert Gumphry, told the Herald, "This parlour is lowering the Heights, so we've formed Victory Against Massage Parlours."*

*That's VAMP for those of you who like acronyms.*

*He told our reporter, "The whole tone of our*

*neighbourhood is being undermined. The next thing we'll have massage parlours popping up all over the place. The Council had no right to allow such a business to start up in an area where children play and families walk."*

*Glade District Council Planning Rights and Obligations Manager, Rex Feather, declined to comment other than to refer the Herald to the Council Planning Regulations. The regulations state, "small businesses may be run from residential properties provided they do not attract more than four customers at any one time, nor permit undue noise or nuisance in the course of that business."*

*Our man on the spot pointed this regulation out to Mr Gumphry and asked him if he didn't think that the regulations implied the massage business was legitimate. Mr Gumphry's view is that while certain businesses may be strictly permissible in residential areas, and we quote:*

*"The fact of the matter is, and it's important to point this out for the uninitiated who are none the wiser in these situations, the law is the law and the conducted business on the said premises must be lawful conduction in the first place and not some licentious activity that would, in the normal course of ongoing events, be illegal. In short (sic)," Mr Gumphry told the Herald, "the legality of this illegal practice – and I have endeavoured not to have any preconceived ideas about this – is tenuous in the extreme as I have earlier indicated and we will not be letting this matter drop despite the inadequate*

*response from the responsible authority."*

*We ask our readers: Does this cause deserve to be aired? Are you able to fathom what this fuss is all about? Are our complainants just massaging their egos? We would love to hear your comments.*

*Reactions please, to the Editor.*

"Oh my goodness, Mary. What did I tell you?" Sally gave her a worried look.

"But this is libellous. The *Herald* shouldn't print this sort of stuff."

"I agree, it's appalling."

The women stood in silence for a minute. Then Sally made a suggestion.

"Look, shall I call James and ask him what you should do? You mustn't be hasty. This needs careful thought. Why don't I come over to yours. You and Judith and I need to plan some sort of strategy? I am utterly sick of the McGregor woman. It's time she was put in her place. As for those awful Gumphry people, they're weeds that need to be stamped on before they invade the whole neighbourhood."

Shock waves from the *Herald's* bombshell had already lambasted Judith.

She was waiting in a worried state at the door when Mary got home. The phone had rung several times. It was of some comfort to know their clients had their interests at heart and wanted to help to discredit the allegations, but

Judith was not confident it was their clients who should be writing to the *Herald*. It might make matters worse if they were the ones trying to rebut the suggestion that lascivious acts were taking place at *Number 71* Glade Heights.

"It's going to do us so much damage, Mares. Just as everything appeared to be humming along."

Sally soon joined them. It soothed Judith a little to have her there. Sally had been right all along, they should have taken steps to prevent this happening.

"I don't understand, though," she fretted. "Who is this Gumphry person? And why is he involved? He doesn't even live in our street, does he?"

"Hubert Gumphry," Sally explained, "is one of Miriam's cohorts. I understand he's got a maddeningly enthusiastic wife who, if it's possible, is worse than he is. They're new to the neighbourhood, and they have embraced Miriam and she's embraced them. Now Miriam's got someone she can send into the line of fire without risking her own skin.

"Trust me, she'll be staying safe in HQ and planning her strategies from there. The thing is, unlike Miriam, who long ago lost the plot on a serious level, I think the Gumphrys are just dotty. That may work in our favour. We just have to be certain we've worked out the very best next step."

Mary was impressed. "Goodness, Sally. You've given this quite a lot of thought, haven't you? But how do you know all this?"

"Well, I've lived here long enough to know who pushes the buttons and for what reasons. I've seen those Gumphrys darting up and down to the McGregors in their car. They're in league, all right. You can feel the urgency of their mission in the way the tyres swish."

Judith managed a laugh. "But surely you can't glean all that just from the swish of their tyres?"

"Oh – well – and there's James, who did happen to tell me a thing or two about what's up with Carrie."

Reminded of Carrie and what she might be suffering at the hands of these awful neighbours, Mary and Judith agreed they should consult James. Sally rang and arrangements were settled. Mary and Judith would meet James and Sally that night to plan a counter-attack. If Miriam wanted war, they all agreed she would have it.

# CHAPTER THIRTY THREE

## THE OPPOSITION

As a soft dusk fell on Glade and the lights of the town began to ignite a yearning for home in the hearts of Glade's commuters, Stephen decided to make his way back to Glade Heights. His day had been distracted by thoughts of Carrie and Astra encased in their warm glow of catch-up.

He had joined them the previous evening and he thought it had been a success, even if Astra still treated him with a degree of suspicion. On the whole, though, he was encouraged to think, given time, Carrie's daughter would let him stray past the line she had drawn in the sand. He had known it was unwise to stay too late, but he was far too smitten to stay away altogether, and he had accepted Carrie's suggestion they get together again that night.

Light steps took Stephen to his car.

He drove on to Glade's main street. It always amused him, this street with its plethora of sixties mock-exteriors designed to add substance. Glade always looked clean and accessible but it lacked real character, the building frontages looking as if they could be snapped, like so many thin sheets of polystyrene.

It was what was on offer beyond the buildings that kept Stephen living in Glade. He could cope with ersatz architecture when the natural features of the district were so beautiful.

He passed the *Herald* offices and waved to James Brimsmead, who was too deep in conversation with *Herald* editor Colin Grimshaw to notice Stephen glide by. He came up to the lights just as they turned red, and stopped. He was intrigued to see Miriam and Angus turn across his path on their way into the Town Hall car park. Miriam had noticed Stephen, too, and in her determination to gain his attention, almost rear-ended the car in front of her. He pretended he hadn't noticed them.

The lights changed and he edged off. The smallness of Glade had an appeal. He spent enough time in the bustle of large cities without needing to immerse himself in one of them full time. He liked seeing the familiar faces. Not far ahead Mayor Whyte was hurrying away from the Town Hall and crossing the road. He gave Stephen a cheerful wave as he passed.

Yes, it was pleasing to belong.

The road turned out of town towards Glade Heights. Spring was still young, the night still impatient to close the day down. A deep crimson sunset, which had spread out from the distant shore, was laced together by the fine dark-purple clouds of twilight, lending an air of calm expectation to the early evening.

"Wonderful uncomplicated place," Stephen said out loud, without a hint of irony.

Stephen reached home at last and darted in to change. Before he headed out again, he saw he'd missed some calls. He checked his voice mail. Just three calls, one of them from Miriam.

He went to cut her message off short, then hesitated. This new-found repulsion for some of his neighbours, he was discovering, made them far more interesting than they ever were before. So he let the message play out.

Miriam's voice seemed more shrill than he remembered.

"Miriam here, Stephen, dear. I know you are frightfully busy so I'll make this quick. I just wanted to say we were so pleased to have you with us the other night. Thought you'd like to know, the DPB mission is about to enter a new phase. Hubert has correctly recognised the need to inform the police about young Carrie Thompson. They'll know what to do about the children.

"Well, between you and me – and you of all people will have grasped the fact, of course – these ideas need a little push from those of us with a wee bit more nous than dear Hubert exhibits. But I'm sure Hubert is capable of carrying out the less imaginative side of the mission, now that the seed of a suggestion has been sewn by yours truly. Ha-ha!

"We'll keep you in touch with what eventuates, dear. Must be off. Hoping to get to the do at the Town Hall before the Mayor leaves. Something I need to discuss with him. Byeeeeeee!"

"Whoa!" Stephen stared at the phone for a moment. He shook his head then deleted the message with a sharp prod.

He grabbed his keys, headed out the door, and jumped into his car. In no time he had swung down the hill, remembering to leave the car out of sight of nosy neighbours. He sat for a minute, simmering, then hurried around the corner to Carrie's house.

It was not difficult for Astra to see something was up when she opened the door to him a few minutes later.

"You OK?" she asked. "You don't look too brilliant."

"Astra. Hi. I'm beginning to wonder how I ever doubted what Carrie was telling me about these awful neighbours of ours. Has she told you what they're up to?"

They made their way through to the kitchen where Carrie was feeding the boys.

Her beaming face dropped when she saw his expression. Stephen repeated Miriam's message, pacing to the window and back again as he did so.

Looking directly at Carrie he said, "Can you please explain this madness? Honestly. We have to do something urgently about this problem. The woman's a true menace. I saw James Brimsmead in town. He's your lawyer, isn't he? I suggest we call him tonight."

Carrie found her voice. "Are you telling me they're still trying to get the children taken away from me? I mean, that's obviously why they got that CPS woman around in the first place."

"I don't know, Carrie. Sounds like it. But clearly we must do something – now."

Astra could see how upset her mother was, but she was confused. "How's this escalated so far?"

"I have no idea how, Astra. Your mother hasn't provoked this. It's loopy. It's just so hard to understand."

But Carrie knew exactly what was at the root of it.

"When you've been battered, as I have by Craig, you get good at recognising other batterers. I don't know why I collect them, but I honestly think Miriam McGregor is a batterer. She's a natural. All right, Stephen, I know she's had hardship in her life. How could you not feel sorry for any parent losing a child? But it seems she is now taking her misery out on me. How she shows it is different, but that woman is just as much a batterer as Craig will ever be. To make matters worse she now has these dreadful Gumphry people encouraging her.

"I'm beginning to doubt myself. I feel as undermined by that awful woman as I do by Craig."

Astra had been watching her mother, not wanting to interrupt. Now she spoke, her voice flat. "Trouble is, Mum, it's less visible than Craig's abuse, isn't it? Other's can't see it happening, so it's difficult to prove. In a way it's worse. It makes me feel as if someone has taken my brain and spun it into a whirlpool."

The three of them sat for a time, silenced by a feeling of impotence. Finally, Stephen pulled out his phone. "I'm calling James," he told them.

Sally happened to answer James's phone.

"Oh, Sally? This is Stephen Tiehurst."

"This is a surprise, Stephen. How can we help?"

"I was hoping to get a bit of advice from James."

Stephen attempted to explain what had happened, realising as he spoke he must be sounding slightly unbalanced. "Sally?"

"Yes, I'm still here. Just trying to digest it all. Look, Judith and Mary Naysmith are here too, as it happens. They are the McGregors' neighbours."

She hesitated. "You know what? This is getting very tangled. I think it might be best if we all had a drink together. James is about to give the Naysmiths a bit of advice, and it makes sense if we all join forces. I can quickly sort out a babysitter for the children. Why don't we come over to you?"

As far as Stephen was concerned Sally was talking in riddles, but he was so altogether out of his depth with all the social and emotional toings and froings, he was quite prepared to have the forthright Sally Brimsmead involved. Thus, fifteen minutes later Carrie's doorbell rang heralding the Brimsmeads and the Naysmiths. They brought with them a degree of good humour and a quantity of wine. James was quick to sum up the facts in a way everyone could understand and he began to outline a plan.

The effect was exactly what Stephen had hoped for. Worry gave way to sense as a happy conspiratorial atmosphere took over. They were all new to this kind of plotting; weren't the types to gossip; weren't particularly interested in the aberrations of neighbours. Tonight, however, they entered new territory, drawn in by Miriam and her band who, in contrast, were experts at turning and grinding the rumour mill.

"This is great," Stephen grinned. "We might be novices at this game, but Miriam's lot will see we're not going to be messed about."

The others toasted their agreement. With the instinct of reasonable people wronged, they understood their new resistance movement required shrewd and covert action. The enemy had been allowed to dominate too long, and underhand and undercover tactics in response seemed the best way to deal with the situation.

They were positive they would overcome the enemy, had no doubt whatsoever, and having started the evening fearing for the consequences of the war their neighbours had chosen to wage, they were now almost looking forward to seeing how it played out.

Carrie sat quietly, keen to hear what James had in mind. His plan was twofold. Mary and Judith's problem could be sorted out through the newspaper, he told them.

"We'll get nowhere trying to convince these idiots to understand what the massage business is really about. So I had a word with Colin at the *Herald* after you rang, Sally. Once he understood the circumstances surrounding Hubert's so-called *Victory Against Massage Parlours,* he saw the potential to sort out those trouble makers and do you both a favour at the same time.

"Actually, he was mortified his newspaper might have inadvertently undermined the business. What he wants to do – with your OK – is run an editorial response in the *Glade Tidings* column. You know – one of those glorious... pompous...self-opinionated dogmatic-y editorial thingies."

"Dogmatic-y what?" Judith asked, her eyes wide.

James laughed. "You know. Newspapers are always doing it. Telling their readers they know what's best for them. He'll do it well though. The creative liberal showing the conservatives up for what they are, sort of thing. And better than that, he's told me he'll run a feature on alternative therapies and their benefits. Turns out he's quite a fan. Naming your business specifically, and of course in a favourable light."

This was more illuminating, and Mary and Judith grinned back. The others couldn't help it either, it had a lot to do with the wine. They all cheered.

Carrie's problem, James admitted, was a little more difficult to dismiss. Grappling with the police was never straightforward.

"Look, I've learned in the past if trouble threatens, you're best to make your own trouble happen first.

"My advice is we pre-empt a visit from the police by contacting them first. Let me ring on your behalf, Carrie. You know, lay an informal complaint about the Gumphrys harassing you.

"I know the local sergeant reasonably well. Bill Howard. He'll know how to handle things. No charge, by the way. I'm beginning to enjoy myself. We need to hit these people and hit them hard."

Carrie smiled briefly at him. She too had been caught up in the excitement of the evening but beneath the surface she felt very raw.

"Thanks James, although I'm not sure how much good it will do. Don't you think you should include Miriam in the complaint?"

"No. If Miriam is telling Stephen the facts as they are, she's got Hubert to do her dirty work, and he's the one who will call the police about you. They'll be more sympathetic if it's him we mention. They can cope with that – the tie up between the Gumphrys and you.

"You have to admit, bringing Miriam into the picture is mind-bogglingly complicated. We won't need to worry about Miriam if we can shut her up through the Gumphrys."

"I still think you're underestimating what she's capable of," Carrie insisted in a quiet voice.

Stephen moved over to put his arm around her.

"We won't let her get the better of us, Carrie. We just have to stay alert to further developments but let James take this course for now. It makes sense."

A chair scraped back on the kitchen floor, and Sally

rose. She grabbed the last bottle of wine.

"Come on you lot. Let's drink to defeating those dreadful people."

She topped up their glasses and held her own aloft.

"Here's to those who wish us well, and all the rest can go to hell!"

## CHAPTER THIRTY FOUR
## FUTILITY

Angus thrust his hands into his jacket pockets and hunched his shoulders.

The hour was late, and the function his wife had insisted he attend, a disaster on every level. Not only was there nothing in the way of refreshments, it had provided not a modicum of diversion for his wife. Not a single person of wide reputation, good or otherwise, had she identified in the crush at the Town Hall. Even the Mayor had been called out to some unexplained urgent matter just as they arrived, meaning Miriam had not had the satisfaction of baling up Glade's first citizen as she had intended.

As they walked to their car, a heavy cloud settled on Angus's head. It leaked permeating dampness. Miriam was out of sorts and on the war path. These war paths of hers cut swathes in many directions, but because of his proximity they invariably touched upon Angus most of all.

On this unfortunate evening Angus felt sure the immediate repercussion of his wife's bad temper would be the cancellation of the one pleasure he had been looking forward to all evening.

Normally, while Miriam insisted on being the driver of their car on the outward leg of any excursion, Angus was usually the designated driver for any return. He would have liked to have been the driver more often, but at least he was given the occasional opportunity to enjoy that little bit of self-determination he so lacked in the rest of his life.

Getting into the driver's seat was his great pleasure. He would wrap his hands around the steering wheel, caressing its circumference. For a brief moment he would cancel the reality of Miriam and imagine a buxom young beauty with abundant blonde hair in the passenger seat beside him. For Angus, cars were nubile, budding, ready to bloom. Behind the wheel he would drift away into a nook of happiness. Tonight, however, he sensed he would be denied this momentary pleasure, and it was a cruel blow.

Miriam snapped him out of his daydreaming.

"For goodness sake, Angus. It's cold. Hurry up. Give me the keys, come on."

As he had predicted, he was not even to be granted his one small liberation. A steady drizzle seeped from his cloud, making his shoulders slump in submission.

"I'll drive, Angus, thank you. I will not put up with any more mucking around. You were of absolutely no use to me at all this evening."

"You were the one who wanted to go, Miriam. I was not keen, as you know," was all the defiance he could muster.

"You'd never go anywhere, given the choice. Without me, Angus, you'd be a nothing."

So deep was Angus's hollow at that moment, he offered no further protest. Miriam snatched the keys off him, unlocked the car door, and instructed him to get in. As a small compensation Angus understood the drive home would be in silence.

The streets were now deserted and a little forlorn. The orange light from the street lamps lent a surreal glow, making the scene seem like a stage setting. Angus felt there must be substance beyond what he could see, yet it looked like a façade, and as such, was dreamlike.

Miriam stopped for the traffic lights. Dispirited, Angus leant his head on the car window. Little stacks of cardboard boxes waited in neat piles on the side of the road, ready for the rubbish men in the morning. He stared at them. They reminded him of *The Rubbish Tale* and he shuddered. That had been a crushing humiliation, so he had thought at the time. Miriam at her blinkered worst.

Angus was jolted back to the present by his wife accelerating away from the lights with a pointed thrust of irritation. He turned to look at her expression. It gave nothing away. She had worn a similar impenetrable expression when she had marched with purpose into the Council offices to suggest rubbish trucks were unsightly and were no longer required inside the Glade Heights Estate.

When they had walked in, Angus noticed the Public Enquiry Clerk shrink into his chair and swivel in the other direction. The Rubbish Clerk was made of sterner stuff. He stood his ground as Miriam informed him of her rights.

"Look, young man," she had told him. "If you don't organise for collections within the Heights itself to cease forthwith, I shall sue the Council for negligence. And it is on your head the awful consequences will finally fall. You mark my words."

The clerk had been a young chap, Angus remembered. Thin, pimply and sharp-eyed in that oily way thin, pimply people can appear to be sharp-eyed. A flicker across those sharp eyes was all Angus caught before the chap risked his clerical all.

He leant across the counter and told her in a loud voice, "Sue then, madam, sue."

Miriam had gasped, then reaching her full height, proclaimed, "How dare you be so rude young man. I shall go to the *Glade Herald*. They shall know exactly what to make of the sort of treatment the Council dishes out to rate payers. It's a disgrace. I shall have them publish the facts exactly as they have happened."

Angus had twitched. But the Rubbish Clerk, apart from letting his lips curl up slightly at the edges, had remained motionless. While he could not be given credit for originality, he had stated still more firmly and with a triumphant gleam, "Publish then, madam, and be damned."

Miriam had stormed out of the Council offices knowing her wishes would not, on this occasion be satisfied. As he was swilled out the door in her wake, Angus turned. With a look of pleasure on his face, he had doffed a daring flick of his hat at the Rubbish Clerk in a rare display of defiance.

It was a regret for courageous opportunities not grasped

that consumed Angus as Miriam turned the car into their street and accelerated up the hill. He should show more courage.

He looked up at the stars tracking their perpetual path across the chill sky. Indifferent to his plight, they compounded the cold exuded by the icicle wife sitting beside him.

## CHAPTER THIRTY FIVE
## THE COMPLAINANT

The frigid starlit night gave way to a blustery day. Leyla looked at her garden with disgust. Her early roses were being tossed about in the wind, the full blooms disintegrating into bare heads as she watched. Swathes of young leaves were being stripped from the plum tree and lay wilting on the ground.

"At least it's not raining," she thought. "but I simply cannot abide bruised-brown petals in my garden."

"Hu-bie?" Her shrill voice reverberated through the house.

Hubert did not respond.

"Hubert!" she called again, impatient for him to share her frustration with the weather. But when there was still no reply she left the window and went in search of him.

She found him in his office, deep in composition and unaware of the bluster outside or in. She hesitated and for a moment stood marvelling at the talent of her husband before calling to him.

"Hubert?"

Hubert turned, startled, taking a moment or two to realise his wife required his attention.

"Hubert, dear, I need your help to secure the roses."

Hubert was patient "Leyla, my love, I have such weighty responsibilities at the moment. Can't they wait?"

Leyla realised immediately her garden must take second place to the important work Hubert had at hand.

"Oh Hubert, how thoughtless of me. Of course you must continue. Are you composing a summary of what you intend doing about those young hussies up the road?"

"That, of course, is equally important and is crowding in on me along with all these other matters. But no, I am dealing with those Waste Collections people first."

"Wonderful, I've had enough of those awful trucks coming through here. Miriam informs me Council promised long ago to set up a proper collection point for the rubbish outside the Heights gates. You need to remind them of their responsibility."

Hubert gave her a tolerant smile.

"I am a step ahead of you, my dear. We've already seen how hopeless the Council can be by the way they handled the parking business."

"But wasn't that because Miriam had already organised a different arrangement?" Leyla asked.

Hubert didn't like to be reminded Miriam had been a step ahead of him.

"Oh, she's got fine intentions, that one. But this time we must be doubly clever," he said. "I intend to ring Waste Collections and tell them they are not to continue collecting the rubbish from inside the estate, and that Council agrees, and our rubbish can be collected at a central collection point at the end of White Water Road."

"Will the other residents go along with that, Hubert?"

Leyla didn't like to be disloyal but she could see problems with this plan.

"I've thought of that too," her husband told her triumphantly. "The potluckers have already agreed the plan. And I will put a notice in all the other letter boxes informing residents the collection is now at White Water Road. If anyone is disagreeable enough to put their rubbish out on the street, you and I will be out to collect it before the rubbish trucks arrive. If Waste Collections don't find any rubbish at the Heights it won't take long before they stop coming around altogether and we'll have won this little battle."

As Leyla considered this plan she wobbled. It appeared to involve her in some form of physical exertion.

"What do you mean, you and I will be out to collect it before the trucks arrive."

"We'll go out on the four-wheeler bike, Leyla, and whip it away on the trailer."

Her tone became plaintive. "Hubert, I don't want to be a rubbish collector."

Hubert rose from his desk and came to his wife. The firm hand he placed on her shoulder made her buckle slightly.

"All you will need to do, my dear, is drive the bike. I will tote the rubbish. It is a sacrifice I am prepared to make for the greater good of the community."

Leyla looked up at him, tears of affection welling in her eyes. "Glade Heights does not deserve you Hubert Gumphry."

It was true. Glade Heights had never done anything to deserve Hubert Gumphry, or what he was preparing to dish out. Leyla left her husband to pursue his urgent business, noticing, as she returned to her kitchen, the wind had calmed down a little and the few roses left unbattered were looking less vulnerable.

"The comfy Gumphrys. That's what we are," she trilled as she went to the bench in order to whistle up some triple chocolate and raspberry friands.

Buoyed by his wife's approval Hubert wasted no time. Leyla's Magimix had barely begun its buzz before he was in conversation with the manager of Waste Collections Limited.

"What are you trying to tell me, Mr Gumphry?" the manager asked.

Hubert explained.

"It has been drawn to my attention Mr Canwell, that your company was under a contractual obligation to the Council to refrain from inordinate intrusion on the district in general and at Glade Heights in particular, and that this entailed your trucks refraining from collecting the rubbish where such an intrusion was likely. In short, Mr Canwell, when your company did not adhere to the obligations imposed on you by the Council you were then in breach of those obligations and consequently not adhering to the contractual obligations you were obliged to adhere to."

"Eh?"

"Am I going to have to spell it out, Mr Canwell?"

"Clearly you are, Mr Hubert."

"Gumphry. It's Gumphry. The Glade Heights Estate no longer requires a rubbish collection from the kerb-side, Mr Canwell. Is that clear? As the official residents group we are advising you that your intrusive practice of bringing pink trucks into this green and natural environment is indeed inordinately intrusive and must cease immediately by stopping. Next week the rubbish will be stacked en masse, Mr Canwell, outside the gates on White Water Road, and from that point in time, then, and in the future the said en masse collection site will become the official collection site for Glade Heights refuse."

"Is that right?'

"It is, Mr Canwell. Now I have no wish to continue this discussion further. I am sure you understand me. Good bye."

With that, Hubert hung up the phone with great pointedness and sat for a moment considering how satisfactory his conversation with the Waste Collections chap had been.

He looked about his office, savouring its air of authority. He had fitted special shelving to accommodate his file boxes and they sat in tight uniform rows beside him. An old set of statutes graced the top shelf. Hubert reached across for one of the tomes and thumbed through it. He felt an affinity with these books. They not only suggested his missed vocation, they spoke of the old ways, better ways, when servility was respectable; as did the photograph on the wall behind him, which showed Hubert receiving a silver-plated tray from a much younger and slicker looking individual. Inscribed, 'With thanks from all at Cameron Radiators Ltd. Hubert Gumphry – loyal employee for 40 years', it captured the defining moment of Hubert's retirement party.

Hubert put the volume of statutes back and went to the kitchen to report on his activities to Leyla. He repeated his conversation with Mr Canwell of Waste Collections Limited. She managed a doughy congratulations between piping hot friand mouthfuls.

"Magnificent, Hubert." A few crumbs flew out of her mouth and landed on the table. "Simply magnificent! Mmmmm 'magine what nefarious types they are. Ummf. Haf a friand while they're hotf…"

Hubert sat down with a cup of tea and basked. It was important to show a united front with Miriam in this war against decrepitude, but he could see it was possible, if he played his cards right, to become the chief strategist himself. He had been overlooked at Cameron Radiators. Leyla had often told him – and he could not have agreed more – he was far too undervalued at the firm. He was not going to remain some adjutant johnny this time.

Miriam would see she had met her match. What she had been unable to achieve, he would sort out. All of it – prostitutes, ungrateful solo mothers, rubbish – the lot.

At that very moment up the hill Hubert's rival was standing in her sitting room surveying her domain, not through her binoculars, but with her own eyes. Getting an overview.

It was not often Miriam broadened her horizons in this way. For a woman who was so intently interested in other people's doings she was remarkably unaware of what made other people tick. Consequently, she had not calculated the effect the Gumphrys might have on her plans.

She did register, however, something alien, something unpleasant creeping into her world. Carrie Thompson, she had started it all. Her arrival had caused the painful knot in Miriam's chest to tighten. Before she arrived on the scene Miriam's life was manageable. Of course there had been one or two minor setbacks over the years. They were to be expected. But generally, she had been able to keep her environment in tight controllable compartments.

Carrie Thompson had brought instability. Those awful sisters moved in next door at about the same time, and even the Gumphrys were beginning to feel like a worry. Of course she needed some energetic cohorts. They were unquestionable allies. She just hoped they weren't too energetic, hoped she hadn't unleashed something she couldn't control.

"Hubert could be a challenge," she told herself out loud. "I'll need to play him just right."

Hubert was useful as the public front for her own activities. As long as she didn't allow him too much leeway, he would remain manoeuvrable. It would also make him the fall guy if things took a turn for the worse, leaving her unsullied and blameless.

She took a deep breath and exhaled slowly, dispelling the uncertainty. Things were on track. She should not worry. Putting the binoculars to her eyes she scanned the houses below in more detail. Above her the clouds moved at pace and their shadows bustled across the neighbourhood. Carrie's house was bathed for a second in bright sunlight before it slid back into gloom.

"You watch out, young lady," Miriam muttered. "I've got my sights on you."

Miriam had good cause to feel disconcerted. Encouraged by his earlier conversation with Tom Canwell,

Hubert was back on the phone introducing himself to Sergeant Bill Howard of the Glade Police.

This was, in fact, what Miriam wanted. However, it was not about Carrie he was calling, as she expected. Hubert decided he would first clear up the prostitution problem instead. So he was calling the Glade Police Department to lay a formal complaint, not against Carrie but against Mary and Judith.

"That didn't take long," Bill remarked when Hubert came on the line.

"I'm sorry?" Hubert asked.

"Nothing, ah, Mr Gumphry, is it? How can I help?"

"Yes, well, I've rung to complain about two women in our neighbourhood using their house for a prostitution racket."

Bill Howard was matter of fact. "What do you mean prostitution racket, Mr Gumphry. Are you aware that prostitution is legal these days?"

Hubert knew only too well the law on prostitution had changed and he was ready for this.

With a tone of loathing he reserved specifically for immoral conduct, he said, "A racket, sergeant, is a racket whether it is made in the execution of a legal business or an illegal business. I am talking about flagrant behaviour, amounting in my considered opinion, sergeant, to a breach of the peace. I said, a breach of the peace."

"Ah. That's a breach of the peace, then, I take it? So you're not objecting to the prostitution. It's the racket that's in question here, is it?"

"Don't take me for a fool, sergeant. We live in a peaceful place where people are law abiding and morally upright. Prostitution is a vulgar immoral activity, which, if I had my way, would be reinvested with the status with which it had previously been invested, by which I mean, for laymen such as yourself, made illegal once more."

"Eh?" asked Sergeant Howard.

"These girls are creating a considerable disturbance," Hubert said succinctly.

"Could you be more specific Mr Gumphry?"

Hubert considered this question briefly, knowing he must hit the mark or the moment might be lost.

"Let me give you just a small example. There are comings and goings from that house at all hours of the day and night..."

Bill Howard remained silent, waiting. Hubert scrambled for something more substantial.

"...with their activities conducted in full view of the neighbours."

With the sergeant still maintaining his disconcerting silence, Hubert could have been tempted to abandon his pursuit. But he was determined not to be diverted, and he began to outline a series of events even he acknowledged stretched the truth. He hadn't lied exactly. Indeed, he told Leyla later, what he had said was an "inspired piece of ex tempore eloquence, my dear."

And she had known it was.

What Hubert said to Bill Howard was this: "Naked bodies exposed in all manner of expositions, visible to children let alone adults, is hardly the kind of behaviour normally tolerated in our society, sergeant."

It was a baseless provocative picture but it at least spurred Sergeant Howard on to promise to send someone around to have a chat with the parties concerned at *Number 71*.

"Once the police arrive," he reported to Leyla, "they will be able to deduce the rest for themselves. Those

Naysmith women will be unable to continue their unsavoury business a moment longer.

"Needs must, as Miriam herself would say, when matters fundamental to the well-being of the greater community dictate that we commit to the description of an event that will end up taking place in the future if we do not deal with the particular problem in the here and now."

And while Leyla blinked, she had known, indeed needs must.

## CHAPTER THIRTY SIX
## WHAT RUBBISH

It is one of life's greatest ironies that at the very moment events seem to be coasting along in slow motion, they are in reality whipping past at alarming speed. Thus not even the arrival of a sunny indolent weekend had been able to put a brake on the momentum that had been set in place at Glade Heights.

On Sunday evening, just on dusk, Hubert and Leyla Gumphry drove out of their garage on their four-wheeler bike and darted on to the street, narrowly missing Mary Naysmith who was driving past on her way home from the gym.

They were towing a small trailer, Leyla driving. Her head was low and furtive, but in order to grasp the handlebars her large frame had forced her elbows wide, giving her a paradoxical look that was both embarrassed yet defiant. Hubert sat on the bike's back tray and signalled for her to turn first towards the lake.

"We must tackle this matter logically, Leyla. I have plotted the correct path to minimize your inconvenience, my dear. Don't worry, we will be through in no time."

The plan was to pick up any bags left on the kerbside and cart them back to a larger trailer Hubert had at home. This process would be repeated until the whole estate had been cleared. The rubbish could then be taken in one load out the gates, down the road, and left in a convenient turnaround spot where the Waste Collections men would see the bags and take them away from there.

Not many residents had heeded Hubert's directive to take their rubbish down to White Water Road. All the same, Leyla's reluctance to be involved gave way to a more co-operative mood as the evening progressed. She watched with admiration as her angular husband grappled with the heavy piles. She didn't go so far as to get off the bike to help him, but she did begin to scan the darkening streets for bags and she encouraged him with a beckoning of her stout arm.

"Oh good. Over here, Hubert. Here's another one."

Hubert had rather underestimated how long they would be at the exercise. The sordid undertaking jerked its increasingly grubby way around the streets, clearing the neighbourhood of its weekly trash, and not until nearly midnight did Hubert and Leyla fall exhausted into bed.

On Monday morning Glade Heights was bathed again in sunshine. Much to the bemusement of the Waste Collections Ltd truck driver and his mate, however, it was not bathed in rubbish.

When their brief drive around the area uncovered no rubbish bags, there was nothing else for them to do but turn around and head back to town, picking up a surprise pile of rubbish on White Water Road as they went. They were not to know one solitary bag, obscured by an overhanging bush, still sat outside the McGregors' house at *Number 73*. Hubert, in the excitement of planning, had forgotten to tell Miriam he had put his monumental plan into action.

By 11:00am, with the sun shooting sparkles off the lake, an ebullient Hubert completed a reconnoitre of the neighbourhood.

He had driven around the whole of Glade Heights and out to White Water Road and back, and not a jot of rubbish was to be seen. He speculated it may take a number of weeks before all residents made the connection between collection day and White Water Road, which would require his Sunday evening sortie to be repeated. He was confident, however, Glade Heights would soon be rid of smelly, noisy, pink rubbish trucks polluting their way around his pristine neighbourhood.

"We've done it," he told Leyla as he drank his morning coffee.

Leyla chomped into her slice of home-baked carrot cake.

"I knew we would, Hubert," she confirmed. A white line of cream-cheese icing ran parallel to the smile on her lips. "You were astonishing last night. Astonishing."

"We've got her, you know," he continued.

"Who? Carrie Thompson? What's she got to do with this?"

"No, Leyla. Miriam. I haven't wanted to say too much to you before now, but I do feel the Heights needs better guidance than it's been getting. Oh, I know Miriam has made a super effort so far, don't get me wrong. And she is unquestionably a wonderful friend. She needs, however, the strong hand of a mind that has the legs to go the extra distance. When one is in a position to view the extended picture and envisage the consequences of so many interrelated relationships, one understands how important it is to help all the little people out from time to time. Miriam has many attributes but I would call her light weight in comparison – and I know you won't think me egotistical, my dear – in comparison to yours truly."

Leyla loved it when her husband talked like this. She would ring Miriam the minute they finished their morning coffee. Why not bolster her husband's successes by rubbing a little salt into the wound Miriam would invariably have incurred? Hubert might be right, perhaps she was a wonderful friend, but it didn't hurt her to know the Gumphrys were just that little cut above, and from now on her role as majordomo had been usurped.

Angus was seeking solace in *The Hidey-hole,* letting the sun irradiate his conscious surroundings. He did not ask for much from life. The tittle tattle stimulated him enough, especially when contrasted with the dry existence he had experienced in his work days. So why this emptiness?

He was pondering this question and just how he could find a way out of his dilemma when the telephone interrupted. He dragged himself up to answer the call, cursing Miriam for not considering the use of mobile phones.

"It's Leyla, Angus. Miriam if you wouldn't mind."

He shouldn't have been surprised to be relegated by

Leyla in this way. Clearly everyone saw him as existing simply to do Miriam's bidding. And yet, while Leyla's rudeness was confirmation of his lack of importance, he did recognise its positive gloss. Perhaps, if he were such an unnecessary cog in Miriam's wheel, he could exempt himself from duty permanently.

He grunted a monosyllable down the phone and went to find his wife.

"Your cohort's on the phone," he said when he found her. "No doubt she'll whet your blades."

Miriam glanced at her husband.

"I'm no longer in any doubt whatsoever you need help, Angus," she huffed, and left to answer the phone.

Surprisingly, Angus did not put Miriam out of sorts. Thriving as she did on the opportunity to pass judgement on aberrant behaviour, by the time she reached the phone she was in a most positive frame of mind.

"Hello? Oh Leyla. How are you?" she sang down the line.

Leyla cooed back. "Dear Miriam. Isn't it a most magnificent day. Especially when things are going along so successfully."

Successfully? What successfully? Miriam hadn't expected any successfully to be in the offing. She was on her guard.

"Oh yes. A most delightful day. I, myself, find these mornings are most conducive to delving into a leee-tle light gardening, Leyla. It does the figure such a lot of good. Not that you would need to worry. Ha-ha!"

Leyla let this barb go. "My Hubie has finally done it," she continued, undeterred.

"You mean he's phoned the police about that girl?"

"Oh no. You misunderstand me Miriam, dear. Hubie's finally done it. Got the rubbish people to collect the rubbish from the end of White Water Road."

There was brief silence.

"What are you on about, Leyla?" Miriam demanded, her voice growing sharp.

"I mean, Miriam," she snapped back, "my husband has managed to get action where you couldn't. He advised the rubbish people to go no further than White Water Road to collect the rubbish, and that is what they have done this very morning."

"You're not serious, I trust?"

Leyla became more conciliatory.

"Oh Miriam, don't be too sore at him. He should have let you tell Waste Collections when the new scheme was to start. I'm sure he meant to. But he is so good at sorting these things out and what with one thing and another, events obviously just hurried along.

"I have to say, I was quite surprised to find how smoothly it went given the Waste Collections man's response to Hubie on the phone the other day. But there you are. He's so very adept at these things. And as Hubie says so wisely, 'needs must'."

*Needs must? Needs must?* Surely that was Miriam's own phrase. Miriam's brewing discomfort with the Gumphrys bubbled to the surface.

"Smoothly?" she cried. "I'll give you smoothly you stupid woman. I've just spent a good part of this morning ticking off the Council Rubbish Clerk because our rubbish wasn't collected this morning, and now you tell me I've been made to look a fool all because of what you and Hubert have done. And done without any final clearance from me?"

Leyla was valiant. "Why should we get clearance from you, Miriam? You're not the only one with brains around here. And compared to my Hubie you're a nothing."

"Well, really!" Miriam's snort was truly heart-felt. "You two think you can come to Glade Heights and run the place as if you own it. It's been a step up the ladder for you, but I would suggest it is a rung too high. You should go back to where you can manage affairs better.

"All I asked Hubert to do at this stage was sew the seed of a revamped rubbish collection with the Council. I didn't think for a minute he would be so insubordinate as to go so far as to cancel the collection yet."

Miriam ignored Leyla's spluttering. "Furthermore, he was instructed to ring the police and he can't even manage that small job. One should never delegate. I shall have to do it myself."

As Miriam finally drew breath, Leyla was able to get a word in – and she quivered with self-satisfaction.

"Well, let...me...tell...you, Miriam know-it-all McGregor, Hubie has rung the police, and not because you say so. He's a step ahead of you, you see. He's already told the police about those two disgusting girls next door to you. It's us you'll thank for getting rid of that trash once they've gone. Left to you they'd be there forever." And with that, Leyla hung up.

Miriam gave three fast and furious blasts through her nostrils before rushing off to fire more fury at her husband.

"Angus. Angus!" she shrieked. "Where are you when I need you?"

She found him in his retreat where he frowned and

stabbed his pipe at her to ward off a further advance.

"'Hubie'. She called her husband 'Hubie'. I knew that woman was trouble. The very minute I saw her."

"No you didn't," Angus told her. "You thought she was wonderful. And her telegraph pole deluded husband, you thought he was wonderful, too. For myself, I never thought they were wonderful. You've got what you deserve."

"What's this? Are you choosing this moment of all moments to be pettish and perverse, you ungrateful little man?"

He got up to leave.

"I don't want to hear the latest, to be honest. I'm going into Glade for an hour or two," he told her, pausing only to shroud her in a cloud of pipe smoke.

Miriam knew, she had been right to suspect an unpleasant change was in the air. Now she had absolute proof, not just of one threat, but of many. It was ironic the most immediate threat came from her supposed friends, the Gumphrys. She chastised herself for thinking they were controllable. What had caused her to get so drawn in? She should dump them immediately and have nothing further to do with them.

She was standing by one of Angus's pot plants and noticed it was overrun with weeds. A wave of exhaustion washed over her as she tried to stem the insidious creep of self pity. Why were there always so many weeds?

"I want that Thompson woman gone," she muttered, crossing her arms to squeeze out the pain. "Out of my life, gone. She's nothing but trouble."

For one of the few times she could remember, Miriam felt stymied. The course she had set out on had taken an unpredictable turn. She couldn't think straight. The Gumphrys had seemed so useful. It was inconceivable she might have made an error of judgement where they were concerned.

At the same time she sensed they were key to carrying out her audacious plan. But what to do? She had now gone and offended Leyla. Perhaps it was not too late to regain the initiative. It would require eating a little humble pie, but – well – needs must.

She hurried into the sitting room and took up her notebook. Time for *Itemizations* – a decent list to get everything back in perspective.

A fierce intensity burned in Miriam's face as her pen flew across her notebook:

> *Gumphry woman - completely out of control. Hubert Gumphry also in too high a gear. Make phone call and rein back in.*
>
> *Thompson initiative imperative – must not get so sidetracked. They simply must get on to police to maintain pressure but not straight on heels of Naysmith call. Will have to hold them off for a week or so or everything will blow sky high.*
>
> *Call GP about Angus. Needs referral to psychiatrist.*

Leyla did not tell Hubert immediately about her phone call to Miriam, anxious her husband might think she had intruded on his territory. Not until she had garnered some courage from her afternoon's baking did she advise him of the latest turn of events. They were seated once more at their kitchen table.

"Miriam has her nose right out of joint," she braved between bites into an ANZAC biscuit.

"Oh?" Hubert had his head down attempting to fit a battery into his small transistor radio.

"Yes. She had no idea the rubbish routine was changing this week, apparently."

"Ah well. Not even Miriam gets it right every time, my dear."

"She accused you of not getting on with things, actually."

"Well, that's where she is wrong, isn't she, my dear. I have got on with things and that is why her nose is out of joint."

At last he looked up. "I wouldn't worry your pretty little head about it if I were you."

Hubert was taking this well, but despite the thrill of flying the colours for her man, Leyla remained unhappy. On one hand she couldn't bear how domineering Miriam was. On the other hand, Miriam offered a fast track into respectable Heights society. It would be a shame to have to throw that connection away. Besides, they did agree on what was appropriate neighbourly behaviour and what was not. She just didn't know whether she should make up with Miriam.

Having weighed up the pros and the cons, Leyla finally settled on the path of appeasement just as the phone rang. She could hardly believe her luck. It was Miriam. And Miriam was ringing her to do the apologising.

"So that's the way it is, Leyla. Angus is just in another world, you see, and it is such an awful preoccupation one is inclined to forget oneself. You can imagine."

"I quite understand," Leyla oozed sympathy. "I would be beside myself with worry if Hubert tended that way. Of course Hubert is never likely to lose his marbles. He keeps them far too organised in that mental pouch of his."

Miriam was all sweetness.

"Of course he does, ha-ha! I suspect he is far too busy with important matters to lose his marbles. So, having rung the police about the Naysmith girls he won't be wanting to call them about Carrie. Perhaps it's better if I do that, do you think?"

Leyla hesitated. Was Miriam paying Hubert a compliment or not? She thought not but could not quite calculate why. She hated it when her grey matter hurt like this. It always put such great demands on her, causing her to want to gravitate towards the biscuit barrel.

What should she do? She was reluctant to jeopardise the truce she and Miriam had only this minute made, and yet Hubert had told her they must retain the initiative.

She faltered. "Well, Miriam, you are so very able. I am sure Hubert would consider it perfectly acceptable for you to make the call."

Miriam dripped more treacle. "Well, dear, we shall leave it for a few days, shall we? No point making the police touchy with too many complaints. I will give you a call and we can talk about it again."

Leyla walked away from the phone with her anxiety greatly relieved.

She found Hubert in his study. "I've just spoken to Miriam, Hubert, and she has apologised. Quite right, of course. She thinks she ought to take on the responsibility of ringing the police about Carrie Thompson.

"Of course, it should be you who does that. You are so very much more adept at these things. But Miriam has agreed to leave it for a few days and then discuss it with us again. Very reasonable I thought."

Hubert indulged his wife. "I'm glad you are happy, my dear." Then he added, "However, I intend to keep abreast of events over the next few days. I intend to act the minute my involvement is at that moment called for."

CHAPTER THIRTY SEVEN
## BALANCE V

A few days later on his return from his walk, Angus noticed a police car disappear up the Naysmiths' drive. He registered curiosity and attempted a mental *Itemization* for Miriam but got no further. His heart was not committed to observation duty any more. Nor had his head been cleared by the walk as he had hoped. It ached in the afternoon's warm oppressive air.

"Miriam will have to figure that one out for herself," he decided. He watched the car, then turned up his own path without any further interest.

The police car stopped at the Naysmiths' front steps. Two officers unfolded themselves, placed their hats on their heads with official deliberation, and walked up to knock on the door. Mary showed no surprise at seeing them there.

"Afternoon, miss," the older officer said. " I'm PC

Burwood, this is PC Stewart."

"Mmmm. We thought you people might be paying a visit," she told them, opening the door a little wider.

"Oh?" PC Burwood sounded wary. "And why might that be then?"

Mary was uncomplicated. "About our massage business. Or should I say," and she threw her voice into low theatrical tones, "massage parlour. We knew you'd come eventually."

"Sounds like we had better come inside then, madam."

"Not madam, George," his younger colleague hissed through the side of his mouth as they passed into the hall.

They were soon joined by Judith.

"Ah... we've had a complaint laid about your business, Miss," George said to Mary. "What do you girls get up to here, exactly?"

"Women, thanks very much," Mary retorted. "We run a therapeutic massage business. Strictly legal according to Council."

"Even a brothel's legal these days, Miss. But what does go on, eh? No cavorting round the garden or anything like that?"

"Hey," Mary began to protest, but Judith gently placed her hand on Mary's shoulder.

"We would be perfectly open with you if this were a brothel," Judith said in a more business-like manner. "But it's not. We're ex-nurses and what we have here is an alternative health facility. Strictly 'non-explicit therapy'," she added, describing two fat quotation marks in the air. "We're aware our neighbour doesn't like us running a business from home, but frankly we don't cause a disturbance, and we have the Council's blessing."

PC Burwood did not looked convinced. "What hours of

the day do you conduct your business then, might I ask?"

"We have the odd client come around 7:00 at night if they can't get off work to come earlier. And I suppose that means an 8 o'clock finish. But otherwise it's, what, Mary? 9:00am to 6:00pm?"

"About that," Mary confirmed.

George Burwood persisted. "No romps take place, then?"

This time Mary got in before Judith. She was livid.

"What romps? Oh, honestly! We massage people's tired muscles on massage tables in our respective treatment rooms. They dress and undress in private and when they leave they are fully clothed. OK?"

"You won't mind if PC Stewart has a little look around, then?" he asked her coolly. "We don't want any holes in our story, do we?"

"He can search my bloody knickers drawer for all I care. The only holes he'll find will be in the ancient old ones I've worn threadbare."

PC Chris Stewart slipped out and Mary was aware of him working his way in and out of each room. She glowered at George Burwood. When the younger policeman returned he signalled an impassive nod.

"Right," George said. "We'll be off then."

"Off? And...?" Mary prompted.

"We'll be in touch in due course, Miss."

Mary and Judith watched in silence as the two policemen walked to their car, but once they had disappeared, Judith was fretting.

"Good Lord. What a visit. I had hoped we'd seen an end to all this. What are we going to do, Mares?"

"Don't worry about it." Mary perked up. "They're satisfied we're legit, Judith. You can tell. You handled it well, by the way."

And when her sister still looked doubtful, "Truly. That young guy had his head screwed on right. Don't think our friend George was too pleased with him though. Did you hear George call me 'madam'? What a hoot." Then after a short moment to reflect, "What an idiot."

"I hope you're right, Mary. I am so sick of all this stuff."

They closed the door.

"Come on," Mary laughed. "Come and have a cup of hot coffee, and I'll read out the *Glade Herald* apology once more, to soothe your weathered brow."

Down the road Hubert was finding it difficult to concentrate in the stuffy atmosphere of his study. He decided to get some fresh air. He was not a happy man. The previous day's *Glade Herald* had published an apology for printing his comments about the Naysmith women. It was outrageous. Made him look like a fool.

He found Leyla, generous bottom skyward, pulling out weeds from the rose garden.

"I feel restless, Leyla. Restless indeed."

Leyla pushed herself up from her compromising position, her face blotched with exertion.

"What's wrong, Hubert?"

"That apology in the paper, yesterday. The editor is without doubt acting in a manner which is beyond the bounds of decency. We cannot let these people jeopardise our perfect lifestyle, Leyla. How dare they get involved in this matter, dictating the way people should feel.

"And look at that most unsettling article they've published. Alternative health therapies? I'll give them alternative health therapies. Leftie, pie in the sky ideas."

"What are you going to do about it, then Hubert? Shall I go and make a cup of tea?"

Leyla pulled off her gardening gloves and dropped them into her garden-tool carry-all.

"I've made scones," she encouraged him.

She began to walk towards the house but Hubert didn't move. His eyes remained fixed on the middle distance, his mind appearing to be likewise. Leyla came back to his side and cradled his elbow in her hands.

"Come on Hubert. There's nothing like a good hot cup of tea and a scone for sorting out a problem. I'm sure the minute you sit down you'll know which way to proceed."

When he still didn't reply she nudged him gently and led him back inside. What had struck Hubert dumb was the awful realisation people might be laughing at him. He, who single-handed had sorted out the Glade Heights rubbish troubles. It was preposterous.

Once back inside, and with a reviving cuppa under his belt, he seemed to come round. His cup clattered down on its saucer, and sitting bolt upright, he spoke with great deliberation.

"You know, Leyla, we're not going to let Miriam handle this Thompson business with the police. Why should she take advantage of a situation we've created, and through sheer foot slogging? Why should she get all the praise at the end? No, this unfortunate episode with the paper has led me to believe in the belief that it is imperative for the community that the campaign for moral rectitude be waged to the bitter end, and that it is I who must now go forward at this point in time and wage it."

Leyla licked the butter off her fingers and decided to make this her last scone. She had licked her fingers and made the previous scone her last one, too, but she knew in her heart this statement of Hubert's was too monumental to be dismissed without some form of consolidation.

Leyla really did believe the Gumphrys' position consolidated, but over the next few days the balance of power at Glade Heights began to shift.

Ironically, it was Hubert's impetuous complaint to the police that was finally going to relieve Judith and Mary of all the interference they had been suffering. PC George Burwood may have been suspicious when he first arrived to investigate the sisters, but after a brief discussion with PC Stewart, even he conceded there was nothing untoward going on at *Number 71* Glade Heights, and he intended filing a report to that effect.

However, the fact that the heat had been turned off Judith and Mary meant it was about to be turned full blast on Carrie.

# CHAPTER THIRTY EIGHT

# DIVISION

Since the get together with the Brimsmeads and the Naysmiths, Carrie's life had regained a degree of normality.

She was still beset with her worries. James had rung to tell her he had arranged a meeting with Craig and Craig's lawyer in ten days time. Less than two weeks' grace. But having Astra still at home had been a blessing, and in any event, worries of the Craig kind were somehow more straightforward because they were real.

As she had suggested to Stephen, "The trouble is these awful neighbours have fabricated a situation then nurtured it until they believe it's true. How can you fight a nothing?"

Stephen was a calming influence. He was spending most of his spare time with Carrie and her children, and even Astra was warming to the man who was so clearly building Carrie's confidence.

"When I can get him to lighten up, Mum – and not concentrate on admiring you so much," she told her mother, "he's actually really good company."

Astra at last saw Stephen as an effective protection for

Carrie against Craig and the frightful neighbours.

Carrie was glad to be able to show her daughter a happier face – knowing how much more relaxed it would make her about returning to university for her exams.

At least the manageable calm that had settled around her meant thoughts of neighbours were not constantly in her head.

The events that were to shatter Carrie's short peace began with Hubert's scone-induced epiphany. Miriam's plan was to wait until the massage dust had settled, then she would flatter Hubert into ringing the police about Carrie. She was sure her instructions had been understood. Despite this, the following day she was eager for reassuring signs all was well.

Unable to trust Angus's competence as a deputy, she hurried her breakfast and, after grabbing a few gardening essentials, hastened into the garden to station herself near the gate.

She had her *Itemization* notebook secreted in her garden carry-all; one never knew when it might be needed. She wanted to be on the spot when the police made their raid on the Naysmiths' house. She would contrive a word with them without making it look too obvious, to add substance to Hubert's complaint. Once that was achieved, she would call Hubert and get him to make the next call about Carrie.

When the morning had crawled by without results, however, a dispirited Miriam decided to retire inside for some lunch. She found Angus sitting at the kitchen table.

"You've been out there a long time," he observed.

Miriam was in no mood to be pleasant. "If it weren't for you Angus, I would not be put to such trouble."

"What do you mean?"

"Just that. It's your job to note down these things. Needs must. You know that. My job is to coordinate all *Itemizations* into an intelligible form. I suspect, however, even if you had been obliging enough to do this minor undertaking for me, you would have fouled the whole job up. Probably it was your ineptitude that caused the Arts and Crafts Show to flounder. You never were supportive over that matter, Angus. I cannot understand what gets into you at these times."

Angus stared at his wife for a moment without comment. His lethargy left him reluctant to offer much resistance, but at last he mustered a response.

"You know, Miriam, I never understood it myself until recently. It turns out I have something of an intuition after all. From the beginning I thought that stupid Artsy Crafty scheme of yours wouldn't work and tried to tell you so at the time. You only have yourself to blame it all went pear shape."

"How dare you," she sneered. "I suppose you also think *intuitively* that it's perfectly acceptable for those two next door to be carrying on as prostitutes. Just you wait until the police turn up to interview them. I'll add a thing or two to make their files hum, just you wait and see."

"What do you mean, 'when the police turn up'? They've already been."

Miriam gasped. "The police came – to this street, to the house next door – and you didn't tell me? What is wrong with you? You were supposed to be on duty these last few days. What were you thinking of?"

Miriam didn't wait for Angus's reply, not that he was about to favour her with one. Her cheeks flushed as she turned heel and swept out the door, her wide frame whipping the air into turbulence. Angus stared after her, fascinated as the curtains were sucked into the vacuum left in her wake. He found her tragic in that moment.

He remembered – there had been one fateful time, an incident she would never let Angus mention, when he had seen her in the same light. *The Mayor's Tale* – she had made such a fool of herself, and it was not so much a defeat she experienced. Rather, he saw her take a harrowing glimpse at her own truth.

Malcolm was paying a rare visit to his parents. He told Miriam Mayor Whyte, who had just been elected Mayor of Glade for the first time, had been at school with him.

This scintillating piece of parochial connection thrilled Miriam. She already had tickets for the glittering dinner to be held in Mayor Whyte's honour. But she had found it impossible to get a VIP ticket to sit at the High Table, and it was at Glade's High Tables Miriam believed she should be stationed.

"It's the least we should demand, Angus. I'll ring the Mayor's secretary immediately and have her seat us on the Mayor's table."

"But Miriam," he had protested, "she won't be authorised to do that."

"Angus! Where's your social awareness. Malcolm is quite the best friend Darryn ever had."

"Who's Darryn?" Angus asked.

His wife shook her head. "We may not have voted for him, Angus, but he is not to know that."

Without any compunction she called the Mayor's office. Angus found it terribly embarrassing; Miriam's ingratiating voice, her blunt instructions, the theatrical hand flourishes. There appeared to be a little confusion, Angus had thought, but his wife assured him all was in train and he was a lucky man.

Her exuberance over the following few days and in particular on the day of the mayoral dinner had been almost unbearable.

"Why did you have to go and tell your mother the Mayor was at school with you?" Angus berated Malcolm.

Malcolm just shrugged. "Scarcely know the guy, actually. Mother'll make a bloody fool of herself if she doesn't watch out."

"But apparently she's secured tickets to the High Table and I'll have to suffer her handing out of potluck dinner invitations to fire chiefs and civil defence executives like there's no tomorrow."

"I wouldn't worry about it," he had told his father with a slow yawn. "High Table? I doubt she'll make it past the kindergarten chairs."

Malcolm had been right. Angus did not have to suffer the insistent offer of invitations, nor any brief brush with the fire chief's brassy wife.

With Angus trailing behind her, Miriam had marched up to the security guard at the VIP entrance and announced, "McGregor, Miriam. Oh, and my husband, Angus."

"Tickets please, madam," he had prompted.

"No you misunderstand, young man. My name is McGregor, Miriam. My son and the Mayor are like this," she added pinching her fingers into the tightest of squeezes. "Darryn's secretary has organised it all."

Angus shrank into the shadows. A number of the town's glitterati stared as they edged past his wife and made their way through the VIP entrance, waving their gilt-edged tickets at the guard as they went.

But against Miriam's assault the guard was resolute.

Angus longed for the earth to swallow him up. His wife seemed to know no bounds.

"Surely Miriam will crumble under the security guard's steely resolve," he thought as he watched with horror.

Miriam had by now risen to her most imperious, and in the loudest, most censorious voice she could muster she told the guard, "Young man, I no longer have any patience with this matter. Go and fetch my son's dear friend, Mayor Darryn, and have him sort this out in person."

And in his loudest voice the security guard said, "The Mayor's name, madam, is not Darryn but Daniel."

This was the moment Stephen Tiehurst had slipped past. Miriam saw him too late, saw her own social error too late. Not only did she fail to bask in the reflected sparkle of Glade society, but Glade's most sparkling, her very own Stephen, had heard her make this most dreadful social gaff. She had turned from the marquee and, ignoring Angus, fled into the darkness.

Angus knew his wife had felt a true humiliation that night. Her manner with him was cold but for once, indirect. He had even been allowed to drive them home.

What had left the greatest impression, however, was not so much the picture of his wife wrestling with the socially-impervious security guard. The following day Miriam had picked up the phone and called the Mayor's secretary.

"Do tell Daniel, will you," she told the secretary in

the most cheerful and confident of voices, "Angus and I are so very sorry we were unable to take up his invitation last night. We were suddenly called away. I'm sure he was sorry, but I know he'll understand."

What was it reminded Angus of the Mayor's dinner? Was it Miriam's reaction to not being told of the police visit next door? Probably. Her behaviour was as out of proportion and ludicrous now as it had been at the Mayor's dinner.

He had felt sorry for her on that occasion, and the vestige of affectionate sadness he had remaining made him care his wife had become so hardened. "Would she have been any different if Cynthia had survived?" he wondered.

He didn't know. But he did fear her blind determination would lead her to take a terrible fall.

He watched as she picked up the phone on the far side of the sitting room. "Doesn't want me to hear," he told himself. "Hasn't realised I no longer want to."

Angus rose from the table and made his way past her. She snatched the phone from her ear and clutched it to her chest, giving him a discouraging scowl.

He ignored the slight. He was after *The Hidey-hole* and fresh air.

# CHAPTER THIRTY NINE
## NON-COMPLIANCE

The call Miriam was making was to the Gumphrys, and she had Leyla on the line.

"So what I am saying, Leyla," she continued once Angus was out of earshot, "is that it would be advisable not to ring the police about Carrie Thompson in the meantime. It might be overload, if you understand my reasoning."

"But Miriam, Hubert could never overload anybody. He's very clear in what he says."

"You misunderstand me. I don't think Hubert could over*load* anybody, I just think he can be rather too clear at times.

"If only I'd been able to intercept the police when they called on the Naysmith two the other day this whole strategy would have had more substance. We need to wait for the outcome of that police investigation before we can set them on to Carrie Thompson. We need to know they have confidence in Hubert's credibility. Surely you see that?"

"I do understand, Miriam. I am not stupid. There is no need to be quite so dictatorial or to question Hubert's credibility. He has quite the most subtle appreciation of these things. If he chooses to ring the police it will be because his incisive mind has told him it's the right moment."

Miriam had spent enough years of manipulation to know how to time an approach to officialdom. She was the master. They must not rush the gate. However, she was so concentrated on this, and the worry that all her hard work undermining Carrie Thompson might go to waste, she failed to consider the effect her own behaviour was having on Leyla.

Just like at the Mayor's dinner, in her blind pursuit it was her own behaviour Miriam forgot to check.

"For heaven's sake woman," she cried out in desperation. "Do as you're told!"

With that, Miriam brought the conversation to an end, satisfied the Gumphrys would do as instructed.

Down the hill Leyla stared at her phone. So outraged was she, she abandoned any thought of taking refuge in her normal sanctuary of tea and the new batch of ginger gems. She must speak to Hubert at once.

She found her husband at his desk, hunched over his computer and humming *We Are the Champions*. She was loathe to interrupt, he seemed in such a productive mood. But the burden of her conversation with Miriam was too much.

Hurriedly she outlined the conversation.

"I mean – Hubie, who does she think she is? I..."

Hubert carefully pinched the corners of his eyes with one hand and held the other up to silence his wife.

"My dear. My dear," he said quietly. "You know my mother and father christened me Hubert. Let us not get too carried away, shall we?"

"Sorry, Hubert," she corrected herself, holding her head sideways in apology and throwing him a sugary smile. "It is only because I love you so that it slips out from time to time."

"That's all right, Leyla," he reassured her, though she could see the pain remained in his eyes. "Now, let us look at this matter of Miriam carefully. My own view of this, Leyla, is that Miriam is a rainbow."

"Rainbow? But Hubert she has been so awful. Rainbows aren't awful."

Hubert etched a tight smile for his wife. "Hear me out, my dear. She is an arc, as I say, of many colours. She is the yellow of jealousy, jealous of her control on Glade Heights. She is the green of envy, envious that it is I who have stolen the thunder."

Leyla began to thrill to this metaphor. Here was eloquence indeed from her 'Hubie'.

He found more. "She is the red of anger over the loss of it all." Then he paused, unable perhaps to call many more colours into his overtaxed brain.

"What I mean precisely, Leyla, is that our own strategies have shown up the unmitigated failure of the strategisation of our now fallen general and we must pick up the cudgel and hit a blow for the good of all. It is true that she is unreasonable – indeed misguided in her judgement over this whole matter. We must go forward poste haste at rapid speed and without undue delay in my opinion."

Leyla got a little lost searching for her pot of gold at the end of Hubert's last verbal rainbow, but whatever had just been proposed by her husband was perfect as far as she was concerned.

"Oh Hubert. I couldn't have said it better myself."

By the time the sun had gone and rainbows had dissipated the Gumphrys had resolved to lay a complaint about Carrie Thompson to the police first thing in the morning.

# CHAPTER FORTY

# THE LAW'S LONG ARM

Another brooding spring day offered the following morning. Poised by the phone in his study, Hubert registered a few storm clouds on the horizon, but they in no way distracted him from his main purpose.

He took the phone and called Glade Police Station. His call was answered promptly, and the officer on the front desk advised Hubert he would put him through to the police sergeant on duty. Inadvertently, Hubert was not put on hold as his call was transferred, as a consequence of which he was able hear the officer announcing his name to the sergeant.

"Who?" the sergeant asked.

"Some guy called Human Gumphry. Something like that. Sorry, Serge, didn't quite get the name."

Hubert heard the sergeant give a distinct sigh. "Don't worry," he told his junior. "You didn't need to, I know what this guy wants. Put him through."

"I am through," Hubert interrupted, and he was answered by a rapid clearing of the throat.

"Ah, Mr Gumphry, Bill Howard here. Yes, um...Mr Gumphry. I was just about to give you a call. Look, I don't think there is any substance to your concerns. I've had a goo..."

Hubert didn't let Bill Howard finish. "Now look here sergeant, we can get back to the prostitution matter in a minute, though I must say it's far too early for you to be making assumptions of innocence. I'll have you know that Section 16 (iii) (x) of the 1996 Crimes Amendment Act makes it a crime to..."

It was Bill's turn. "I don't need you to read me the Crimes Act, Mr Humphry. The next thing you'll be reading me my rights."

"It's Gumphry if you don't mind. And that is precisely what I mean. You police can never get these things right. I am of the firm belief that any hereinbefore investigations with regards to the safety of the proximate residents of Glade Heights to the illicit activities will need to be followed up again in due course and in the ordinary order of things."

A pause followed, but when Bill added nothing, Hubert continued. "In any event it is with much greater concern that I am ringing on this grave morning to bring to your attention, since you are as a force as a whole so inattentive yourselves to matters which the force, yourselves, ought to be being attentive to."

"Get to the point please, Mr Humphry." Bill Howard's voice sounded stifled.

Hubert let the mistake go. "There is, sergeant, in our very midst, a young mother who is daily abusing her children to within an inch. You must send someone over there forthwith."

"Have you rung the CPS?"

"Yes. The CPS have been and I am without doubt sure they will be around to that house within the shortest time to collect the children but I fear it will be too late. It is essential, Sergeant, that you send someone around there urgently to rescue these children."

"Are they in immediate danger?"

"Are you not listening to me, Sergeant? I have said they are."

"Are you not listening to me Mr Humphry?"

That was one time too many. "Gumphry." Hubert was terse.

Bill did not correct himself.

"Look. Have you any reason to suspect the children are being physically endangered by their mother right at this moment? Why are you ringing in particular, right now? Should we not wait for the CPS? I need a straight answer, Mr Gumphry, and not some spiel of evasive innuendo which has absolutely no substance."

Hubert was affronted. "I won't have you talking to me like that."

"And I will not have you talking to me like that. Any more spurious calls and I will have you charged with wasting police time. Good day, Mr Humphry."

And with that, the sergeant was gone.

Hubert held his phone out at arms length and spluttered. There was nothing left to do – apart from speaking into the ether – but hurry into the kitchen where Leyla was preparing the way for a bake-up of Afghan biscuits.

"Wasting police time. That is what the man said. What an absolute outrage, Leyla. They will have blood on their hands, I know it. I shall contact the Police Complaints Authority. That will take the too clever sergeant by surprise. He thinks he's got the better of me."

Leyla was aghast. "But those children, Hubert. It's shocking."

"I couldn't agree more. Give me a moment, Leyla. I just need a little fresh air to digest this unfortunate discourse that amounts to police misconduct while simultaneously constituting the endangerment of two vulnerable minors."

He swept the back of his hand across his weathered brow and, leaving Leyla in a high state of agitation, walked out to get the mail from the letterbox.

Hubert's mind was rather distracted as he walked slowly towards his gate. A moist breeze slipped over the fence and having circled him a couple of times, darted off to shift the few leaves that had been allowed to gather about the Gumphrys' doorstep. Reaching into the letterbox Hubert pulled out a number of letters. He registered only routine and disappointment. Then, seemingly out of nowhere, hope glimmered in the shape of a manilla envelope with a government emblem printed on the top and the words *Children's Protection Service* on the bottom.

Immediately Hubert lifted his head and, with the letter unopened, strode back inside holding the letter aloft.

"I've done it, Leyla," he cried. "Here's what we've been waiting for. That woman will finally get her comeuppance."

They sat together at the kitchen table as Hubert placed the envelope in front of them. Neither moved to open it immediately. Instead they took their time to stare at it and enjoy the anticipation of a positive response. Finally, Leyla sat back, wrapped her hands around her floury tea towel and nestled them in her ample lap.

Hubert unfolded the letter and began to read.

*Dear Mr Gumphry,*

*Thank you for bringing to our attention the matter regarding Mrs Thompson. Our field staff have investigated this matter...*

He started with vigour, but his voice quickly trailed off – ending in bitter anticlimax.

*...and have no cause for concern whatsoever. We will not be taking any further steps in this regard. Investigating unsubstantiated claims wastes valuable resources.*

*sincerely, etc etc*

Hubert lowered the letter and stared into the middle distance. Leyla waited for some sort of guidance from her beloved, but it was not forthcoming.

"Hubert," Leyla declared at last. Worry had prodded her into anger. "This cannot continue. You have not been wrong. You have infallible judgement. The authorities are so stupid they are going to allow these children to be abused right under our very noses. But I for one will not have blood on my hands.

"Come on, we have to do something about this ourselves. I'm going to ring Miriam. She might be bossy. She might be rude. But three heads are better than two, as the saying goes."

Having remained impassive and motionless up to this point, Hubert slowly turned his face to Leyla. He looked at her for a brief moment, blinked, then without a solitary word, turned away again.

Leyla knew what she had to do, and she had to do it quickly.

Miriam answered the phone and was given the news both of the letter and Hubert's second call to the police. At no point did Miriam interrupt nor remind Leyla the Gumphrys had ignored her advice about reporting Carrie to the police.

"And the CPS haven't even got the decency to explain why it is they will take no further steps," Leyla told Miriam. "One wonders how they can be so blind. The woman they sent around to view the children will need to be disciplined. It's a disgrace. Do you know, Miriam, they can't even get Carrie Thompson's marital status right."

Miriam could not suppress her curiosity. "Oh?"

"No. They referred to her as Mrs." Then Leyla hesitated. "Gosh, Miriam, you don't suppose that's right?"

For a moment Miriam said nothing.

"What if Carrie Thompson is married?" she sneered, eventually. "Does it make any difference? Is she any more desirable as a neighbour? No, Leyla, I think Carrie Thompson is more sinister and clever than we have given her credit for. We must rescue those children at all costs. Even...even...even if it means we have to uplift them from their mother ourselves."

The thrill of Miriam's suggestion shot through Leyla. It hadn't occurred to her it might be possible to rescue the children themselves.

"Of course," she cried. "Once we get those boys to the police and their plight is recognised, the authorities will understand exactly what needs to be done. Brilliant, Miriam. Let me talk to Hubert. I'll call you straight back."

Hubert was still sitting thunderstruck, and Leyla went to him as gently as her bombastic nature would allow. Having outlined her conversation with Miriam she waited for a moment, but when there was no reaction, she leant forward.

"I've spoken to Miriam, Hubert," she yelled in his ear.

This was more effective. Hubert started, and turned to face her. His eyes narrowed.

"I have been doing my own deep thinking, Leyla. Yes, we must act. But I must insist, Miriam is not to share this glory. I have worked tirelessly for a decent outcome for those children and it is I who will go into the fray and bring them out unscathed."

His eyebrows lay heavy with responsibility.

This is what Leyla wanted to hear. Her husband would find the resolve he needed to bring this matter to a proper conclusion. Would Miriam resist? She hoped not.

However, she must let Miriam know immediately what Hubert had decided, and considering the mission too serious for the telephone line, she hurried to her car and swept up the road to the McGregors.

Where this idea to spirit Carrie's boys away from their mother had come from, not even Miriam knew. But she soared within. Common sense had yielded to her overriding desire to see Carrie gone. The plan might be outrageous but it was perfect.

She greeted Leyla at the front door with eager expectation but remained wary, keen to be sure the Gumphrys understood their role.

"Miriam," Leyla told her friend, "I do believe we should leave this most serious undertaking in Hubert's capable hands."

Excellent. Miriam would keep her hands clean. For Leyla's benefit, however, she put on a decent appearance of disappointment at having to defer to Hubert.

"Oh it is so good of Hubert. I will console myself, Leyla, with the thought of organising a congratulatory get together," she said, clasping her hands submissively in front of her.

As Leyla got back into her car to leave, Miriam felt the need to reinforce the arrangement one last time.

"So, Hubert will uplift those children from the property tomorrow morning, and I will endeavour to organise Sunday night's potluck crew to celebrate success. It's the least I can do, dear Leyla, the least I can do."

## CHAPTER FORTY ONE
## NABBED

It was more than a week since Stephen had warned Carrie of Miriam's threat. The strain of being on constant alert was exhausting. But with no attack eventuating, she began to relax. She was not happy Astra was due to go back to university the next day, but she could ask her to stay no longer. With her first exam on Tuesday, there was no choice.

It was Saturday and Carrie was still in bed. Stephen had spent the previous night with her. He had slipped off to attend to some urgent issues at the office, leaving Carrie to stretch and enjoy the early morning sun that bathed her bed. She reached out her arm to stroke the sheets where he had lain.

"Sort things out with Craig," he had whispered, "then marry me. Be with me always."

She pushed the duvet back. The warm morning shimmered its way across to the distant lake shore. Tight clouds formed flying saucers above the mountains telling of a speedway of wind high in the sky, but below, only a light breeze tapped at the trees in her garden. Busy noises issued from the living room where Jake and Tom were already playing.

She grabbed her robe and went to fix breakfast.

Jake was keen to go outside. She opened the French doors wide and lifted their bikes down to the grass. Tom scrambled up on his and with a push from Carrie was soon manoeuvring it across the lawn with his feet. She stood a while to watch, her arms folded. Then hearing her landline ring, she pulled her robe a little tighter around her and turned to go inside.

"You boys be careful," she called to them. "Come in before long and have some breakfast." And she rushed off to get the call before it rang off.

"Hello?"

"Hello. Is that *Miss* Thompson?"

"Who is this, please?"

"It's *Mrs* Gumphry from across the road. I can tell you young lady it makes me most uncomfortable to ring you like this, but I have lost an important document and it is probable it fell out of my handbag when you..." and Leyla coughed a couple of times, "...ah, when you so unkindly threw it down the path at me."

"Look Mrs Gumphry, I don't want to have anything to do with you I'm sorry."

"I can well appreciate that. The feeling is mutual, let me assure you. But the thing is I must have that document."

"I haven't seen it," Carrie told her bluntly.

"Well, ah, would you please check it didn't fall out in your hallway or anything of that sort. I know it was in my bag before I went over to your place and it is very important," Leyla persisted.

Insufferable woman, Carrie thought.

"Oh, all right. Just a minute will you."

Carrie went into the hallway and had a look behind the chest, then got down on her knees to ensure nothing was lying underneath it. "Nothing there, of course. Stupid woman," she muttered.

As she came back to the phone she could hear Tom and Jake making a terrible din out in the garden and her heart leapt.

"I've got to go, Mrs Gumphry. I'm sure there is nothing of yours here."

As she went to hang up she could hear Leyla still gabbling down the phone.

"I simply have to go. Sorry."

Leyla continued to stall.

"No but look here, one moment, I, now look, ah..." and then after a further unintelligible muttering she suddenly cut Carrie off short. "No, no – you're quite right. Goodbye."

Perplexed and not a little irritated, Carrie put the phone down. There was no further noise from the garden, but she thought it best to go and check on the boys. She stopped to slip on some old flat shoes and walked into the kitchen. Jake and Tom's bikes lay on the lawn but the boys were nowhere to be seen. Perhaps they were hiding behind the bushes. As she made her way down the steps her heart began to thump. Still no sign of them. She quickened her pace, a knot tightening inside her. Where could they be? Behind bushes. Behind the trees. Around the side of the house. She couldn't find them anywhere. That was when she noticed – the side gate to the garden was wide open.

"Jake," she cried. "Tom. Where are you?"

Craig. They couldn't possibly reach the gate latch. It had to be Craig. She raced out to the road but there was no trace of anyone. No boys, no Craig, no cars. Nothing.

Trying not to panic, Carrie ran back inside, pulling her bathrobe even tighter around her.

"Astra! Astra, quick! Craig's taken the boys. They've gone. What am I to do? I left them for just a few minutes in the garden, and I heard them crying out, now they've gone."

Her daughter came flying out of her bedroom.

"Mum. Calm down. What's happened?"

"I knew this would happen," Carrie wailed. "I know it's Craig, Astra. He's found out where I am and he's taken the boys. I heard them calling out to me. I didn't get there in time."

Astra grabbed her mother by the shoulders and held her gaze. "Mum, listen. We've got to call the police – now."

"What? And tell them that the boys' father has taken his children. Legally. Don't be mad, Astra. I'll not get them back. The police will think I stole them away from him in the first place. What am I going to do?"

The equilibrium Carrie had managed to maintain over the long weeks since she had left Craig collapsed. She could hardly speak, barely think. She sank to the floor and buried her head in her hands.

Astra hesitated only a moment. Leaving her mother where she was, she went outside to have a look for herself.

"OK," she told her mother calmly on her return, "you're right. They are nowhere in sight and they didn't answer me. So I'm going to call Stephen – I think you need him here, Mum."

She grabbed the phone and rang Stephen. Then she called James Brimsmead.

"James is coming down. He and Stephen have both said to call the police. So that's what I'm doing. OK?"

All the time Astra spoke with even deliberation.

She put through the emergency call and explained the situation to the operator. There was now nothing else she could do except tend to her mother and wait.

Carrie let Astra help her up and lead her to the garden steps. They sat close, staring at the garden where the boys had just been playing.

"They'll be fine, Mum," Astra said with gentle reassurance.

Carrie looked at her daughter. How strong she was. She put her arm around her and pulled her daughter's head to rest on her shoulder.

"I hope so, darling."

They sat in silence, hugging the interminable minutes away, until at last James arrived. Appraised of the facts, he told them to stay where they were while he stationed himself outside to meet the police. Soon Carrie could hear him talking to someone at the front door.

"Stephen!" She ran down the hall and flew into his arms.

"It's all right Carrie." He held her close. "I'm sure he'll not have got far with them. They'll be safe. Let's leave James to meet the police. Come inside and tell me what happened. There must be something we can do before they get here."

He managed to soothe Carrie as he led her into her living room, but the toys scattered over the floor, taunted her.

She let out a wail of absolute misery.

"Oh Stephen. It's my fault. I've been such a fool. I should never have run away from Craig. I should have stayed to face the music."

"Mum, don't be mad," Astra cried. "You had no

choice, did you? What would have happened if you'd stayed."

Carrie let her head drop. "I don't know. I just don't know," she whispered.

The three of them stood in a huddle, unsure what to do next, when a noise outside warned them the police had arrived. In a moment James was back followed by two police officers.

Carrie sized them up. How would they react to this situation given her own actions in leaving her husband? One was an older, kind looking man – she was grateful for that – and with him was a young policewoman.

"I understand you have an estranged husband, Mrs Thompson?" the senior policeman asked her. It was Bill Howard

Carrie explained her circumstances, expecting a censorious response from both officers. But no rebuke came.

"But I'm so confused," she added. "How would he know where I was living."

"Private detective, possibly."

She shot a desperate look at Stephen.

"He'd take them home, would he?" she asked, turning back to Bill Howard. "I mean, is that what normally happens in these circumstances."

"We don't even know for certain if it's him, Mrs Thompson. They've probably just wandered off down the road."

Carrie's misery burst. "But I know it's him. He told me I'd be sorry I'd ever lived."

She turned to James. "I should have told you about it, James. He sent me a letter through your office – a horrible threatening letter. He's so dangerous. I know him. It's why I ran off without telling him where I'd gone. I'm so frightened that in his anger he'll go over the edge."

Having learned as much as they were going to from Carrie, James and Stephen went out of the room to discuss the situation with the police.

"What's the best approach, Bill?" James asked.

"First thing is to check with the husband. We can only assume it's him. If he's got the kids it will make things easier with any luck, provided the chap's not as canon loose as Carrie suggests.

"You stay here with her. I'll just do some checks with the station. I'll be back in a moment. We'll also need to get some extra officers out here to do a neighbourhood check. Despite that letter, it's quite possible they're not very far away at all."

Bill hurried off to his patrol car while James and Stephen rejoined Carrie and Astra. Now they had to wait until the police got in contact with Craig.

# CHAPTER FORTY TWO

## NABBERS

In the meantime, across the road at the Gumphry residence, things were hotting up. Having put the terrible events in motion, Leyla was back on the phone again, this time to Miriam.

"Oh Miriam, what a to do down here," she spluttered. "We've uplifted the boys. I have to say they are a wild pair."

It had not occurred to Leyla two small boys might be indignant at being summarily whisked away from their sunny morning play.

"Hubert has told them they have to come with us, but they don't seem at all co-operative. And now I'm in a complete frenzy – their mother has called the police. For pity's sake what are we to do? I suppose I had better take them home. The whole thing is getting out of hand."

Miriam was soothing. "Yes, it is rather a muddle. But don't be too hasty, Leyla. I'm sure it will sort itself out properly."

"I need you down here, Miriam," Leyla urged.

"Ah. Down there. Mmmm? I'm not sure that will help immediately."

"But Miriam, surely you are..."

"No no. Let me make some phone calls, Leyla, and I will call you back shortly," Miriam told her without further explanation.

Remarkably, this ambivalent suggestion seemed to satisfy the alarmed Mrs Gumphry.

"Oh yes. Please. You pull those strings of yours, then Miriam. You must help get us out of this situation."

Leyla was not to know Miriam had other plans. Angry she had allowed the Gumphrys to colour her judgement and engineer this disastrous escapade, Miriam knew she must regain control. She decided it would be a good idea, after all, to go down and assess the situation for herself – but she would go unseen, incognito.

Without letting Angus know where she was off to, she got the car out and drove down the hill. When she reached the Gumphrys' street, she slowed and parked away from the tangle of cars outside Carrie's house. From there she was able to observe operations from a distance without herself being seen.

Inside the Gumphry house, matters were going from bad to worse.

Hubert had experienced some difficulty nabbing the

boys, with the older boy yelling out as hard as he could and the toddler biting his arm. Finally, he succeeded in spiriting them across the road, where he and Leyla decided they were best locked in the front room while he got the car ready to take them to the police station.

As they were taking the boys to the front room, Hubert had received a couple of hefty kicks from the older boy, who had looked alarmingly pleased with the results. Leyla's answer to that was to let him know she would spank his bottom if he continued to behave so badly, and since this threat had made the toddler cry, it had a quieting affect on the other.

The arrival of the police across the road, however, created a complication neither Leyla not Hubert had anticipated. Over an hour had passed since his foray into Carrie's garden.

"Hubert, we can't just leave those boys in there. Think of something."

"Leyla," Hubert declared, "think of something is what I do as a matter of course and having you nagging at me is stifling the superior cognitive function that is my particular forte."

Despite the confident manner in which Hubert peeled off this wisdom, his brow was creased with indecision.

At that moment an enormous noise summoned Hubert and Leyla to the front room. To their horror, both boys were standing on Leyla's finest green velour armchair, pounding on the window and hollering like there was no tomorrow. But not until Leyla lunged at them did she understand the full scale of their predicament. Outside the window, gazing straight in at her, and no more than Leyla's protuberant nose away, was a policewoman.

"Ho!" the constable called out and banged on the

window. "Let me in – now."

Instead of moving further to shut the boys up, the Gumphrys found themselves transfixed by the enormity of what was unfolding.

"Hubert!" Leyla screeched at her husband. "They'll think we took the children deliberately."

To which Hubert, with uncharacteristic clarity was able to reply, "But that's exactly what we have done, Leyla."

The loud banging on their door failed to stimulate either of them into action but Jake had had enough and was ready to move. He grabbed Tom by the arm, and ducking around the two flustered adults, reached the front door and opened it to a delighted looking police woman.

"Jake? Tom?" she asked.

And they replied with great solemn nods. As she took them by the hand and led them down the path towards home, several other policemen ran past them and through the Gumphrys' front door.

Leyla watched, aghast, as the two boys were taken across the road. The last she saw before she was grasped firmly from behind was Jake running up the steps into his own house, with Tom carried up behind in the policewoman's arms.

## CHAPTER FORTY THREE
### RELIEF

Bill Howard beamed. He had no immediate luck locating Craig Thompson, so he had put in train the next move, which was to ring in some extra staff for a door to door enquiry. He knew that would net the most information, he just hadn't bargained on getting the issue resolved so promptly.

"Very satisfactory," he told his team. He watched Carrie gather up her boys and smother them in kisses. But he was impatient to get over the road to find out why these boys had been taken in the first place.

"I'll need to talk to you again, Mrs Thompson. But you just look after those little chaps of yours for now. PC Hobbs will stay with you," he said nodding at the policewoman who had come with him earlier. "I'll be back later."

He turned to James Brimsmead. "Can you give me a moment, James."

The two men stepped outside, joined by Stephen.

"It seems the boys were shut up in the neighbour's

house," Bill said. "The older boy told our officer they had been locked in, so it wasn't a case of them just wandering off. Who lives there, do you know?"

"I do," Stephen offered. "It's those new friends of Miriam McGregor's. What's their name, James. Unusual. Oh, I know...Gumphry."

Bill's eyebrows shot to his hairline. "Well, well, well! That's a turn up for the books, then, isn't it? Think they could take the law into their own hands did they? We'll see about that."

He explained how Hubert Gumphry had phoned him, just as James had predicted.

"I gave him the bum's rush, as a matter of fact. Think I'll go and have a little chat with my friend Mr Gumphry."

Bill walked into the house across the road to find an older couple well and truly restrained by his officers. The man was the physical antithesis of the woman. While her scarlet face erupted when she saw Bill, showering the room with her saliva, he stood erect – thin, taut, and white knuckled. At the sight of the sergeant, however, Hubert found his voice.

"How dare your men detain us, sergeant."

"Well, actually...Mr Gumphry is it? Actually, they have every right. I think you and Mrs Gumphry have a lot of explaining to do. From where I am standing, you're in line to be charged with kidnapping and assault."

At this, both Gumphrys detonated. The room rocked with noise and flaying limbs, and while Bill's constables were fighting to subdue them, Bill folded his arms and waited for an explanation.

At last the room was quiet again, and, despite being pinioned by a muscular young constable, a dishevelled Hubert managed to draw himself up to full height.

"If you people had done your job we would not have had to intervene to save those children," he rasped.

Bill was livid.

"Far be it for me to suggest the two of you are doomed from now on to become part of a shady Glade criminal underworld, Mr Gumphry," he barked. "But I really do dislike opinionated people like you. Bigoted, self-appointed arbiters of society's morals. That's what you are. The arrogance of it all. It boggles my mind. I'm not going to deal with this matter here. We'll go down to the station and do it properly."

He put his face right in front of Hubert. "Hubert Gumphry?" he said in the most solemn voice he could muster. "Hubert Gumphry, I am arresting you for the …"

Hubert's face tightened into utter disbelief as Bill proceeded to read him his rights.

Leyla, beside him, but restrained by one of the arresting officers, let forth an unintelligible spluttering. "… Miriam? …promise … disgusting … phone calls … Hubie!!!"

The formalities finished, Bill had them both handcuffed for their march to the waiting police cars outside. The mortification for the arrested pair was complete when they walked out to a sea of neighbours' faces and the flash-flash of *Glade Herald* cameras.

James had not wasted any time letting his friends in the press know what was up that Saturday morning at Glade Heights.

In her confusion, Leyla found it hard to focus, but in the distance, clear, defined and apart from the main crowd, she detected one familiar face. For a moment, relief flooded over her and she let her shrill cry for help rend the air. But the figure turned without responding and retreated.

The Gumphrys were to face the music on their own.

James and Stephen left the sergeant to it, and after making his own check to ensure Carrie was safe with her sons, James went to leave, too.

Carrie walked with him to the door.

"I can't tell you how grateful I am James. For everything. I'm ready for that meeting with Craig. I know I have to front up to the cold hard facts."

"Well, as long as it's a meeting where his lawyer and I can act as intermediaries, Carrie, you won't come to any harm. I think all this lunacy has to have an end, don't you?"

Stephen had joined them, and he placed his arm around Carrie's waist as they watched James drive away. The emotion of the morning had drained them both.

"You won't leave me, will you, Carrie?" he asked without looking at her.

"No," she said.

# CHAPTER FORTY FOUR

# DEPARTURES

The downfall of the Gumphrys was not what Miriam had anticipated. She had used them as an artillery buffer to prevent any harm coming to herself, but she had not foreseen such a calamity. Where was her victory? The victory celebration? She had organised the usual crew to present themselves and their potluck contributions at her house the following night for a thorough debrief and congratulatory dinner. That was when they were to have planned the final strike against Carrie Thompson. Instead there had been a complete collapse – her right flank routed. She was facing ignominy and shame.

She had abandoned the battlefield in haste, leaving the Gumphrys engulfed in the flames she had ignited.

Her hurried departure had not gone unnoticed by Leyla, Miriam realised that. The woman had bellowed her unseemly cry for help across the crowds. Perhaps Leyla had known the cry would go unanswered, because as

Miriam had turned away the poor woman lost all control of her dignity. The last Miriam heard as she left was a tirade of foul language cutting through the clamour with megaphonic efficiency.

Miriam made her way back to the sanctuary of her sitting room where the familiar surroundings acted as an instant salve. She sat in an armchair, eyes closed, breathing deep soothing breaths and letting the cool chintz permeate her being.

She considered her position.

Thank heavens she had avoided any association with the morning's débâcle. That Leyla Gumphry would certainly now dislike her, she could cope with. Her original summary on that first day in the domain had been spot on. Leyla was an insignificant nobody. As for Hubert, she decided he was a snivelling, loquacious, ex-stock control clerk who had never amounted to anything and never would. There would be no further challenge to her supremacy from that quarter. The Gumphrys were finished.

She had the grace to think she may have played a small part in their downfall. And while it was impossible to ignore the fact her army had suffered a trouncing, Miriam did not feel daunted.

Rather than deflate her ambitions, the turn of events had the opposite effect. Deep inside her, the bitter righteousness that had long been spreading, began to consume her. Recently, she had caught glimpses of this nemesis in her soul but she had refused to recognised it for what it was, did not appreciate the danger that lay within.

So, on this eventful day, instead of accepting defeat and withdrawing gracefully, she plunged into the abyss.

The news of the morning's activities had already reached Angus by the time Miriam found him in the kitchen. He watched his wife's face carefully as she entered. He could see the crazed determination, could guess what was unfolding in her mind. He was almost past caring. What did she matter to him any more? But he made a final effort to push himself outside his comfort zone, to warn his deluded wife, for old times sake.

"For goodness sake, Miriam. Stop now," he entreated. "It's time to stop. Before it's too late. How can you still have any appetite for this sort of thing after what's happened this morning?"

He realised immediately his efforts were fruitless. Such was Miriam's hunger, she was never going to be able to sate her quest for revenge.

"I will find something, some fact, that will finally topple that girl," she hissed.

Angus turned to avoid the spittle. His voice was low, depleted. "This time Miriam, I think you must let go. She's actually done you no harm. It's Cynthia, isn't it? You haven't got Cynthia so why should Carrie have her children? That's what this is about, isn't it?

"You know, she may not lead the kind of life you would choose, but it only harms you because you contrive to let it."

Miriam stared at Angus. Her colour had risen and he could almost feel the pulsing veins in her temple.

"What would you know about the way I feel, you worthless mongrel?" she spat. "You're a nobody Angus. Nothing but grey and flat. You were able to lose Cynthia then move on. It was obviously all right for you. Manageable for you. But why should I have to go through all that pain. Why me?"

She turned away for a moment, then bared a cold steel face to him.

"I don't expect you to understand. How dare Carrie Thompson be part of this community? How dare she? The Heights is supposed to be exclusive. Can you understand the meaning of the word? Ex-clus-ive. No riff raff. Let's not invite in the plebs."

"Exclusivity? You can talk about exclusivity." Angus tried to keep his voice level. "Exclusivity doesn't mean special. It doesn't make you a cut above the rest. All it does is keep others out. And that's what you do. You shut yourself down and keep everyone else out. Me, Malcolm, your brother included; you don't even let yourself inside yourself. All you do is carry around some precious shadow of our daughter – *our* daughter, Miriam – locked up where no one else can touch it."

Until this point he had been seated. Now he stood and his voice rose.

"But Cynthia's death touched me just as much as it touched you. I haven't put it behind me. I've just learnt to deal with it. You can damned well deal with yourself any way you choose. I'm past caring. But it has nothing to do with Carrie Thompson and you don't have the right to keep others out of Glade Heights."

Immediately she answered his challenge. Any restraint she might have exhibited towards him over the years, for fear he might not support her campaigns, evaporated. She hurled her anger, hate, unhappiness at him, all of it spilling out, her voice growing louder and more shrill until it caught in her throat, causing her to retch as she gave Angus her final foul reading of his pedigree.

His own response surprised him. He looked at her with sudden calm and managed a sad smile.

"I loved you once Miriam," he told her. "But I can honestly say it's been a long long time since I liked you. And now any love for you has died, leaving you will be a piece of cake. All this conspiratorial potluck manip-u-nonsense. It sickens me. Leaves me nauseated, the way that awful dessert you always insist on cooking leaves me nauseated.

"I'll miss my garden. Nothing else. You'll have to shift for yourself once the house is sold, because sell it you will have to. I'll need my half to buy my own place, away from this town. And what a glorious place that will be. No nagging. No itemizing. No peanuts on side tables. And best of all no potluck dinners."

"What nonsense are you talking now, you clot? Where did all this rubbish suddenly come from?"

Angus winced at the word 'rubbish' but let it pass. Miriam's silence as she waited for his reply was startling. It sliced through the room. But Angus was no longer intimidated.

"It's not nonsense. It's not sudden. Probably been brewing for the last ten years when I think about it, but this last month has done it finally for me. I can begin to see the insanity of it all. For you, I think it's addictive. Perhaps you'll never be able to stop. Me? I want something better from my life, and you're not capable of understanding that. Can't be part of it any more.

"God moves in mysterious ways, Miriam – you've shown me the light. I'll be packed up and gone by tomorrow evening, potluck or...," and he let forth a final explosion, "...no cursed potluck dinner."

Early on Monday morning Mary and Judith Naysmith sat at their kitchen table, their noses deep in the folds of the latest *Glade Herald* news.

*Hubert and Leyla Gumphry, a retired couple from Glade Heights, have been named as the couple responsible for writing to the CPS regarding unfounded accusations against an unnamed mother of Glade Heights. The Gumphrys have been cautioned formally by the police...*

Mary was reading aloud.

*... who have indicated they will not be pressing charges for wasting police time. Nor will they press charges for kidnapping against the pair following their aborted attempt to take matters into their own hands. However they wish it to be known that unprovoked attacks of this kind on defenceless and innocent members of the community are not to be tolerated.*

"Ooo, and look. Here's a separate piece in the *Glade Tidings* column. Quite delicious."

*The Glade District Council reports that rubbish collections have been reinstated in Glade Heights as of today.*

*Commenting on an unfortunate breakdown of communication between Council and Waste Collections Ltd, the Mayor told our reporter there was never any bad feeling between the two parties. The Mayor says, while the problem kicked up quite a stink at the time, it was now all sorted and everyone has come up smelling roses.*

*We say: What rubbish!*

The sisters roared with laughter. "Those Gumphrys must be nuts," Judith said finally as she wiped her eyes.

"I suppose so," Mary reflected. "What staggers me, though, is how the Dragon has managed to keep her name out of all of this. She started it, I'm certain. I'm also certain we won't have any more trouble. But, I tell you young Judith, my instincts tell me Carrie's chances of staying out of the fray aren't good at all."

## CHAPTER FORTY SIX
### UNRAVELLED

Mother and daughter stood bleary eyed, waiting for the bus. The morning had the slight chill of a day that promised better once the hour was more sociable. People stood in small desultory groups. They passed only occasional comments to each other, imminent departure signalling topics of conversation had been exhausted.

Astra had delayed her return to university for a day. Now her need to get back for her first paper had become urgent. Carrie cast an objective eye over her daughter. It may not be many years before Astra herself would have a permanent partner in her life. They would be lucky, whoever they were. She had even sensitivity. Understood the way people worked. She was ambitious, also. Perhaps she would succeed where Carrie had failed, to get life sorted while she was still young.

"Not that I'm old," she blurted out.

Astra turned. "What are you on about, Mum? Rabbiting on to yourself as usual. You are feeling OK now, aren't you?"

Carrie was. Stephen had stayed close by for the rest of the weekend. He was at home at that moment looking after the boys while Carrie and Astra had a last quiet moment together.

"Stephen's good for you, Mum. I like him. I wasn't sure at first, to be honest. But now I just think that's because he's so nice and we're used to Craig being so awful."

Carried smiled. She looked at her daughter and thought of Astra's father. It was time she told Astra about her father. She was sick of hiding things, of telling lies. She had often told herself lying was the safest thing to do, the kindest thing. But it complicated life too much and Carrie was so tired of all those complications. She would not put off telling Astra much longer but she had decided to wait until exams were over. The emotions of the last two weeks had been distracting enough without the poor girl being landed with that piece of news.

"Stephen has hidden depth, Astra," she suddenly told her daughter.

"I know. I mean it – that he's so nice. Actually, I think he's lovely, and I'm sure he'd see Craig packing if he had to."

Carrie shuddered. It had been a gruelling two days. She wasn't sorry when Bill Howard told her the Gumphrys were not to be charged. She could not begin to describe her anger towards them, but she knew how much they would have suffered from such a social and public humiliation. She had no desire to go to court and relive the awful morning when she thought Craig had struck a final blow.

"I think I'll be able to deal with Craig out in the open now," she told her daughter. "Yes, having Stephen helps. I don't care if Craig finds out about us, either. If I have to, I'll go to the courts for a non-molestation order. All the same, Astra, I'd be much happier if he would realise he needs treatment. I did care for him once and I can't bear to think of him hurting too much."

Astra just shook her head. Her daughter obviously thought she was too close to it all. Certainly Craig needed treatment. But he was unlikely to seek it for himself and she was just going to have to buy time until she and the boys no longer represented a source of agitation.

The bus was pulling in and the other passengers shuffled towards the curb.

"I'd better go. Love you Mum. Call you at the weekend, eh? But you call me any time of the night or day if you need me. Promise?"

Carrie promised. She had seen Stephen and Astra exchange mobile numbers. They were looking after her like so many mother hens. She gave Astra a firm hug, one she hoped told her daughter she was mother and back in control, then she waited until the bus drew out before returning to her car and heading home.

A brief moment on her own. How often did that happen? She looked in the direction of Glade Heights. Perhaps this really would be her permanent home from now on. There were worse places, she thought, and she could run her part of the business from Glade. She'd been too long away from work. She needed to start thinking about practicalities. Tom into day care – Jake almost at school.

She daydreamed her way home, town giving way to countryside unnoticed as she traced the line of the lake. Not until she was turning into her own street did she register the trauma of the previous days and see it as a turning point. Her life was getting back on track. She would be OK. But there was one last difficult task she had to face.

She parked the car in the garage, took a very deep breath and walked inside.

Stephen was reading the paper. He heard Carrie open the door and looked quickly at his watch. It was time he was off to work. He put the paper down and walked out to meet her in the hallway.

"How did it go? Did Astra get off?" he asked.

"Yeah. I'll miss her."

"I know you will," he sympathised. "But look, I'd better get in to work. Will you be OK now?"

Carrie put her arms around him. He felt an urgency about her as she hugged him.

"Stephen, I need to talk to you."

"What's this, Carrie?" He was laughing but as he gently held her at arms length he saw how serious her expression was.

"What is it? What's happened?"

Carrie looked down for a moment, then she turned her face to him and with an effort she said, "It's best if we sit down. Come on."

Stephen let Carrie take his hand and lead him away from the boys and into her bedroom.

"You're not going to tell me you're leaving me, for Christ's sake? Are you?"

Stephen was finding Carrie unnerving.

"No. Of course not. No look, it's Astra."

"Astra? What's wrong? Is she sick?"

They were sitting side by side on the bed and Carrie

turned to Stephen and put her hands on his arms.

"Stephen, there's no subtle way of telling you this, so I just have to spit it out. I've been going to tell you ever since we ran into each other. But then I was so uncertain whether things would work out and I didn't want to jeopardise our chances together. And what with Miriam complicating things with her awful vendetta. And having to sort out the CPS woman. Then this appalling business with the Gumphrys and dealing with the police. Well, my head's been too full of other stuff to..."

Stephen put his hand on her lips. "Carrie, what are you saying to me? You said you'd spit it out. Spit what out for God's sake?"

"Astra," Carrie said again. "Stephen, you're her father."

The words punched him in the stomach. He looked at her, trying to register what she had just said. A sharp wave of emotion welled up inside him and rushed to his head. What was Carrie saying? He couldn't take it in.

"What do you mean?" he asked her.

She put the back of her hand on his cheek but the touch of it shocked him and he brushed it aside. He could see the hurt in her eyes, but he was confused.

"What do you mean?" he snapped

"I am telling you," she whispered, "Astra is your daughter. You are her father."

As Carrie's words began to make sense, Stephen put his hand up to his eyes and without warning he found himself weeping. The tears came from nowhere. This information Carrie was giving him – he had felt this way when told his father had died. An overwhelming surge of affection overlaid with indescribable hurt had taken him over. Hurt. It was mostly hurt – a physical pain.

Somehow he collected himself enough to look at Carrie.

He registered the shock in her expression, but as she started to put her hands up to his face again, he ducked his head away and stood up.

"Carrie, what have you done?" Stephen's voice cracked. "Why have you never told me? Are you sure she's my child."

"Yes. She's your child."

"But why did you run away? Why didn't you tell me?"

In an instant Stephen's hurt turned to anger. He strode over to the window then turned on her.

"Why did you run away, Carrie? What must you have thought of me? What do you think of me now? I'm not just some passing item to be toyed with because it suits at the moment. Is that what this is about? Is it convenient to tell me, now your marriage is on the rocks? You need to be cared for? Is that it?"

He was shouting at her now. Carrie sat motionless on the bed, her head bowed.

"God Carrie, you're telling me that all these years I've had a daughter and I've not once had the opportunity to care for her, to get to know her, love her. Look at me. Have the guts to look at me."

Carrie turned her head towards him. Quiet tears traced the line of misery down her cheeks. Stephen started to pace, taut and agitated. He drew his hand through his hair and looked back at her. When he next spoke, Carrie started, his voice was so hoarse and flat.

"How can I believe you? How can I believe anything you've said to me?"

Carrie was sobbing now. "You must not doubt me, Stephen. I do love you, truly. I've not known what to do over the years. I know this is a terrible shock for you, but I was so young and frightened."

Stephen had turned to look out the window. He could hear what she was saying but it sounded like a dream.

"I didn't know I was pregnant when I went to Australia," she was telling him. "My parents were hassling me and I just needed to get away from home. So I went to Sydney and that's where I found out I was pregnant with Astra. Truly I didn't realise before that.

"I knew no one, had no one to help me, but because I was so alone I decided it was better to keep it that way – I thought I was showing strength not weakness. I know, that sounds daft, but it's true. And as time went by and I got myself a job after the baby was born, and began to find my own way, I thought it would be more hurtful to you if you found out you had a child. I thought you'd hate me for ruining your life and your chances.

"Certainly that's what my father thought. He told me no man would want to help. I thought it was up to me to look after her. I believed," she said finally, then hesitated before continuing in a low voice, "I believed it was my problem, my fault."

Stephen was silent for a while, then he faced her again.

"Why couldn't your parents have told me? You'd think they'd have wanted me to help, to take responsibility."

"I never told them or anybody who her father was."

"Then you've not told Astra?"

"I want to tell her, now. Now that she's met you. But not just before her exams, Stephen. It wouldn't be fair."

Suddenly he yelled at her.

"Fair? When have you ever considered what's fair? You're unbelievable Carrie. This isn't just your life, you know. This involves a lot of people – and not just you and Astra and me. It's too incredible."

Turning to snatch up his jacket, which was lying on the

end of the bed, he began to stride towards the door.

"I can't handle this," he snapped. "I'm going."

Carrie jumped up and chased after him, but he pushed her off.

"Stephen, please. I know this has been a shock but it was never going to be easy and we have to talk it through."

"You know what, Carrie," he told her, a sharp edge wrapping around his voice, "I don't care what you need. I'm worried about what I need, and I don't need this right now. I don't even know I can trust what you say is true. Why should I believe you? How do I know she really is my child? Everything else seems to have been a tissue of lies."

As he made to leave the room, Carrie pleaded with him to stay. But anger and unhappiness enveloped him. A daughter – he should be rejoicing – but this was all the wrong way round and in that moment he looked at Carrie and he really didn't like what he saw.

He loved her – at least, he thought he did. But this was such a betrayal, and he found himself hating that love.

"Leave me alone," he said, shoving her roughly aside. "You sort your own damned life out. I sure as hell won't have a hope of doing so."

Leaving Carrie grief-stricken in a heap on the floor, he walked out the front door and slammed it shut behind him.

Carrie broke. She heard Stephen's car start up and roar away. What had she done – now, then, in all the years in between? She sobbed until she thought her heart would break.

She was unaware of the time passing, but slowly the

shadows in the room shifted and cold crept in. As she continued to lie there, something soft touched her arm, just a gentle light stroke, and lifting her head she saw Jake, wide-eyed, kneeling beside her.

"Mummy?" he was quiet, anxious.

Carrie pushed herself up until she was sitting cross-legged beside him and drew him into her lap. At that point Tom ventured into the room, and he, too, climbed into her lap.

"Will Stephen come back soon, Mum?" Jake asked.

She buried her face in his hair to smother a sob.

"I don't think so, darling. I don't think so."

# CHAPTER FORTY SEVEN

## LIFTING THE CARPET

At the McGregor household an unreal calm had settled. Miriam's sleep had been fitful. She had not thought her husband would have the courage to walk out. By Sunday evening, however, he had gone. She managed to head off the Pattersons and Holbeins before they turned up for the potluck victory dinner.

"That Patricia Patterson woman had better watch herself," Miriam had hissed when she got off the phone. "What did she mean, she thought I'd be calling? Strike her off the list."

Then her night had fallen quiet and she had taken herself early to bed with a cup of tea and a large dose of self-justification. It had been a welcome relief to see daylight creep in.

She made her way into her sitting room and gazed at the lake. The mountains had a dusting of snow, an icy-thin unseasonal smattering. It did not occur to her to enjoy the view, admire the expanse of sparkling water. Her focus was too concentrated on the immediate, the human activity between her gate and the foreshore.

A few, unfamiliar, stirrings tapped at her shrouded soul, but she ignored them, not wishing to heed any lessons. Instead, Miriam needed a fix as soon as possible.

She looked over at her binoculars, the conduit through which she fed herself her drug. She picked them up, placed them tight against her glasses. The flood of relief was immediate.

Where was that house? Awful woman. Then she had it. It stared back, mocking her. Try to undermine us now, it said. Miriam snorted in reply. What was it the police told her on Saturday morning? When she had seen the officers rush into the Gumphrys' house she had gone to find out what was going on. They had mentioned something about a husband. They first thought he had taken the children? Something like that. And what was it Hubert had told her last week? He had found out on the internet Carrie had been living in Milltown before she moved to Glade. That was it.

She wondered if the husband might still be living there, whether he'd be traceable. Miriam did not have any adjutants to help any more, but who needed them? Hadn't she developed quite enough skills herself? Oh yes. If they thought they had done for Miriam McGregor, they were wrong.

Miriam kept her focus on Carrie's house and narrowed her eyes. They could not charge the husband with kidnapping, could they? Let him come and collect the children, then see what that strumpet did with herself. Miriam turned to pick up her notebook and made a couple of frenzied *Itemizations*:

*Milltown. Find number. Must be Thompson.*
*Approach: ask if Carrie is at home.*

*If no luck – Malcolm. Have him do internet check.*

Her life-blood coursed as she reviewed her notes, the *Itemizations* giving her an appetite.

In the kitchen she threw some breakfast together, then hurriedly set up the kitchen table as her working desk, impatient to start. Efficiency was critical. Note pad at hand, she picked up the phone and rang telephone directory assistance.

"Yes, hello," she sang in her most appreciative tones. "I am so silly, but I have no idea of my daughter's new address. I'm looking for a Thompson in Milltown. C Thompson."

The operator was silent for a minute.

"No C Thompson, sorry."

"Oh. Any Thompsons in Milltown? That's with a 'p'."

"There's about 30 of them. I can't run through the lot, you know."

Miriam clenched her teeth. These people drove her to distraction but she didn't want the operator to cut her off.

"Ah. Well, what am I to do?" she asked.

"Try the post office," was all he said, and he was gone.

"Oh honestly," she huffed.

There was no way Miriam was going to go all the way down to the local post office. She'd have to resort to Malcolm. She wasn't too keen to be calling him just yet as she would have to tell him about Angus. It must not look as if he had left her.

She sat, thinking for a minute. Finally, she nodded and picked up the phone again.

Malcolm was at work and she got him straight away on his direct line.

"Mother here, Malcolm."

"Mother? Don't talk long, I've a lot to get done."

"No. Well, look. An urgent matter has come up and I do need your help."

She explained a little about Carrie and how she wanted a number to contact her husband, adding that Carrie was fast and loose.

"That will spur him on," she thought.

"See what you can find out for me on that internet thingy and call me back, would you."

She didn't have to wait long. She had been right about Malcolm. He was a chip off the old block.

"Turns out she is the brains behind some food industry based in Milltown with operations all round the country. Quite the local celeb," he told his mother. "Good looker, too. Photo's on the site. Think I might look her up myself, as a matter of fact. This ex of hers, by the way. Name's Craig."

Having been given the business phone number and Craig's name, Miriam no longer had any patience with her son.

"Don't go getting any ideas about her, Malcolm. She's a good-for-nothing waster of government funds."

"Doesn't look like that from where I'm sitting."

"Just because the girl has had a success of some sort doesn't put her into the category of acceptable in a superior neighbourhood like this, Malcolm. People are not what they seem. Look at your father," she continued, seizing the opportunity. "I put up with him, thinking he had a modicum of sense. But no. I was wrong. I've had to tell him to leave, I'm afraid."

"What? You've kicked the old man out?" Malcolm was mocking her.

"That's correct. I know it's hard on you as our child, but there you are. I couldn't live with the trials any longer."

"Yeah, right. Look, do you want this husband's number or not? His mobile number's on the website," was all her inadequate and disconnected son added.

And it was as easy as that – getting Craig Thompson's number; shifting gear into her new status as a wronged and separated woman.

Miriam began to hum, and soon a foreboding mixture of tremolo and gusto filled the room.

If anyone had thought the falling out of the Gumphrys and Miriam McGregor would cause the storm they had spawned to lose momentum, they could not have been more wrong.

It simply slipped out west for a moment in order to gather strength over warmer waters. Miriam had time on her side. Hadn't she always got her organisation right in the past? She would take the day off and get down to dealing with this husband the following morning.

Even though the weather of the last few days had become increasingly oppressive, she thought a little gardening would be in order. In fact, she decided with enthusiasm, she would rip out those awful rengarenga lilies Angus had planted in pots in *The Hidey-hole* and replace them with something a little more colourful. A little late for bright polyanthus. Gazanias then, perhaps.

Once she was in the garden Miriam had time for contemplation. Her first thought she would have considered treasonable coming from anyone else. If what Malcolm had said was true, she pondered, perhaps Carrie Thompson had been worth cultivating. What if the girl was rich and not a blight on society after all?

It discomforted Miriam to think she may have made a mistake, and she dug deeper in search of justification. Of course, any woman with children from several fathers had to be questionable, didn't they?

Then Miriam shuddered. That older girl. Oer! She had spotted her when those boys were being carried back into the house. She was dark skinned. Just think. Could not have that lot at Glade Heights.

Satisfied on that count, Miriam then began to assess the damage to her own reputation. Of course the public at large had no idea of her involvement in the Gumphrys' fiasco. Her position was quite secure as far as the Mayor was concerned, for instance. Maisie Holbein? Oh Maisie would stand by her, she was sure of that, and no one else held any particular importance. All Miriam required to be fully fuelled was a willing audience. Who constituted the audience didn't matter.

Stephen. Ah, now there was a thing. She hoped she hadn't made a mistake by involving him in the dinner to depose Carrie. Her strategies to ingratiate herself with Stephen had resounded with success up to this point and she must hang on to his good opinion no matter what. Even the Mayor paled into insignificance beside such a captain of industry.

Miriam broke away from her tilling to look skyward for a moment. She sighed at the thought of Stephen stepping out in the world of commerce, then turned to stab furiously at the soil.

"What if Stephen were still interested in Carrie?" she mused. A loud snort trumpeted out of Miriam's nose. Of course he wasn't. Couldn't possibly be. The Gumphrys would have noticed him visiting and would have let her know. Or she would have spied him through her binoculars, drawing up in his car. There had been no sign of him during all that activity the other morning. And anyway, Stephen was far too moral to be wanting to have anything to do with a girl like that.

Having satisfied herself on all counts, the rest of Miriam's day was quite mundane. No phone calls, no departing husbands, just a small *Itemization* or two to whet the appetite. Then dinner and bed.

Unlike the night before, when her head hit the pillow on Monday night Miriam slept the deep sleep of innocence.

# CHAPTER FORTY EIGHT

## CLUBS

Promptly at 9 o'clock on Tuesday morning Miriam McGregor picked up her phone to put in place the fateful meeting between Craig and Carrie Thompson. She emitted a glow of vindication. Carrie had brought chaos and disaster to Miriam and her neighbourhood. At last the moment of Carrie's downfall had arrived.

She tried the business line first. "Hello. Miriam McGregor here. Craig Thompson, please."

To her surprise she was put straight through, and while the phone rang she lifted herself up in preparation.

A firm male voice answered. "Thompson."

Miriam settled into her chair and delivered her ultimate broadside.

"Mr Thompson, my name is Miriam McGregor. I live in Glade. Glade Heights to be precise. I'll get straight to the point. I am concerned about your children who are living here, too."

Craig was quiet on the end of the phone.

"Mr Thompson? Are you still there?"

"Who are you?" he growled.

"I've already told you. My name is Mrs McGregor. I..."

Craig cut in. "I heard what you call yourself. What I want to know is what the hell is your involvement with my children?"

"Don't you get impatient with me, young man. At Glade Heights we do things politely and I have had just about enough of you young people. I suppose you don't care about your own children, in which case I will say goodbye."

"No. Wait. Where are they? What's their address?"

"Ah yes, I thought you might not know. You see, you need me. And to be frank, Mr Thompson, I need you. I am fed up with that trollop of a wife of yours."

"Hey!" Craig interrupted. "What the hell are you saying? Just tell me where the kids are."

Miriam took a more soothing tone. "Well, Mr Thompson, if you will guarantee to remove the children from her shocking care, I will give you her address."

"I'm not guaranteeing anything, you stupid interfering old bitch. Just give me the address. Where did you say you were from? Glade Heights?"

"Well, really...I... now you just watch wha..."

But Craig was gone.

Miriam replaced the phone and stared at it for a minute, astounded by the abruptness of the exchange. Had this call been a success or not? She couldn't tell.

She paced her sitting room for a few minutes, still undecided, then hurried back to the phone and dialled once more.

"Miriam McGregor again. Craig Thompson if you will."

"I'm sorry Mrs McGregor. Mr Thompson has just raced

out on urgent business. May I tell him you called?"

"Oh. No thank you," she replied and hung up. After a moment she tried his mobile, but the call went straight to voicemail and Miriam was not going to leave a message.

All she could do now was wait to see what came to pass. If Craig remembered Glade Heights, he'd have no trouble finding out which house Carrie lived in.

With little further she could do, she decided she would go into town, run the errands she had neglected over the last few days, and fetch a few things from the supermarket.

She collected her handbag and keys and walked down to the car. As she lifted the garage door, the wind burst in, scuttling leaves and dust into the corners. Miriam squinted at the elements. What a wild day.

She drove down to the lake where the wind picked up the waves and sent them rollicking. Distant clouds banked up in a looming crowd behind the mountains, appearing to congregate before making their start towards Glade.

The elements, however, never held much interest for Miriam other than as a source of inconvenience when it was too wet to garden or too hot and dry to do without irrigation. She had been met by the gusts in her garage but was oblivious to their portent.

Stephen Tiehurst, on the other hand, was particularly struck by the day's agitation. He had driven into Glade distracted and unhappy. His car radio was on and he heard the weather forecast with a sense of foreboding; gales with thunderstorms and occasional torrential rain.

"I know how it feels," he muttered.

He couldn't bear the thought of going to the office yet. He stopped for a takeaway coffee at the waterfront cafe. Normally he loved driving down to the lake for ten minutes meditation before work, but on this morning everything around him looked flat and unreal. An echo across an empty space.

He took his coffee back to the car and went to park looking out over the water. He had hardly slept the night before. For hours he had relived his conversation with Carrie, unable to fathom the hurt he felt. He placed such faith in honesty, in facing up to reality. Carrie's deceit was beyond his comprehension.

His coffee was finished without him being aware of having drunk it. Waves broke on the lake shore and rattled up the gravel. Thunder reverberated around the mountains. A pair of mallard ducks negotiated their way over the whitecaps.

"If only," he thought, "I could feel so safe on such rough waters."

Lunchtime came and went. Carrie Thompson had been over and over the previous day's conversation with Stephen. She had tried to keep busy with Jack and Tom who were oblivious to their mother's ache.

From time to time as she passed a window she would stop and look out, transfixed by the brewing storm. She was surprised by the force of the wind as it raced unimpeded across the water and slammed into her house. As the morning had gone on the rain had come in, and now it was smashing against the window. Almost horizontal.

Obliterating the outside world and locking her in. She released a deep shudder of sadness.

"I will simply have to survive in my own world," she murmured.

She had just put Tom down for a rest and Jake was on the living room floor colouring in some frightful monster when she heard a rap on the door. Her heart missed a beat. "Stephen."

She threw down the laundry she had in her arms and hurried to open the door, holding it hard against the tug of the storm. She barely had time to register the sight that greeted her – the thin rain-drenched figure, shoulders down, arms and fists taut and ready. A chill stabbed its way down her spine.

"You Bitch!"

The pain was instant.

Craig slammed the back of his hand into her face, sending Carrie reeling down her hallway and crashing into a heap against the wall. She tried to recover and protect her face.

"Bloody Bitch," he yelled at her again, striking her with his boot this time.

"Craig, stop," she pleaded. "Please stop. We need to talk, Craig, please."

"Talk? You never gave me a chance to talk. I'll teach you how to talk."

"But Craig," she reached up to him, "you'd agreed to a meeting. Please. Stop. Please."

"Weren't going to tell me where you were, eh? Well you can thank your lovely neighbour, Mrs McGregor. At least she had the decency to ring me and tell me where to find you."

"Mrs McGregor? Craig – no. Leave me, please!"

With cold and systematic efficiency, Craig Thompson began to pick Carrie up and strike her back down again. Pummelling. Pushing. All the time thrusting her further back into the house. Carrie tumbled about, crying out, begging him to stop.

Jake had reacted to his father's first words with terror. He made to go to his mother, but his father's violence was so great he turned and ran to hide, cowering behind the sofa. The ferocious thud of beatings continued, punctuated by Carrie's screams. The wind and rain crashed against the window.

He held his hand tight across his mouth. But he began to cry and his crying grew into a crescendo of fear.

Carrie fell silent. Deep in Jake's hiding place everything grew dark. He tightened his hand over his mouth even more, trying to stifle the sobs. Then the shock as his shirt was grabbed and he was yanked up, still crouched in a ball. He let out a harrowing cry.

"You little shit."

His father had him. Jake fought, pleading for Carrie. He was falling, crashing to the floor, curling his arms into a shield over his head and bracing, bracing for his father's fury.

But it didn't come. Instead, Craig was flying backwards over the sofa. Then Stephen – inflamed, unbridled.

Jake ran for cover. Stephen fell on top of Craig, landing a cracking punch to his jaw.

"111, Jake. Call the police! 111." Stephen yelled.

Jake knew exactly what to do. His Mum had taught him. He grabbed her mobile and punched in the emergency number. A man answered immediately. Jake told the man through gasps what was happening. Managing to cry out his address. Sobs racked him. The storm raged around him, dark and out of control. Over and over the man said, "Stay on the phone, Jake. You're doing so well. Stay on the phone. Someone is coming to help."

But Jake could see his mother slumped on the floor by the French doors. Dropping the phone, he ran to her. Stephen and Craig tumbled over each other, rolling and punching. Then up again, careening towards Jake and Carrie, threatening to trample them both.

He fled to the cover of the table, then back to Carrie. Why wouldn't she wake up?

"Mum! Wake up. Mum!"

The thunder, the wind, the lashing men, and through it all Jake strained his ears and listened.

"Why don't they come?" he sobbed.

First, a distant siren. Then closer. Then loud, near his house. Then people, so many of them, bursting into the room. All rush and noise. Closer and closer. They were going to trample on him.

"Mummy!" he screamed.

Without warning he was jerked up from behind. His terrified cry cracked the air. Then in the chaos he saw his father – far away, on the other far side of the room, struggling with two policemen.

Stephen, his own chest heaving, had Jake clasped firmly in his arms.

"You're OK now, Jake. You're OK."

He lowered Jake to his feet and a calm of sorts descended. Finally Stephen felt able to let go of him. He bent over Carrie. She lay lifeless, her face battered, her clothes torn. He didn't speak to her, just reached straight for a pulse. Faint. Just alive. The room was filling with more people. Police officers. Then paramedics. He stood to let them get to Carrie, lifting Jake into his arms again as he watched them take over.

And then he remembered.

"Oh my God – Tom."

Still clinging to Jake, Stephen rushed into Tom's bedroom, and there, incredibly, he found Tom, still asleep. Emotional exhaustion engulfed him as he crept quietly from Tom's room and placed Jake on the sofa. He crouched down beside him.

"You all right, old man?" he asked. Jake didn't speak. He simply nodded; deep, serious nods. "Your Dad, Jake, I don't think he knew what he was doing."

Without warning, Jake started yelling, "He did. He did know. He hurt my Mummy and he was hurting me. That lady told him. That lady told him where we were."

"Shush, Jake, it's OK."

Stephen held him tight, rocking him back and forth, needing the reassurance as much as Jake did.

Slowly Jake's sobs subsided, and when he had got his breath back enough to talk he whispered between hiccups, "She did, though Stephen. That M-M-Mrs McGregor. I heard Dad say. Mrs McGregor r-rang him. That's how Dad found us. M-M-Mrs McGregor told him where we lived."

Stephen hovered nearby while the paramedics stabilised Carrie as best they could and prepared her for the journey to hospital. He used the time to ring Astra. The poor kid. She was just out of an exam and surprisingly calm once he had reassured her – her mother was in the best possible care. As he hung up he thought about her all those miles away, fretting and anxious, and willed her journey back to Glade to be quick.

Across the room PC Julie Hobbs waited with the boys until Sally Brimsmead could get over to collect them. Tom was now awake, and Stephen bent down to talk to them both. They looked at him, dazed, Jake's face streaked with drying tears.

"I'll come to see you very soon," Stephen reassured them. "We just want to make sure your mummy gets all the help she needs and then I'll come back. Don't you worry. She's going to be home and smiley in no time. And Astra will be here in the morning. Promise." He put his hand on Jake's cheek. "You saved her, Jake. You're a hero."

Stephen closed his eyes for a moment to dam his own threatening tears. He had gone to work but been unable to settle. He loved Carrie too much. She had hurt him terribly, and not just once. But he knew in his heart he had to talk to her and sort through the emotional mess that had unfolded. So he had got in his car and driven out to find her.

What if he had decided to stay at the office instead? What would have happened then? He stood up and went to her. The ambulance staff were ready to leave.

# CHAPTER FORTY NINE
## DIAMONDS

Miriam got home from town rather late. She had taken her groceries up and unpacked them, grateful to be out of the frightful storm. Having sorted the kitchen out, she proceeded to the sitting room. It was time she made a quick check of the activities below.

She picked up her binoculars and trained them on the prow of Glade Heights. What she saw astounded her. Police cars, a couple of ambulances, people flying everywhere.

She moved the binoculars to take in the Gumphrys' house across the road, but apart from the trees flinging themselves back and forth in the garden, there was no sign of any activity there. Even the curtains were drawn. Carrie's house was where everything was happening.

Miriam grabbed her coat and hurried down to the car. This she had to see at close quarters. As she edged out of the comparative shelter of her garage, the rain lashed against her windscreen, forcing her forward to peer through the beating wipers. She negotiated her car through the storm and arrived at Carrie's house in time to see a lean, dishevelled looking man being led out of the house. He was shackled to a couple of large policemen, his head hung low, preventing Miriam from getting a good view of him. She could guess who he was, though. She struggled out of her car, wrapping her coat tight about her and hunching up against the wind.

A woman she didn't recognise was already braving the weather to watch the drama unfold. Miriam made her way across to her.

"What happened here?" she asked, raising her voice to be heard above the wind.

"Young woman pretty knocked up from the sounds of things."

"Is that so? Who's that then?" Miriam pointed at the man.

"Couldn't tell you to be honest, though I wouldn't mind betting he's the husband. Always is the husband."

The woman pulled her hood further over her head and moved away to the other side of the street, leaving Miriam fully exposed to the tempest. Miriam took herself closer to Carrie's house and poked her head over the fence.

While she was taken aback by the sheer magnitude of the events she had set in motion, she continued to justify her own position. The girl had it coming to her. She had no right to carry on a life of no responsibility. And if the husband had turned out to be a little brutal, probably she deserved it. He was the children's father after all. Well – father to the younger pair.

As for that young girl, Carrie's daughter – she came from another hue. Carrie Thompson couldn't disguise her daughter's dark blood, and this was a respectable neighbourhood.

It was when she turned to watch the activity at the front door that she was met with a wholly unexpected sight. Stephen Tiehurst, his suit torn, cuts to his face, his tie – his tie of all things – askew. Stephen was coming out of the house beside the stretcher that bore Carrie. He held her hand, was talking to her as they made their way down the path.

"Steeee-phen," Miriam shrieked out across the raging elements. "What in heaven's name are you doing here?"

Stephen looked up, startled. Leaving Carrie for a minute, he marched across to Miriam. A sudden gust of wind caught him, forcing him to reach for the fence. He pulled himself straight, ignoring the rain that belted in and ran off his face.

"You, Miriam," he yelled at her, "you conceited, self-serving, ingratiating, repulsive...witch. There's no other name for you. If you had even a modicum of intelligence or imagination to understand what you've done, it might help. But you haven't."

"But Stephen, really," Miriam reeled back. It was a hard biting punch he had landed. "She'll be all right."

"I don't know. I don't know if she will. If she isn't, it will be you who will have to take responsibility."

Miriam stared at him for a moment. Had he lost his mind? Instantly she attacked back, her voice turning savage.

"Oh wake up," she spat. "The girl deserves it. She's a sloppy mother, I've seen her."

She pointed her finger at him and stabbed it into his chest where his shirt had ripped.

"And don't forget she has another child. Older. Not even the same father. Stephen, for heaven's sake have some sense, man. That child's tarred. Brushed brown. She's Māori, Stephen. Who knows whose child she is."

Stephen thrust his face at hers. They were calling from the ambulance for him to come. He spoke with ominous calm.

"You have no class, do you Miriam? No class. No grace. And you're the only one who can't see it. The child, you ghastly, mindless woman, is mine. I'm Māori. She is, as you would say, tarred by my ancestral brush."

And he turned to go back to Carrie.

Stephen watched over Carrie through the night.

She had stirred in the morning, had acknowledged him with a weak smile before they sedated her again. She would get better. They had said that. The wounds would mend.

He watched over Carrie and he wondered about Astra. Of course Astra was his child. When he thought about it, he had sensed it the first time he saw her. Her light gait the day she walked up Carrie's path to the door, her arms speaking with the same inflection as his own. Her dark looks were his own mother's. That was why he had felt so unreal the first time he saw her – he was looking at his mother as a young woman, he just hadn't realised until now.

He wondered if Astra sensed it, too. She hadn't given any hints she might. He had to accept Carrie's silence had been a protection both for herself and for him.

How did it really make him feel? That he had a daughter all these years and not known her, had not been able to cherish her. Would he have cherished her, all those years ago? Honestly? At 18 life seems eternal yet opportunities all too fleeting. Would he have resented the demands of a small baby? Because there was no question, he would have felt bound to stay with Carrie, not to continue at university.

If Astra would accept him now, perhaps he would deal with his pain and the awful, empty sense he had of being cheated.

Carrie stirred. A deep furrow dug into her brow and he leant over to brush her hand with his, saw her fretfulness subside.

More than anything he wanted to keep her near him. Hoping. Willing her conscious again, to be able to reassure her. Yes, she had been protecting him by leaving. He hoped it was love that had kept her away, allowing him to go forward. Forward? It was so appalling. He'd spent all those years looking back. So much wasted time looking back. He continued to watch her, knowing he must not look back any more.

At that moment the door to the intensive care unit opened and Stephen turned to see Astra slipping into the room. He stood and stepped back from the bed, keeping his eyes on her face as she hurried across to her mother.

"She's going to be fine, Astra. Truly she will be. It looks a bit scary right now, but the doctor says she'll make a full recovery."

Astra didn't speak. She glanced at him, her eyes spilling with tears, then bent to touch her mother's cheek with her own.

Stephen's whole being sank. He felt so utterly miserable.

"I'm so sorry I didn't manage to protect her from this. I should have been there, Astra."

She turned to him, and for the first time he had known her, she smiled with real affection. A tear-wet smile of understanding.

"No, Stephen, it's been one of those things. Ever since Mum and Craig got together I've held my breath waiting for this to happen. It's a relief in a way to know it's over. It's happened, but she is OK. She's going to be OK. You mustn't think you could have changed it. I tried, too, but I couldn't be there all the time. So please, please don't fret. Heaven knows I've done enough fretting over the years."

She paused for a minute, turning her attention to Carrie. Then she looked back at him, a shy, child-like look.

"I'm quite like you, aren't I?" she said.

## EPILOGUE

Slaying dragons has always been the knight's best path to ultimate glory. That Stephen had slain the dragon and rescued his damsel in distress, his true love, was unquestionable. He and Carrie had reclaimed their love and reclaimed their family. All they had to do now was get on with life and enjoy it, and being in fact the idol Miriam held him up to be, Stephen, together with his Carrie, was likely to succeed at that.

As for the Dragon herself, Miriam stood in her sitting room gazing out at the remnants of her domain. It had been pared to a sliver of its former measure, and what did remain was in tatters. If she was not in fact mortally wounded, she was at least morally dead. So shredded was she, she was not even confident she could rely on Maisie any longer.

She put the binoculars to her eyes and scanned her territory. They trembled as they roved. Gone was the brusque, chest-forward scrutinising. Stephen had shocked her. Like the opening of a can, his words had cut a circle around her whole being and laid bare her inner soul. What was disclosed reviled her. This unresolved, insecure being. That was not her, surely? Miriam was Queen, was in control. Miriam was not this uncertain, this slain person struggling through the worms of the can.

She replaced the binoculars on their table and continued to gaze out. Stephen. Stephen, Māori? Stephen Tiehurst of all people? It had never occurred to her. He didn't look Māori.

She glanced at the note pad sitting beside her binoculars and was reminded of all the babbling potluck dinners, of the fun and energy she had generated in the neighbourhood. Could she say goodbye to Stephen when he had been so much the stimulus for these occasions, when he represented so much, reflected so much?

But what was he really, when she thought about it? He was a father who had never nurtured his baby daughter. His baby daughter.

She gasped as a sharp pain stabbed at her. To think how close she had come to being his quite best friend. She had always known there was something wrong with Stephen Tiehurst. Those inadequate, shifty contributions he made to her potluck dinners.

An involuntary shudder trickled her length, and as it trickled it shook her mind. The lid of the can quivered, straining to close, to shut out the repellent sight within. Miriam picked up the binoculars once more. She tried to ignore the nausea welling up inside her, the tears that stung her eyes.

A target. If she could just give the binoculars a target.

Several weeks had passed by the time Angus drove to the top of the hill overlooking Glade Heights. He had bought himself a little car, a Mazda convertible sports number. Red. The type that was certain to turn heads when he revved past, sure to give him an exhilarating sense of freedom. This trip was to be a milestone. He had decided, once it was over he would not come back to Glade Heights.

He gazed across the lake. A single yacht was set into the chalky-blue horizon. He held his breath for a moment. The weather had recently settled into a languid pattern of clear, still, sunny days and he closed his eyes to make his customary salutation to the sun.

On such a soft day it was hard to imagine the water could ever become rugged and churned up. With relief he knew he wouldn't be around this neighbourhood for the next storm. This was how he chose to remember Glade Heights. Inviting, safe, unreal.

He turned the car and wound his way down the hill, out through the Glade Heights gates and to the water's edge. Council workers were busy erecting signs along the road. He was curious and drove to take a closer look. The 'No Parking' signs had been removed. But what Angus saw next filled him with unexpected pleasure.

Instead of the 'Residents Only Parking' signs he had been expecting, the workmen were erecting signs that said 'Parking 120'. The District Council were cocking a snoot at Miriam. Full parking was being reinstated and the public were to be allowed to enjoy the beach below Glade Heights to its fullest once more.

He let out an involuntary snort in what was to be his final repudiation of Miriam's campaigns. Then, car in gear, and with his retired foot hard to the boards, Angus released the clutch.

In 0.5 seconds he was speeding away from Miriam McGregor's shadow forever.

Made in the USA
Las Vegas, NV
28 November 2021

35529168R00206